D0556268

Me and Jinx

SKEET WILL

ISBN: 978-1-09831-356-2 (print)
ISBN: 978-1-09831-357-9 (ebook)

Book One

CHAPTER ONE

The slightest brush of a whisker across my cheek and a low "meow" and I was awake. In the moonlight coming through the only window in the stable, I could see the figure of a man carrying something that looked like my saddlebags. I swung the barrel of the shotgun I had lying beside me into position and cocked the double hammers. He froze at the sound.

"Is that your Pa's shotgun boy?" he asked, and I recognized Dub Cross, one of the no accounts who hung out at the saloon down the street from the livery stable where I slept. He'd heard I had come into some money and decided to try his luck. I guessed someone might, so the shotgun was there, just in case.

"It's a double barreled ten-gage, loaded with double ought buck, and I'm not a boy," I replied. "But I am wondering how much of you it would take through that wall behind you if I pulled both triggers."

Everyone in town knew that gun, and they knew I had fired it before. "Put it down and walk out of here, Dub," I said. "And if you make any moves I don't like, I'll make sure they get your name right on the tombstone."

He stood still for a few seconds, maybe calculating his chances, then slowly lowered the saddlebags to the floor where they made a crunching sound in some straw scattered around. Smart man. Within a minute he swung open the stable door, and I watched him walk away down the street.

When he entered the saloon, I closed the door, stretched out on the cot again, and welcomed Jinx, my little black cat, back on my chest where he usually slept at least part of every night. We settled down to sleep again.

"Thanks, little buddy," I murmured, and stroked the coal black fur that made him invisible in the dark. Always alert, his senses were with me every night.

The runt of the litter, he had never gotten very big. I called him my "little buddy" and we were together most of the time. He had been born in one of the hay lofts above the stable two years before, smallest of four, and his mother would not let him nurse. I had taken to him from the first and took to feeding him by dipping a cloth into warm milk and letting him suckle it off. When I cradled him in my arms and fed him, his eyes would fix on mine and I believe he looked at me as a mother. I think they call that bonding

His eyes were green even then, and overlarge for the rest of him. As he grew into them, we became close companions. I think he thought of himself as sort of human because he never acted like any cat I'd ever seen. In the saddle with me as soon as he could hang on, he and Rusty, my roan gelding, became buddies too. Many times, while I helped Pa in the stable, he would snooze on Rusty's back and occasionally on his head and neck.

Sometimes in the morning, while I dressed, he would wait until my pants were half on and pounce on my foot causing me to topple over, usually onto the bed. Of course, I'd call him all manner of bad names, but in the end, it always came back to "little buddy". That's why I loved him so much; he made me laugh ten times a day.

I had weighed him on the scale Pa kept for weighing grain and such, and he came in at about five and a half pounds full grown. My constant companion, he was the best friend I had in the world, and all I had to love now that Pa had passed.

I found it hard to go back to sleep and lay thinking of the past and of the future I suddenly had before me. It had just been a week since Pa died, his body wasted by the tuberculosis that killed him.

He had been born on a hard scrabble farm in the Ozarks of northern Arkansas and grew up poor with two brothers, two sisters, and a neighbor boy taken in when his parents died of cholera one winter. Growing up, he learned thrift and hard work, and at eighteen became a rider for the fledgling Pony Express, an adventure that also paid well. After that, most of the hundred dollars a month they paid him went into the bank in Junction City, Kansas, a new town where he had settled after leaving home.

At 5'4", an orphan and skinny as a rail, he fit the requirements demanded by the company for its riders perfectly. By the time the company folded in October 1861, John Fry had become a solid, respected young citizen of Junction City.

When the War broke out two months later, he joined the Union Cavalry and served with Grant and Sherman as a scout through most of the actions of the War in the West. Wounded twice, he mustered out in North Carolina in May 1865 after Joe Johnson surrendered to Uncle Billy Sherman.

Back home he took a job as a shotgun guard for Wells Fargo. After one incident where he fought off three robbers to save a payroll, the company rewarded him by presenting him the ten-gage. He sawed off part of the barrel to fit his short stature a little better and kept it close for the rest of his life.

In 1864, home on leave, he had married his childhood sweetheart and the following year, I came along. They settled in Junction City, where he took his savings from the Pony and the War and opened a livery stable, the second one in town. Two years later she died, along with the baby girl she'd given birth to, and he and I were left alone.

He never remarried and spent most of his time with me. I grew up in the stable learning the business, caring for horses and mules, carriages and buckboards, and cleaning up after the horses and other livestock that came and went. He also did some blacksmithing and tack and saddle repair and was the best gunsmith in town. I learned the rudiments of all these trades and at seventeen, when he passed, had a way to support myself.

With the end near, we talked about my future. He decided to sell the business, and I would take the money and go to live with one of my uncles, Bill, the boy the family had taken in back in Arkansas. A carpenter in Sacramento, California, Bill had invited me to come and stay many times before.

In addition to the money from the sale, most of which went into the local bank, I had my horse, Rusty, a small, compact roan gelding I had raised from a colt, a nice bridle and saddle with large saddle bags Pa had made for me, a Colt Peacemaker with holster and belt, a Henry rifle and the ten gage. And of course, Jinx.

Pa and I had practiced with the weapons and, beginning about age seven or eight, I had gone with him most times to test-fire the guns he worked on. At seventeen I had been drawing and firing a pistol of one sort or another for almost ten years, and it felt as natural as scratching my nose.

I would miss my Pa, a sturdy little fellow who had thickened a bit over the years. Blacksmithing had given him the shoulders and chest of a much larger man. I once heard someone describe him as "tough as a hard road over the cap rock". At almost eighteen, I was taller than him by a few inches but not so thick and heavy, though work in the smithy had given me muscle in my shoulders and upper arms.

Sadly, by the time he died he had shrunk to less than a hundred pounds, his face gaunt and stark. He had always been there for me after Ma died. John Fry's son, Johnny I would always be, and proud of it.

Though the tracks ran all the way to Sacramento, I had decided to ride the route of the Pony Express to get there. Uncle Bill had ridden the Pony with Pa and when he had visited, the three of us talked late into the night about their adventures when they had been but little older than me. Bill once showed me a map of the Pony Trail and I think that's where the idea for the trip came from. Both he and Pa were proud of the time they had spent riding for the company.

The Pony Express riders took about ten days to cover the 1900 miles from St. Joe, Missouri to Sacramento. It would take us considerably longer. We wouldn't have express stations every ten to fifteen miles for provisions and rest, or ride twenty-four hours at a stretch, or cover seventy-five miles in a day's time.

Since we were in no rush, I would take my time and aim at safety for me and Jinx. Getting there in one piece was important, not how fast we did it. Now a days, though there were railroads and telegraph wires all the way, there were still a lot of wild country and wild men between here and there.

Pa liked for me to read and he had a surprisingly large and varied library for that time and place. He also had many magazines and never threw away a newspaper, so I had much to choose from. Many nights I read by lamplight deep into the late hours.

When I left in the morning, I would not be able to carry much, so I chose a book to help me get there: a guide to the Oregon and California trails. I had read it through, and it would be a good friend to have by the campfire, at least as far as Salt Lake City, and something I could discuss with Jinx while we rode.

Though there was light in the sky when I opened the big double doors of the livery the next morning, the town was mostly still asleep. I led Rusty out with Jinx sitting on the saddle and my equipment loaded on the roan's back. Jinx had been riding with me since just after he was born and was used to hanging on when he had to and yowling to let me know when he occasionally fell off.

Over time he had learned to adjust to a change in gait and an occasional leap over a creek or rut in the road. I always left him a space between the saddlebags and the cantle with a blanket secured under the saddle so he wouldn't dig his claws into Rusty's back, but for some reason he never did. He just used whatever was handy, including me sometimes.

On long rides he liked to sleep behind the saddle, but mostly he rode in front of me with his forepaws on the saddle horn, or sometimes around my shoulders. He was so small I sometimes forgot he was there, though I usually wore a leather vest as proof against his claws. Town folks were used to seeing us loping down the main street together, on our way somewhere.

I stopped at the watering trough in front of the general store to give Rusty and Jinx a chance to drink before we set off and nodded to Mister Rodgers where he stood on the porch, leaning on a broom. He had never seen me with the Colt belted on in town or the ten-gage in my hand as I pumped water into the trough. I had no idea where Dub Cross was, but the shotgun made me feel a little safer if he decided to try his luck again.

"Well Johnny, it looks like you're ready to hit the road," he said, and held out his hand. I had known him and his wife since I was a nubbin following Pa around town. Junction City was the only home I'd ever known, and though a little sad to leave it behind, I was excited about the adventure ahead.

He winked at me. "I'd offer you some licorice, but you look like you're a bit old for that," he said.

I grinned at him. "Never too old for that."

He disappeared into the store, returned and held a large glass jar out to me. "Take a couple," he said and, as I did, he reached up to scratch Jinx's ears. "Goodbye Jinx, you take care of this fellow, ya hear?" He paused for a minute and said, "Your Pa was always proud of you, Johnny".

I nodded and turned away so he wouldn't see the tears forming in my eyes. I mounted Rusty and as I turned away from the trough, Mrs. Rodgers came out carrying some vegetables in a box for display on the front porch of the store. She waved to me and called goodbye as I rode off down the street.

The Pony Express route left St. Joe, Missouri and ran through Marysville, Kansas, a town about two days ride north of Junction City, where I planned to pick it up. My route took me past Ft. Riley and north along the Big Blue River. The early morning June sun was just beginning to heat up as I passed the last house in town and lifted Rusty into a lope to get the kinks out before we settled into a steady walk.

Conversations with Jinx were a part of riding, so I explained to him where we were headed for the day and how long before we got there. He swiveled his ears towards me, and sat on the saddle, paws on the horn, seemingly ready for anything.

About an hour north of town we passed Fort Riley and I stopped to let a squad of cavalry gain the road ahead. I recognized the sergeant leading the patrol as one of our regulars at the livery stable and raised my hand in greeting as they passed before me at a canter.

Most of the soldiers spent some time every week in town. They were important customers for the merchants and businessmen, and I knew many of them by sight. After the war the fort had been home to George Custer and the 7th Cavalry for a while before that unit was wiped out at Little Big Horn.

I remembered standing holding Pa's hand, watching Custer in his blue uniform, long hair streaming out behind him, leading his men down Main Street in town, riding a big white horse. He looked very tall.

The road bent east a bit to pass around the fort and a few miles on we came to the Big Blue River. I had forded the river near here a few times and paused for a minute to gauge the current and spot where I wanted to climb out on the far side. The mud and rush of the spring thaw was long gone, and the river sparkled and flowed lazily in the early morning sun.

Before I put Rusty into the ford I dismounted and made sure everything was secure, then remounted and, with one hand on Jinx, urged the roan forward into the water. It was cold and swirled around us. I kept an eye out for snakes on the occasional tree or branch floating by. A confrontation with a rattler or a cottonmouth in mid-stream was something to be avoided if possible. Within a few minutes we were scrambling safely out on the far side. I stopped and looked back at the life I was leaving behind, then turned my horse and rode north to Marysville into the future.

CHAPTER TWO

Because he was a gunsmith, Pa was careful with his weapons and he taught me to give them the same care. Shortly after we crossed the river I stopped in a clearing on the east bank for some hard tack and jerky, and sat under a tree and dried, cleaned, and oiled all three. The Colt was a .44 caliber Peacemaker with maple handgrips Pa had bought new after the standard bore was altered in 1880. He had given it to me, and I had learned to use it at a range we had outside of town where we test fired guns he was working on. With a five-and-a-half-inch barrel it was somewhat lighter that the old .45 caliber, seven-and-a-half-inch barreled model. He liked the gun because it used the same .44 cartridge that fit the Henry rifle, his favorite.

With the seventeen-shot tube magazine and lever action, the Henry rifle was the gun that Confederate raider John Singleton Mosby had said of, "You load the damn thing on Sunday and fire it all week." In any kind of a fight it was a fearsome weapon. Pa had used it during the war and loved it, not only because of the fire power it had, but also because of the memories it carried of his life as a scout.

The ten-gage was a special kind of gun. Because he was some shorter than most men, Pa had taken several inches off the barrel to make it easier to handle and thus increased the spread of the shot so that, loaded with buckshot, it would blow a hole in a plank wall one and a half to two feet across at a distance of six feet. It was a great weapon at close range and was, in effect, a cannon with a fearful recoil. It was the kind of gun to be used sparingly and only in certain situations. I had sewn a pad into the shoulder of my vest as proof against the recoil. Looking down the barrels at close range was a frightening sight to anyone standing in front of it.

The Colt had a slide-off front sight, and I had removed it so it didn't snag on anything when I tried to get the gun into action in a hurry. Pa had taught me to shoot from the hip by pointing the gun like I would point my finger, and with practice, I found it was very effective and surprisingly accurate for close range work.

The two long guns went back into the holsters on either side of my saddle, and with the saddle bags, I still had room for Jinx's box.

When he was a kitten, we were camping, and an owl had tried to grab him, leaving talon marks and a lasting impression on both of us. He still carried the scars and memories of that encounter and tended to stay close to me whenever we were camping. Afterwards I had built a box using lightweight wood and brass hinges that folded and hung by a strap on one side of the saddle. Most nights when we were camping, he slept inside it when he wasn't on my chest.

When everything was stowed again, we mounted and moved out along the river. At this point, the Big Blue was a prairie river, broad and shallow, with low banks and lined with trees, most of them cottonwoods. Just south of Marysville, the Little Blue joined it from the west. When I left Marysville, I would re-cross the Big Blue and follow the

Little Blue west and north into Nebraska, a place I'd heard about all my life but had never been.

A few miles north of the ford, we caught up with a farm wagon loaded with furniture and household stuff. The tailgate was down and the small boy riding on it looked familiar. As we got closer, he waived gaily to us and I recognized him. It was little Jim Radisson, and when I pulled abreast of the wagon, I saw his father, mother and little sister riding on the seat.

Big Jim, we called him that because he was Little Jim's father not because he was very big, was driving and was surprised to see me on the road this early. He was a friend, one who had worked for Pa occasionally when we needed extra help around the livery. Little Jim was a close copy of his Pa, towheaded and blue eyed, as was his sister.

Big Jim was the town handyman who made ends meet by doing odd jobs for anyone around town that needed help. His rickety old wagon always seemed to be hauling something for one farmer or another. Everyone in town wondered how he and his wife made out with the two children, but the kids were always scrubbed clean and looked well fed and healthy.

"Hi Jim," I greeted. I tipped my hat to his wife and said, "Morning Mrs. Radisson. You must have left town pretty early to be this far ahead of us."

He kept the wagon moving and I slowed Rusty a bit so we could walk alongside and talk. Jinx looked curiously at the wagon and seemed inclined to inspect it, but I put a restraining hand on him. He didn't believe in private property, felt everything belonged to him and could be right pushy about it. He remembered the kids from when they played in the loft with him while his father worked in the stable and wanted to join them in the wagon, but he didn't argue.

"I haven't seen you in a while so you probably wouldn't know, but my brother, Henry, was down a few days ago and wants us to move up to Marysville so he and I can go into business together," he said. "He's got some idea of doing deliveries of stuff that people order from the Montgomery Ward. The new catalog just came out and it's got over 400 pages of stuff you can order, and they ship it to you."

"The stuff comes into the station and he figures we can deliver it to people from there if they don't want to, or can't, get it themselves. He figures with that stuff and other hauling and such, with his two wagons and mine we can make a living for both of us and maybe build up a good business."

"That sounds reasonable," I said. "Do you have a place yet?"

"Not yet," his wife said, "But Jenny, that's Henry's wife, said they'll move the boys in with their sisters and we can have that room and we have a tent and such, so we should be ok for a while."

"Henry said we can put our stuff in his barn until we find a place," said Jim. "He and I can work on building us a place on his land when we aren't hauling for folks. We should be able to get under roof before winter."

"Sounds like you got it all worked out," I said. I had been to their home in Junction City and it didn't look to me like they had everything in the wagon. When I said as much she replied, "Jim and Henry are coming back down in a few days to get the rest and then we'll be set."

I liked them. They had invited us for dinner several times over the years and Jim was always cheerful, a good worker and usually there when we needed him. We'd see them at church occasionally, though Pa and I usually read on Sunday mornings or rode out to our target range to practice.

"You just going to visit?" Jim asked and then added before I could answer, "Sorry to hear about your Pa. He was always good to me and helped me out more than once when I was in a tight."

When I told him of my plans he grinned broadly. "I'm not surprised. I remember when Bill was here you all talked all day and half the night about California. And you're going to ride all the way?"

"Yep," I said. "Plan to ride the Pony to about Salt Lake City, spend the winter there, and finish up the next spring and summer."

His wife looked at me skeptically, "How old are you, Johnny?" she asked.

I grinned at her. "I'm almost eighteen and there's no one I have to ask for permission, so it's up to me" I said. And after a pause I added "and Jinx. And he sure wants to go."

Jim laughed. "I reckon I'd have wanted to do something like it when I was seventeen," he said.

I said goodbye and pushed Rusty into a canter for a few miles to make up a little time before we stopped for the night.

Riding away from them, I thought about some of the things I had read about other countries in the world and how most people like Jim and his family, and me and Pa, were born into a place in life and expected to always live in that place, usually for the benefit of others. They wouldn't have had the choice to do what Jim was doing or what I was doing.

I guess that's one of the reasons people came to this country from all over the world; just so they could choose.

Pa and I had been to Marysville several times in the last few years, so I was familiar with the road and the scenery and could skylark a bit, talk to Jinx and enjoy the ride.

Near sunset we stopped at a good spot Pa and I had used before and set up camp. The mild weather meant a pleasant night, and it didn't take long to get supper and relax at the campfire. Jinx usually ate some of whatever I did, and tonight that was bacon and johnnycake washed down with water from the Big Blue. Setting up camp I was reminded of the need for a hatchet around a campsite and vowed to remember to get one at the general store in Marysville.

After supper I tried to read a bit, but my mind kept busy with the trip. Our lives from now on would be different from anything we had lived before, so I just sat and talked to Jinx about where we were going and how we would get there.

Sleeping under the stars beside a low burning campfire was always something I loved but when I rolled up in my blankets, I had the ten-gage next to me and Colt close to hand in case of need.

The next day we were up and on the road early. I was hoping to be in Marysville by early afternoon, so I rode at a canter every other hour for a while and we ate in the saddle, with just a couple stops to rest Rusty and let him water at the river. We rode into town about three o'clock.

The first place we stopped was the Sheriff's Office. Bob Risley had been a friend of Pa's since they served together in the cavalry years before. Bob had been severely wounded at Chattanooga and had lost the use of his left arm. Invalided out, he found the shortage of men at home gave him a chance to run for sheriff of Marshal County. He had won and been reelected every two years since.

He was a couple of years older than Pa but still hale, though his hair was shot with grey and he was a little stooped.

The last time we had seen him, he told Pa of plans to retire after this term was over. Pa and I had stayed with him and his wife Hattie whenever we came to town and he was glad to see us.

He said hello to Jinx, who totally ignored him and proceeded to investigate the office, after which he curled up in a chair in the sunshine. Bob had heard about Pa passing and offered his condolences.

"We went through a lot together, he and I," he said with a remembering expression on his face. He paused for a minute, apparently looking back over the years. "Never had a better man to side with."

"So where are you two off to?" he asked with a smile. "Plan to take the cars headed west?"

"No sir," I replied. "We're going to ride the Pony all the way to Sacramento."

His mouth fell open in astonishment. "Johnny, that's 2000 miles. Have you lost your marbles?"

"Pa and I talked about it before he died. It took him a while, but he finally came around to the idea. I wrote to Uncle Bill in Sacramento about it and he was enthusiastic. I think that's what finally brought Pa around to the idea. You knew he rode the Pony with Pa before the war, didn't you?"

"Yes, I knew that," he said. "I knew Bill before the war, and I remember him being a little scattershoted then. Sounds like he ain't changed much."

He scratched his chin with his good hand and grinned a bit. "Well, it sounds like quite an adventure. When I was your age, I probably would have wanted to do the same thing or something like it."

Then he laughed. "I know damned well I would have, so I reckon it's not so crazy after all. You know Hattie will try to lock you in the barn, so you won't leave. At your age you want to try things, so you'll have something to lie about when you're my age," he said with a smile.

He stood up and stretched his back. "Well, tell Hattie I'll be home for dinner at the usual time. I supposed the cat will sleep in the house with you?"

"What will Hattie say about that?" I asked with a grin.

"She'll probably make a fuss and end up giving him catfish for dinner." He stood in the office door while I lifted Jinx onto the saddle and mounted behind him. When I looked back, he still stood in the office doorway, shaking his head.

I rode slowly through the town noticing some things that were new. The old Pony station had been remodeled and was now a hotel advertising running water and hot baths, and a water wagon drove through town spraying the street to keep the dust down.

On the other hand, I noticed the girls at the Silver Slipper Saloon still hung over the rail above the front porch to greet passersby, and dogs still slept in the sun. Some things never change. In earlier days Marysville had been a 'hell on wheels' kind of place. Now it was just a nice, peaceful place to live.

Since the railroad passed through, the town had grown. Everywhere you looked there were new buildings, houses and businesses. Besides being the supply center for local farmers, it was also the center for entertainment so that Saturday night in town was a nice break from the hard work of farming.

A short way out of town, Bob and Hattie's place sat atop one of the few hills in the area. The hill country of eastern Kansas flattened out the farther west you went, and soon the land spread out in gentle rolls and flats.

I remember Pa telling me Bob had bought some of the adjoining property and planned to do some farming on a small scale when he retired from sheriffing. It looked like he had already started. The lane that led into his front yard was bordered with corn on both sides, tall and well-tended.

Hattie must have seen me coming. She was standing on the front porch shading her eyes against the sun, trying to make out who I was. Finally, she made me out and came rushing down the steps calling, "Well, Johnny Fry, aren't you a sight for sore eyes?"

She waited while I tied Rusty to the hitching rail, then rushed to take me in a warm hug.

"Who's that you've got with you?" she asked. "Why it's Jinx." She clapped her hands and laughed. "Isn't that just like you. Everyone else has a dog, and you travel with a cat. Lands sakes, how'd you train him to sit up there when you ride?"

"He's smart enough not to fall off, I reckon" I said. We stood smiling at one another. "How are you Mrs. Risley?"

"I'm very well, thank you and you can call me Hattie. We've been friends long enough for that." She smiled up at me. Bob had married her after his first wife died. She was about 20 years younger than him, about thirty I'd guess, though I'd always had enough sense not to ask her. She was short, round and pretty. I'd liked her from the first time we met.

She whisked me into the kitchen, and soon I was sitting at the table with a plate of cookies and a glass of cold milk in front of me, listening to her chatter like a squirrel up a tree.

"I was so sorry to hear about your Pa, but not surprised," she said. "He had been sick for so long and working in all that heat and dust probably helped it along."

We chatted about this and that while she continued fixing Bob's dinner and finally, she sat and asked, "So, Johnny, or should I call you John now? You're so grown up. Where are you heading? It looks like you're setting out for somewhere."

"Pa was John, I'll always be Johnny," I said. "We sold the livery stable, and I'm going to live with Uncle Bill in Sacramento. He's got a good business going and I like the sound of California."

"Where are you going to catch the cars?" she asked, and I braced for her reaction to my answer. Her face showed the same expression that Bob's had, and I had to laugh as her eyes widened and her mouth dropped open.

"Well, I never," she said. "You and that cat riding all that way. How far is it?" When I told her she shook her head in disbelief. "Well if you're like your Pa there's probably no talking you out of it. How long will you be staying with us?"

"Probably just overnight and maybe tomorrow," I said. "I just left yesterday, and I'd like to get into Utah, maybe Salt Lake and settle down for the winter, then finish up next spring. I'm not in a hurry but I don't want to drag my feet either."

She shook her head. "Well, we can give you a good feed and send you on your way with some food that will last for a while. What does Jinx eat?"

"He pretty much shares with me unless he catches something on the side. The vet in Junction City fixed him so he won't wander too much. He's two years old and my buddy. He seems to be happy to hang around with me."

By this time Jinx had finished his examination of the house and sat at the back door waiting patiently for it to open, which he was sure it would. I held it for him and watched him pause on the top step of the back porch, survey the barnyard, and begin his tour. I knew he'd be back in time for dinner.

When Bob got home, we sat down to a good meal and afterwards talked for several hours. Every aspect of my plan was gone over at least twice. Bob had been right; Hattie tried to talk me into taking a job at the farm where I could sleep in the spare room and stay as long as I liked. She did give Jinx catfish for dinner, and after eating he rubbed against her leg to thank her. It was the nicest evening I'd had since Pa died.

The next day I helped the hired man with some chores in the morning and after lunch took all three of my weapons out behind the barn to practice.

When I finished, I cleaned and oiled them. Jinx was noticeably absent during this time. He hated the sound of gunfire and instead kept busy in the loft reducing the mouse population.

After dinner that night we all sat in the living room, and I showed them the map Bill had given me of the Pony Express route all the way from St. Joe to Sacramento.

"You know," said Bob, through a cloud of tobacco smoke, "almost all the relay stations are gone, and most of the home station buildings are being used for some business or another, if they're not torn down or fallen down. The Avery House Hotel is the old Pony Station in town, and he had to put a lot of money into that place to be able to use it as a hotel."

Hattie waved her hand. "Bob, I wish you'd take that thing out on the porch to smoke it," she said as she got up to refill our drinks, "especially when we have company."

"Johnny's not really company," he said with a wink at me. "Besides, that's when I enjoy it the most; when I've got someone to talk to."

"I'm not surprised at that" I said stroking a purring Jinx on my lap. "I wasn't counting on anything from the Pony because I know the stations are all gone. I mean, it's been 22 years since it stopped running. Besides, we've got everything we need to sleep out and eat out too, for that matter. I'd like a hotel every few days to clean up a bit and put on the feedbag, but I can live without it."

"There will be places where you have no choice but to sleep out, and probably for more than a few days at a time. West of Salt Lake is pretty tough country, from what I hear, and you've never seen anything like the Sierra Nevada."

He leaned back in the chair and stretched. "Hattie and I went to San Francisco for a few days after we were married. Those mountains are something to see. Going over them on a horse won't be easy, especially by yourself. The country you'll have to cross is one of the reasons the Pony failed. And I'll tell you something else; it's a country to go through as fast as you can without killing your horses."

"The Pony Express lost a bunch of money. From what I hear they never planned it as a money-making thing. They were looking to line up government contracts by showing they could deliver the mail. The Pony was part of a larger outfit. It almost bankrupted the rest of the company, and it took them a while to get back on their feet."

"I know they paid Pa good," I said. "Most of what he put into the livery stable came from money he'd earned with the Pony. He didn't bring much back from the war."

"I remember," said Bob. "A Henry rifle and the clothes on his back was about all."

He stood and stretched, "Time for me to get to bed," he said. "Stop by the office in the morning, and we'll see if we can work out some way to use the telegraph so we can keep up with you. Since telegraph wires destroyed the Pony, it seems like it's the least they can do."

I woke the next morning when the sun coming in the window finally got around to my face. Jinx bounded off the bed, stretched and had a morning wash while I did the same. An hour later we were packed and ready to go. After a last hug from Hattie, we headed back into Marysville to see Bob.

It seemed a little strange it was so quiet. I had listened to Bob and Pa talk about the old days there when the railroad was building, and Marysville had been a right wicked place. Twenty-four-hour saloons, women of the evenings, gambling and other shenanigans kept Bob pretty busy for a few years, but now it was a nice place and had a chance to become nicer with all that was going on.

Bob was sitting at his desk when I walked in. He had been setting up 'the system' as he called it. He wanted me to stop at every sheriff's office on the way and send a telegram so he would know where we were and if we needed anything. He and Hattie would appreciate it if I could drop them a line now and then, so they knew how things were going.

He finally stood and offered me his hand. "Good luck Johnny," he said. "I've got a meeting with the Mayor, so I need to get over to the City Hall." He reached down and scratched Jinx's ears and said, "You take good care of this boy, Jinx." He smiled at me and continued. "Take good care of this man, I make it."

I watched him walk away down the boardwalk and thought, "Now it begins."

CHAPTER THREE

I stopped at the general store to pick up a couple of things including something for Jinx. At home I had fashioned a toy out of some rope and scrap leather. He loved to play with it, but in the excitement of leaving I had forgotten it.

I bought a short length of rope for the toy, a good belt knife, and a hatchet for use around camp. When I went to pay for it, without thinking, I opened my shirt and took some money out of my money belt. As soon as I did it, I knew it was a mistake. When I turned my head to look around me, I looked right into the face of a rough looking man who was peering in the window.

"Do you know that fellow?" I asked the lady behind the counter.

"I don't know his name," she said, "but I've seen him in town a lot. I know he's not a very nice man."

When I came out of the store I looked left and right but there was no sign of him.

I crossed the Big Blue just west of town at a well-used and marked ford in a different kind of river. Here the water was deeper and running a little faster than the last time, but the bottom was firm and in no time, we splashed out on the west bank. A few miles on we came to the Little Blue and turned toward the west, north west. This direction would lead me into Nebraska and the Platte River Road.

The trail led beside the Little Blue. The river was clean and clear and the rushing sounds from it were new to me. I knew I'd be seeing and hearing those kinds of new things all the way across the country. All the new things I would likely be seeing was a prime reason I wanted to take this trip.

We stopped at about ten miles out to check the load and give Rusty a chance to browse and drink. I had been enjoying the morning and not really paying attention to things. I realized my mistake when two men stepped out of the trees with drawn guns and came toward me.

Jinx was sitting in the saddle when they walked by Rusty, but they didn't appear to notice him. With a yowl he suddenly leaped for the tree above and scampered up among the leaves.

The sudden noise caused them both to turn and when they did, I drew my Colt and put a bullet into the tree between them. The rough man I'd seen at the store staggered forward and fell, gun flying out of his hand, while the other man froze. He knew the Colt was cocked and must have had a hunch I meant to hit the tree.

"Drop it," I said, and he slowly open his hand and let his gun fall. I kept the Colt trained between the two and spoke to the man on the ground.

"Get over to that tree," I said. When he started to rise, I said "Crawl". The other man was dressed stylishly with a string tie, a nice coat and a flat white hat with a wide, sweeping brim. From then on, I thought of him as 'the Gambler'.

"You sit beside your friend while I think on this a little" I said to him.

When they were both on the ground and I had collected their guns, I holstered the Colt, drew the ten-gage from its scabbard, cocked a barrel and pointed it between them. "This is a ten-gage, loaded with double ought buckshot." I let them think about that for a minute. "I would guess your horses are tied up back there, because you couldn't have gotten ahead of us on foot."

"Who's this 'us' you're talking about?" The Gambler asked, turning his head to look around him. "Who else you got with you?"

I pursed my lips and called. Jinx immediately hopped down onto the saddle and began to take a bath.

"Oh, my God," the man growled looking down at the ground. "You mean we got out-done by a kid and a cat?"

"Looks like it," I said with a smile.

Apparently looking down those barrels had a weakening effect on the rough man. In a shaky voice he said, "Mister, you let us get on our horses and ride and you'll never see us again."

"That's what I'm thinking about. How can I make sure I never see you again?"

"I'll tell you what," I finally said," take off your boots and your pants."

They looked startled and the Gambler started to rise, "I'll be damned if I will," he growled, but when I cocked the other hammer of the ten-gage, he sank back to the ground.

"It's either that or I pull both these triggers and dump you in the river," I said. The rough man quickly began to pull off his boots, the Gambler a little more slowly. Before long they were both standing on the trail back to Marysville. It was going to be a long walk home in bare feet and long johns. Neither of them had socks on.

"I'm going to stand here and watch you till you're out of sight and then I'm going to take your horses and leave," I said "and don't bother to come back looking for your guns and boots and things. That's all going into the river."

"What's your name kid? Just so I'll know," asked the Gambler.

I just smiled at him and said, "I'm going to send a wire to the Sheriff in Marysville about you two, first chance I get, so you might want to get out of town before it comes."

When they had hobbled out of sight on the rocky trail, I threw their boots and pants into the river. The rough man's gun followed but when I picked up the Gambler's gun I paused and stood looking at it for a moment. It was different, unusual, and I decided, too nice to spend eternity on the bed of a river. I took a piece of oiled cloth, wrapped it and put it in the bottom of one of my saddle bags.

With the two horses trailing behind me on leads, I rode out of the clearing and west on the trail. The rough man's horse, probably a plug from the livery stable in Marysville, was good natured, docile and led easily, but the Gambler's big black gelding was a little harder to deal with. He wanted to lead, and I had to smack him on the nose with my hat a couple of times before he got the idea I wouldn't let him.

Late in the afternoon I found a clearing that might have been the site of a Pony relief station, and we set up camp just west of it along the river.

Looking around I came on some logs and what looked like an old stone foundation, but when Jinx shied away from them, I figured there might be snakes around. He was a good snake detector and I had learned not to challenge his judgment.

After dinner I played with Jinx a while and then examined the roll behind the saddle on the big black horse. Nothing there could be used to sleep out, even for one night. Most of the stuff was to spruce up a man's appearance, such as a razor, shaving soap, a toothbrush and what looked like a tin of pomade to slick hair. All of it went into the river. When I examined his tack and saddle, I could see the Gambler had a good eye for leather and ornament. The saddle and bridle were died black leather with silver trim, and the bit and decorative trim on the saddle were of what looked like silver and very well made.

I picketed the horses on some grass and sat down to read my book, but my mind kept straying to the clearing and what looked like the site of a building with holes that might have been for the posts of a corral behind it. I could just imagine a young John Fry thundering into the yard, pulling his horse to a skidding stop, running inside to grab a bite while the saddle was changed, then spurring away to the next station, probably about fifteen miles away.

When I stopped to consider the operation, it was no surprise the Pony Express never turned a profit. With all the men, horses, buildings, supplies, tack and equipment needed to keep the riders moving along a 1900-mile trail it was hard to see how mail at $5.00 per half ounce for a letter could make it all work.

On top of it all there were Indians to deal with. The tribes along the Platte were pretty much at peace during the eighteen months the Pony ran, but further west an Indian war led to the burning of many of the stations and the loss of one rider whose body was never found, though the mail he carried was eventually delivered to Sacramento two years late. In winter, the wind was almost constant on the plains and the cold and snow were ever present to slow the riders down.

I had heard stories of riders who were frozen onto the saddle and had to be carried into a station to thaw out while another rider took their place. There were also swollen rivers to cross in the spring and the burning heat of the summer sun. Even so the riders accomplished what they set out to do: deliver the mail across the continent in a timely fashion, usually around ten days.

I grew up on stories about the Pony and Pa was always proud that he had been the first rider to leave the ferry on the west side of the Missouri River across from St. Joe and carry the mail for the first 75 miles on its initial trip across the Great American Desert.

One of my favorite stories, told to me by Uncle Bill, was about a young lady, sweet on John, who would make him pastries to eat while he rode. He sometimes came racing by her house so fast he couldn't hold on to the goodies, so she began to make them with holes in the middle to allow him to get a better grip on to them. You still see those kinds of pastries around. They call them donuts.

I've always liked sleeping by a dying fire. For a while, I lay with Jinx asleep on my chest, my mind wandering but mostly thinking about what lay before me. From the reading I'd done about the west I knew the terrain, but today had shown me there would likely be other things that were new, such as men who might hurt or even kill one or the other of us for what we carried without being bothered by it at all.

Thinking such thoughts, I must have fallen asleep, because was it was light when I was startled out of my sleep by something wet and cold on my cheek. I opened my eyes and started; the black horse's nose was what I felt. He was standing beside me with his head lowered, look-ing at me.

When my heart slowed down a bit, I reached up and scratched him under the chin. We were buddies from then on. It was the first time I ever called him Black, but it just seemed right. I had raised Rusty from a colt and he would always be important, but I could feel something special in Black.

I finally pushed him out of the way and struggled to my feet. "Hey big fellow," I said, and reached out my hand to touch him, and walked a slow circle around him. I guessed him at close to eighteen hands with a small head and a deep, powerful looking chest. Actually, now that I looked at it, his head wasn't really that small. It just looked small because the rest of him was so big.

I had seen Pa attach a strap to the saddle horn and use it to help him mount a large horse like this. If I was ever going to ride him, I'd need something of that sort to help me get on his back. I had no trouble admitting to myself that the idea of riding him scared me a little.

Pa had been a daring rider and had raced horses when he was a kid before he rode the Pony, but it was one skill he hadn't passed on to me. If this big black horse were to pile me into some rocks, my trip might be over before it had started. I stood looking at him for a few minutes, slowly realizing he was the most beautiful animal I'd ever seen.

Finally, I shook my head and turned away, ready to get going. Although I had to throw the saddle over his back, he was easy to saddle and had no objections to me loading a few things on his back for him to carry. The other horse had pulled his picket pin and wandered off during the night and I didn't go looking for him. He was probably home in his stall in Marysville by now.

I set an easy pace that morning and one of the nice things about riding in the morning is that it's a good time to think. I had a feeling that the kind of thing that happened, or almost happened, back there was something I would see again before I got to Sacramento. I felt that needed thinking about, but it started raining and suddenly all I could think about was how wet I was getting.

A mile or so down the road I came to a lane that led to a farm-house surrounded by trees, and with it settling down to an all-night rain, I decided to see if I could shelter in their barn until it stopped.

As I rode into the yard, a man and a boy walked out to greet me.

"Howdy," he said holding on to his hat in the rising breeze. "If you'd like to put your animals in the barn, we're about to sit down to dinner. We'd be pleased if you'd join us."

"Am I in Nebraska yet?" I asked.

"Yes sir, you are," the man said. "Since you crossed that creek down the road."

He turned away and strode quickly to the porch where he shook like a dog to get the rain off his slicker. "There's some hay over the stalls. Help yourself," he called, "and don't let dinner get cold."

"Can I bring my cat in?" I said, "He's my traveling partner."

"My wife's not here so we won't tell her," he said with a grin.

I had raised my hand to knock on the door when the boy opened it. "Saw you coming across the yard," he said, and led the way into the kitchen. Their name was Yorkson. Daniel, the father, introduced his twin daughters, Henny and Hannah, who were still putting food on the table, and his son, Dan Jr.

The boy was about my age and I'd guess his sisters at ten. The girls got me a rag to dry Jinx off with. He wasn't happy about that, but he recovered when one of them gave him some chicken and gravy. After dinner he sat on the back porch, with the twins in attendance, watching the rain and inspecting the farm. The whole family helped to clean up after, so I pitched in too. "My wife's sister is about to deliver her third, so we're alone here while she's in Kearny" he said while we were carrying the scraps to the pig pen. "It doesn't seem fair to make the girls do all the work, so we all help out."

The house was unpainted new lumber and looked crude from the outside, but Daniel said his wife made him paint the inside first, so it was bright and cheery in the big room. Jinx was asleep on a rug near the fireplace and what with chicken gravy and all, was probably ready to move in.

"Johnny Fry?" Daniel said, "there was a John Fry who was a Pony rider around here."

"That was my Pa," I said, "He just died down in Junction City and since I got no other family there, I'm going to live with my Uncle Bill in Sacramento."

You going to catch the cars in Kearney?" he asked. By now I was used to the reaction I got from people about my planned trip and he was no exception. His son's face lit up while we talked about it and I knew how his thinking ran.

"You sure you're not biting off more than you can chew?" asked Daniel, "You're going into some pretty bad country and there are some pretty bad men out there."

"To tell you the truth, I may be. I don't know," I said, "but it's something I've wanted to do since I was a kid and saw a map my Uncle Bill had that showed the route."

"Just yesterday I had two fellows try to rob me, so I'm beginning to realize what I might have in front of me," I continued.

"What happened?" Dan Jr. asked.

"I talked them out of it," I said with a grin. His father laughed but the boy's face was serious. "Did you have to shoot anyone?" he asked.

"No, I was able to convince them it was not a good idea," I said. "Last time I saw them they were walking back to Marysville barefoot in their long johns." He joined his father in laughing and I changed the subject.

"I don't want to tackle the Utah and Nevada deserts in summer, so I plan to wait in Salt Lake through the winter and start out early next spring to finish up" I said.

"Know anything about the Mormons?" Daniel asked.

"Only that they had some problems in Missouri and Illinois," I answered. "I figure to treat them like I do other folks and hope we get along. If we don't, I'll have to find some other place to winter."

"They're a strange bunch," he said, "but they're hard workers and they stick together. If they find they can count on you, then you can count on them."

The next morning after breakfast they were all on the porch to see us off. Hannah, a perfect copy of her sister, had drawn a picture of Jinx. She showed it to me and told me she planned to hang it on the wall in her room. When we gained the trail and I looked back to wave, only the twins were left on the porch. Daniel and his son were probably already back at work.

CHAPTER FOUR

T wo days later we rode into Hastings. It was a good-sized town with a sheriff's office on the main street across from the general store. Black had settled down and was leading fine by this time, and we swung into the hitch rail where a man I took to be the sheriff sat on the porch reading a newspaper.

He looked at me and at Jinx and said, "I imagine you'd be young Johnny Fry. I had a wire from Sheriff Risley about you. Said to let him know if you made it here all right."

"Yes sir, that's me," I said and swung down from the saddle. Jinx mounted my shoulder and we followed the Sheriff into his office.

Inside he held out his hand from behind a desk and indicated a chair. "I'm John Tolman, Sheriff of Adams county." He was shorter than me, bald and looked to be about fifty. He looked like he might have trouble handling some of the toughs I'd seen at home, but Pa had told me to look at a man's holster to judge how he handled a gun, and his was worn smooth in the right places. He looked like he'd been sheriff for a while so he must know how to handle himself.

While Jinx explored the office, I explained how I had come by Black and asked him about ownership and where I stood on that.

He leaned back in his chair and thought for a minute while he looked at the ceiling. "If this fellow tried to rob you and lost his horse in the process, I'd say it's your horse. If some questions come up, you may have a spot of trouble, but have them contact me and I'll see if I can straighten it out for you."

"I knew your Pa," he said, something I was beginning to get used to hearing along this stretch of country. "I was a station agent here when he rode the Pony. I was sure sorry to hear about his passing."

"He'd been sick for a while," I said. I remembered a couple of things I wanted to get done while I was here. "Is there a place I can get some saddle work done, and where is the post office?" I asked.

"Bill Service, down at the livery generally does that stuff around here," he said, "and you can mail a letter at the general store across the street. I'll write you up a letter about the horse while you take care of your business and you can pick it up when you get through. I'll also wire Bob that you and Jinx made it this far."

At the livery I ordered a strap attached to the saddle horn to help me mount Black and while he was working on it, mailed letters to Bob and Hattie and to a friend back home. A half an hour later we were riding out of town and back on the trail.

I stopped to camp that day on the edge of a large grassy swale that led down to the river. After I got things set up, I led Black out into the grass and tightened his girth strap. I had decided to try and mount him and didn't want to worry about the saddle slipping. The idea behind the grass was to cushion my butt if he objected too much.

Two days later I rode into Kearney on Black, leading Rusty.

Jinx and Black seemed to get along from the first, which was good because me and Jinx were paired when it came to horses. If he wouldn't get on a horse, I didn't ride it. Though a decent rider, I'm not a bronco-buster so there are some horses I should just leave alone. Jinx seems to sense that and if the horse didn't feel right to him, I didn't argue.

First stop was at the Sheriff's Office and when we walked in a man sitting at a table with his feet up reading the paper looked up at me and then at Jinx who had led me in and said, "You'd be Johnny Fry and that's Jinx, the famous horseback riding cat."

"I suppose that means you got a telegram about us from Bob Risley?" I asked with a grin.

"Yes, I did," he said. He put his feet down and held out his hand. "I'm Jim Hill, chief deputy hereabouts and that good for nothing at the desk is Harry Forth. The Sheriff won't be back until morning, but he told us to make you welcome."

"Well, Mister Hill," I said. "We'd like someplace to get a hot bath, a good meal and a comfortable bed. Can you help us?" I asked.

"It's Jim," he said, "and we thought you'd ask so we got it all arranged. Go down Main St here till you get to Tenth, turn right and down a few blocks on the left you'll see a sign. 'The Dew Drop Inn'. The lady who runs it is expecting you. She's the sheriff's sister and she sets a good table. She also likes cats. She's got a couple of her own."

We followed the directions and within an hour we were settled in a room on the first floor with a window onto the back-porch Jinx could use to get in and out as he wished. For some reason or other he seemed to get along with other cats most of the time, maybe because he was so small. With the window handy, I could keep him out of the dining room by closing the door to my room. He was a shameless beggar when food was on the table.

Mrs. Crosley, the landlady, was a widow. She informed me dinner would be ready shortly and I was welcome to sit in the parlor and visit or read the paper until it was served.

While there I met two of my fellow boarders and soon four of us sat down to eat with Mrs. Crosley, who, I found out, was the sheriff's older sister. Two were men who were drummers who stopped at the Inn whenever they passed through and the other a schoolteacher who lived there permanently. She wanted to meet Jinx so after dinner I introduced him. She thought him wonderful. No wonder he was so spoiled.

The next morning after I'd finished feeding the horses, I walked downtown to see the Sheriff. He was sitting on the porch talking to Jim Hill.

"Glad to see you made it OK," he said, standing and holding out his hand. "You too," he said to Jinx, who was riding on my shoulder. "I'm Hiram Josephson, Sheriff of Buffalo County. People call me Joe."

I followed him inside and after he was seated, he leaned back in an old swivel with his hands behind his head and asked, "How can I help you?"

"Your deputies already have," I said. After a look at the back room, Jinx jumped up on the sheriff's desk and sat looking around. "We've got a good place to sleep and a good cook. Thanks, we appreciate it," I said. I reached to take Jinx off the desk, but the Sheriff shook his head. "Leave him be," he said. "He just wants to know what's going on."

"How long you going to be with us? The wire from Bob said you were riding the Pony to Sacramento, that right?" he asked.

"That's where we're headed," I said. "I think we'll likely be here a couple of days. Just want a break and to look around a little. This is my first new town in a while, so I might walk around and just look."

I glanced at the door and was a little startled. A very large man was standing in the doorway. He had to duck his head a bit to get inside but once in, he immediately sat down and reached out to shake my hand. "I'm Handy Josephson," he said. He pointed at the Sheriff. "His nephew."

"He's down here visiting family and getting his first taste of something outside Minnesota, although not really too far outside," said the Sheriff.

The two deputies joined us, and we talked about my trip and Jinx and the big black horse and Pa's ten-gage among other things until Joe had to get back to work.

Handy and I stood on the porch and I was about to take my leave when he asked me to join him at the little café across the street to talk some more over coffee. He hadn't said much during the talk in the office, but now he began to ask questions about the trip, what I was planning and why I wanted to do it.

"To tell you the truth, it goes back to once when my Pa and Uncle Bill showed me a map of the Pony Trail," I said. "I think I was about thirteen and that night I lay in my bed listening to them talk about the Pony and what it was like. From then on, I've always wanted to ride it. The farther I get the more I realize it's not going to be like I imagined. But for some reason I'm determined to keep going."

"Having Jinx along is great. I can talk to him and play with him and he just keeps me company at night around a campfire. He also doesn't complain much, and he's been a help in a couple of tight spots." I drank some coffee. "I don't really have a plan for the trip. I want to winter in Salt Lake City just cause it's about halfway, and by the time I get there, it's going to be dead summer and I think it would be kind of dumb to try to cross a desert in the summertime. So early next spring I plan to head across Utah and into Nevada to the Carson River and

Carson City, and then over the mountains to Sacramento. Probably to San Francisco too. Always wanted to go there."

"Have you always thought of doing it alone?" he asked. "Does the idea of having a partner give you a problem?" He paused, took a deep breath and said, "Cause I'd sure like to go with you, if you'd have me."

I was a little taken aback by that. I'd never thought of having someone else with me. It made sense though, on a trip like this, to have someone with you in case you needed help.

He went on, "I've got my horse and kit and everything so I wouldn't be a burden and I've been looking for something to do. This sure seems like something I'd like to be a part of."

I looked at him for a minute. He was a striking looking fellow. I'd guess him at better than 6'6" tall when he stood up straight. I think he stooped some to keep from hitting his head on things built for smaller people. His shirt, probably a large size, fit him tightly across the chest, shoulders and upper arms. His almost white blond hair fell to his shoulders and made his blue eyes seem to jump right out of his face.

"You said your name was Handy?" I asked.

He grinned. "Hansford Robert Josephson. It was mostly Handy Bob when I was a kid but now, I just make it Handy. A lot easier to get a hold of."

"Well Handy," I said. "Why don't you let me think about it, and if you can come by the boarding house tonight after supper, we can talk about it."

He grinned again. "I'm having supper there tonight. Aunt Elizabeth invited me."

I laughed. "That's right, she would be your aunt. I had forgotten. All right, after supper we can sit on the back porch and talk."

Actually, we talked a lot during supper. Uncle Joe was there and the main thing we talked about was my trip. He didn't have any problems with Handy going but he wasn't sure what his sister-in-law back in Minnesota would say. Aunt Elizabeth thought it was a crazy idea, but she knew what young men were like and seemed to accept it.

"Are you sure you want to hook up with someone who's prone to trouble, like this young fellow?" Joe asked Handy with a twinkle in his eye.

Handy nodded, "Yes sir, he seems like he's someone to ride the river with."

"There's five years between you two isn't there?" Uncle Joe asked. "It's his show Handy, how are you going to feel about working for a boy?" He looked at me and smiled, "No offense meant."

"None taken," I said matching his smile.

Handy scratched his head and seemed to think for a minute. Finally, he said, "It looks like he's gotten this far without me so he must know what he's doing. And Just talking to him, I can see he's read a site more than me about where we're going and what we'd have to do to get there. I'd say I don't see it as a problem."

Later, on the back porch, Handy asked me, "So what do you think? Am I going with you?"

"I can't think of a single reason why not," I said reaching out to shake his hand.

I had introduced Jinx to Handy earlier in the evening and, true to form, Jinx ignored him. Later, when he had been shut out of the dining room, he sat in the window looking in, trying to make us feel bad, so we ignored him.

CHAPTER FIVE

⁜

The next day Handy and I spent all day together discussing things he would need for the trip and organizing the packing so we could move it easily from one horse to another. Since I had finally ridden Black, I had decided to switch horses every day, both to rest them and to get used to riding Black. This meant we'd be switching the load every day and I wanted to pack things so that it could be done with a minimum of fuss.

The horse Handy had brought with him was a little small for the long ride we were planning, so he swapped him out with the man at the livery stable, working out a deal for a sixteen-hand high, steel dust gelding with a nice gait.

At lunch in the café, we made a list of things we needed from the general store and spent several hours getting all the stuff on the list and figuring out how to add it to the load. Having the extra horse would help us to carry a few things that would make the trip more comfortable.

Late in the afternoon we rode out of town a way and found a place where we could practice with the weapons and talk about how to handle things if we got into a scrap. Handy was good with the Winchester, not so much so with the old .36 caliber Smith and Wesson his father had given him when he left home.

He was impressed by the way I handled the Colt. He had never seen someone draw and fire from the hip and asked me for some help in learning how to shoot that way. He also was impressed with the recoil of the ten-gage and how, from fifteen feet, it almost tore to pieces a target we had fashioned of some old wood.

The next morning, I was finishing getting the horses ready while Handy had gone to the Sheriff's office to pick up his Winchester when I heard the stable door open then close behind me. When I glanced over my shoulder the Gambler was standing there with a drawn pistol in his hand. Another man was standing back closer to the door as though to stop anyone from coming in.

"I believe you've got a couple of things that belong to me," he said. "A gun and that horse you're loading up."

"According to the sheriff in Hastings, both those things belong to me," I said. "When you and your friend came on to rob me you gave them up."

"I don't see it that way," he said and took a step forward.

A small, black ball of fur, spitting and snarling, landed on the back of his neck, knocking his hat off and making him drop his gun. Jinx dug his claws in, all the while growling and drawing blood with his teeth in the skin of the man's neck.

At about the same time, the stable door opened and Handy came in carrying a bag over his shoulder and a Winchester in his hand. He took in the scene at a glance, dropped the bag, reached one huge hand to the collar of the man by the door and jerked him backwards and down where he hit the floor with a crash.

The sound of his Winchester cocking brought most of the action to a stop. Jinx had been shaken loose and had jumped clear and out of reach. The Gambler stood bareheaded and bleeding from a dozen scratches and bites on his head and neck. He was looking down the barrel of my Colt, while his gun had been kicked out of reach in the scuffle with Jinx.

The man by the door started to get up, but a collision with the butt of Handy's Winchester changed his mind. The hostler had come out of his office holding a blacksmith's hammer, too late to join the fray.

Deputies Hill and Forth were standing on the porch in front of the Sheriff's when we came around the corner of the livery. We were a strange looking procession coming down the street toward them. The Gambler and his friend walked in front, slightly the worse for wear. Handy and I came next, rifles in hand, me with Jinx on my shoulder and trailing behind, the hostler, whose name was Jason Redbird, leading the loaded horses.

Jim stepped into the doorway and said something, and after a moment Sheriff Joe came out and they all stood watching us walk down the street. When we got to the porch he turned and led us into the office where he seated himself behind the big desk and said to Handy, "What's happened?"

With all these reinforcements, we had lowered our rifles. "Johnny was loading the horses when these two guys jumped him." He nodded at the Gambler and continued, "He claims it's his horse and that Johnny stole a gun from him."

"That right?" Joe asked the Gambler who was wiping blood off his ear with a kerchief.

"Yes. It happened back in Kansas and I been chasing him for a week," he said. "When I went into the stable to talk to him, the cat jumped me and the next thing I know he's holding a gun on me."

Sheriff Joe looked at me. "That right?"

"He and a friend tried to rob me outside of Marysville," I said. "They lost the horse and gun when it didn't work out. From what Sheriff Holman in Hastings told me the horse and gun are mine."

The Sheriff leaned back in his chair and looked at the Gambler. He held up a telegram that was laying on his desk. "I just got this a little while ago," he said. "Seems your partner in crime back in Marysville got jugged for drunk and disorderly. He confessed to his part in that robbery and pointed the finger at you as his cohort and the instigator of the whole thing."

The Gambler seemed to lose the starch in his backbone while we watched.

"Jim," said the Sheriff, "take these two in the back. Put them in the same cell."

With Jim's hand on his arm the Gambler turned to me and snarled, "This isn't over my young friend. One of these days I'm going to get my horse back and I'm going to kill that damned cat." Another deputy took his other arm and, together, they strong-armed him into the jail. His friend turned to Joe. "I don't know nothing about this, Joe" he said, "He just paid me ten dollars to stand by the door."

Joe nodded, "I figured that, Bennie, but we got to put you through the process."

When Bennie disappeared into the jail Sheriff Joe looked at me. "Bennie's been around here for years. He's usually pretty straight," he said, "but once in a while he does something stupid. I'll have to see what the judge says when he comes through."

"Do we have to do anything in this?" Handy asked his uncle. "We were just getting ready to ride out when this happened."

Joe wave his hand and said, "Go get a cup of coffee and I'll write up this complaint and bring it over for you to sign."

We were just finishing our coffee when Joe walked in. "Sign this and I can hold him until the Judge comes through," he said. "Also, there is the matter back in Marysville so I can hold him until Bob tells me whether he wants him or not. So, one way or another, I'll have him in the back room for a while. Give you a chance to get a good head start in case he's serious about chasing you down. Don't forget though, he can use the cars to get ahead of you if he is determined to."

"I've got to go out to a ranch to serve some papers, so I guess this is goodbye," he said to Handy. We shook hands and a few minutes later rode out of Kearny, Nebraska.

There are few things more enjoyable than riding across the prairie on a beautiful summer day. We rode at a nice walk, occasionally lifting the horses to a lope to stretch them out. The country around us, sometimes cropland and sometimes sweeping grassland, stretched, mostly flat, out to the horizon. We stopped twice during the day to water the horses and late in the afternoon crossed a creek into a nice little glade and decide to make our first campsite.

After dinner, with Jinx and Handy roughhousing and me cleaning the ten-gage, we began to talk about growing up. We couldn't have had much different lives if we'd tried.

Handy grew up as the youngest of five with two brothers and two sisters. His grandparents came over from Sweden before the war with ten others, all aunts, uncles or cousins. They all settled in the brand-new state of Minnesota in a colony of Swedes and were soon making the prairie bloom and having children. Handy could stand on his father's farm and as far as he could see in any direction the land was owned by kinfolks. Most of the men in the family went to war for a few years and some of them came home after.

He told me about Grange hall socials and dances at the church and helping each other raise barns and build homes. He talked about the hard winters, the everlasting snow and constant wind, plowing and planting in the spring, and harvest festivals in the fall.

His sisters had both married farmers. One of his brothers had gone to the new state university in Indiana and come home with some new ideas for the farm, while his other brother had read law in Chicago and come home to help his family and friends strain against the system by fighting the railroads for fair treatment.

I couldn't imagine living surrounded by that many people, being involved in their lives and having them involved in mine.

After Ma died, Pa and I had stayed pretty much to ourselves. I worked with him in the livery stable, and we lived above it in a nice little place he had added on as the business grew. Besides working with the animals, I learned blacksmithing and gunsmithing, and I was pretty good at saddle repair.

I went to school for a couple of years but mostly I read. Pa wasn't inclined to find a new wife, so most nights after supper we read whatever books, magazines or newspapers we could get a hold of. I remember going to an auction in Kansas City one year and Pa buying almost the whole library of a scholar who had died suddenly.

When he had a gun to work on, he would save it for times when I could work on it with him so I could learn. We had our own range out by the river where we tested them and practiced. By the time I was fifteen, I could draw and shoot from the waist and hit most anything I aimed at, and help repair any guns that came in.

I'd never felt lonely before but with Pa gone I knew I would be lonely without him. I think that's a big part of what this trip was about. I wanted to be busy doing new things, meeting new people, so I wouldn't have time to miss him.

CHAPTER SIX

❨❨❩ ❨❩❩

With all the changing landscape we passed over the next few days there were two thing that were always the same: The Platte River and the Union Pacific Railroad.

The Platte River Road had been a pathway to the west since the 1830's and, though the wagon trains were gone, ruts from wagon wheels were visible in many places.

The fur trappers and mountain men were the first to come this way not long after Lewis and Clark traveled up the Missouri, and some returned to lead many of the wagon trains bound for Oregon, Utah or California and points in between. The Pony Express chose this trail because it was a known path through country that wasn't known. The UP chose it because it led through the lowest pass in the Northern Rockies. In the country beyond Casper, Wyoming Territory the trails separated, and the Pony followed the Mormon Trail to Salt Lake City while the Oregon and California trails went their own ways.

As far as the river itself, it twisted and turned, grew out of its banks and shrunk back into them from season to season. Soft bottomed fords, shifting channels and quicksand were a part of life on the Platte and had to be considered by the people who lived or traveled on or near it. It was the source of water for farming and livestock, but for a man to drink from most places in the Platte, the water had to stand to let the grit settle.

The Union Pacific and the Central Pacific Railroads met at Promontory, Utah in 1869 and in the fourteen years since had changed the West almost beyond imagining.

Thousands of people came west from the east, but the railroads also advertised in most European countries and offered cheap land and a different life. So, they came by the thousands and more from all the countries of Western Europe.

Part of the help the government gave the railroads to raise the money to build it all was land. Every other section along the right of way all the way across the country was deeded to the railroads, then sold to farmers from everywhere.

Towns and villages began to spring up along the railroad to provide these farm families with what they needed and wanted. Besides the farmers who came were the businessmen who opened stores and banks, barber shops, saloons and restaurants. In all the towns that were 'end of track' towns the seeds for growth were planted and places like Marysville, Kearney and North Platte had sprouted because of it.

Of course, the gamblers, thieves, con-men, whores and charlatans had come also, but they just provided spice for the lives of the men who did the work. Soon they were a part of the past, and before long there were enough people and new states came into being along the tracks, one after another.

With the states came law and structure, and eventually civilization, but for now all men wore guns and when they felt it was necessary, used them. I knew that sometime in the near future we would cross a line into a land where law and civilization were a thing of the future. if we weren't prepared to defend ourselves and our possessions, we could lose them as well as our lives.

Many of the buildings and structures we saw along the trail were railroad depots, water tanks, coaling stations and bunk houses for section crews that kept the rails repaired and the trains rolling. Many a railroad depot became the center piece for a new town along the right of way.

On our third day out of Kearny, we crossed a creek about noon and stopped to water the horses and fill our water bags. I was riding Black and Jinx had learned to use the strap to get on his back just like me, so he was riding on my shoulder. He seemed to have accepted Black as part of the family and apparently felt the same about Handy. At night, around the fire, Handy would stroke him, scratch his ears and play with him and was always feeding him part of dinner, which was the best way to get on his good side.

Within a few minutes we came to a gate across a lane that led away from the road. The sign over the gate read 'The Orchards', and looked so inviting we decided to visit and see if we could replenish our grain supply for the horses. We crested a small hill and saw a farmhouse in the distance backed by a steep, rocky bluff that seemed to rise directly behind the house. As we rode closer, we could see there was more distance between the bluff and the house than we thought, and that distance was filled up with orchards of several kinds. The bluff was north of the trees and seemed to serve as a wind break of sorts and probably protected the fruit from some of the worse weather.

As we rode into the yard a group of men in work clothes were straggling out of one of the barns and seemed to be headed for the back of the main house.

I hailed one of the older men and asked, "Can we water our horses and buy some grain from you?"

"Surely you can," he said. "Do what you need to and come sit with us. The ladies just took some apple, cherry and peach pies out of the oven and we're going to have some."

That sounded so inviting that we hurried with our chores and were soon sitting with the men being served several kinds of pie by the women, who then sat down themselves and joined us.

The older man at the head of the long table said, "We're the Collins family and assorted cousins and uncles and brothers. I'm Joe and this is my wife Harriet. We all live in this area and when need be, get together to get a job done. We're putting new roofs on one of the barns and several other outbuildings and this is part of the pay." He indicated the food on the table.

One of the women, apparently his wife, leaned forward and said, "These pies are made from fruit we put up last year. We won't get our crop in the barn for a while, so you'll have to come back and join us then."

Handy introduced us and told a little about our trip, which generated more than a few questions. We asked about North Platte, when would we get there and how big was the town?

Joseph Collins answered. "It's about two hours ride and there may be three or four thousand people living there now. One of our local citizens is famous, you know," he said. "You may have heard of Buffalo Bill? He's putting together a show of some sort that he's hoping will go through the East and show the people back there what the West really is and was."

"Actually, I've heard he doesn't like the word show; it's an extravaganza. I've heard It's supposed to be quite a big thing and could put

North Platte on the map. All sorts of people coming into town from what I hear, so I'm sure it will look quite busy."

"Do they have a hotel in town?" I asked, "We'd like a soak and a good meal."

"We've got a first-class hotel," he said, "Back in the winter of '67, the headquarters for the railroad was here while they tooled up to get started the following spring. The railroad built a big hotel for all the people that came to town for one thing and another. All though the railroad people are mostly gone, the hotel's still here, so they can likely accommodate you, though with all the show people coming to town, maybe not."

He thought for a minute and asked," How long are you planning to stay? Cause there's a widow lady that runs a boarding house around the corner from the hotel who usually has rooms when it's full."

"We might try her first," Handy said, "usually get good food at those kinds of places."

One of the men at the table spoke up. "Best meals in town are at the hotel dining room from what I hear."

The men all got up to go back to work but Mr. Collins sat and talked a while. When I mentioned that I had not seen so many fruit trees on one place before, he grinned.

"Few years back one of our young nephews went to the state university at Lincoln and came home with a new idea," he said. "While he was there, he saw refrigerated rail cars and studied how to use them for shipping farm goods. When he came home, he convinced us to switch our main crop to fruit. With the cold cars we ship our stuff all over the place and we're doing right well."

We left the Collins's with a jar each of canned apples, cherries and peaches and were looking forward to eating them right out of the jars. Jinx didn't care for fruit, so we'd get it all.

We rode into North Platte in the early evening of a summer day. The hotel did have rooms and we were soon checking out a bed on the third floor from a room overlooking Main street. Jinx sat on the roof and looked around while we unpacked.

While we were there, we planned to take advantage of the new indoor plumbing by taking hot baths. We also had some clothes that needed to be washed so we stopped at the front desk to arrange it and followed Jinx into the dining room.

It's funny that no one had ever objected to Jinx in a dining room. Maybe because it was so unusual, and he was a pretty well-behaved cat. He usually ate under the table and was content to sit in either Handy's or my lap and take a bath or doze until we got up to leave. He was sitting in Handy's lap when Mr. Cody walked by our table.

He was walking behind what looked like a group of businessmen, and when he saw Handy, he looked startled. I'm sure it was the first time he'd ever seen a blond giant sitting in a hotel dining room with a black cat in his lap. He turned and nodded at me and his smile changed into a puzzled look.

"I know you from somewhere, young man," he said. "Help me out here." He put out his hand and I took it.

"You sat with my Pa and me one night over our livery stable in Junction City, Kansas and talked for a couple of hours about riding the Pony Express when you were a kid," I said, shaking his hand.

"Your Pa was John Fry," he said with a large grin on his face, "You'd be young Johnny, though not so young anymore."

He turned to shake Handy's hand and said, "I've got some business with these gentlemen, but I'd like to sit and talk after we finish. Say 7:00 in the bar?" We agreed and he caught up with his friends.

At a few minutes before seven Handy, Jinx and I were sitting in the classiest bar we'd ever seen. Granted, neither of us were too experienced with bars, but this one looked and felt special.

With all the bad stuff I had seen come out of the saloons of Junction City, I had decided not to go into them. I figured it would save me a lot of grief and heartache. This one was mostly quiet, except for an occasional burst of laughter from some men playing poker in the back corner. Mr. Cody came in almost right behind us, stopped at the bar to order us a beer and sat down across the table from us.

"How's your Pa?" he asked right off.

"Pa died a few weeks ago," I said.

He leaned back in his chair and shook his head. "I'm sorry to hear that, Johnny," he said. "I always felt he was a special fellow. I remember him as a racehorse rider and a damn good one when he was about your age. By the way call me Bill, it's easier than Mr. Cody."

We talked for an hour about this and that and finally he lit a cigar and said. "You may have heard about what I'm doing these days. I put on, what I call, Buffalo Bill's Wild West in Omaha last year and it was a great success so now I'm trying to put together something else; a traveling thing that will tour all over the country, especially the big cities of the East. I have some people backing me so we will have the cash to do it right."

He turned to Handy and said, "Handy, I'd like to offer you a job in my Wild West production"

Handy looked startled, his mouth fell open and his eyes bulged a bit. I slid out of my seat and said to Handy, "I'll see you upstairs and you can tell me all about it."

Jinx and I took a short walk along the board walk in front of the hotel and then climbed the stairs to the room. Handy came in about an hour later.

He closed the door and leaned against it, hands running over his head. From my place on the bed I could see the lines bunched on his forehead, could almost hear the noise of thoughts running through his mind. Finally, he shook his head and said, "Gawd a mighty, Johnny," he said. "He's offering me the moon and the stars."

"It looks like you want to talk about it," I said. "So have a seat and get started."

He took off his shirt, walked to the window and stood looking out into the dark. Suddenly he turned and blurted, "He's talking about $100.00 a week to start, with a raise to $150.00 after he sees how I fit." He paused. "He'd pay for everything; new clothes, the best horses, beautiful saddle and tack, everything first class. And women. The way he talks they'll be lining up at the gate just to get a look at me. I'd live in hotels mostly and he'd pay for everything."

I must have had a big grin on my face at this point. Cowboys and farmhands I knew made forty a month and found and saw a woman who wasn't married or a whore maybe once a year.

"So, what do you think?" I asked. "Sounds to me like the best thing ever to come down the trail."

He shook his head, "Johnny, I grew up on a farm," he said. "The only Indians I ever saw were in the general store back home. I never fired a pistol more than ten times in my life before I joined up with you.

He wants me to be a cowboy, a gunfighter, and Indian fighter and God knows what else. I'd be the biggest fake in the world."

He was pacing by this time and at a pause on the far side of the room almost moaned, "Johnny, he's hiring me because of what I look like and I'd got to learn to be all these other things."

He stopped pacing and stood in the middle of the room with his arms folded across his chest. "There's two things I been thinking about," he said. "First, I'd have to become a whole different me. What I've been up to now would be gone, completely covered over by this new me. I'm not sure I like that idea, and second, I'm not sure I could do it if I tried. I mean, what if I let you go off by yourself and I can't do what he wants? Then what? I'd be giving up something I'll never have a chance to so again for something I'm not sure I want to do anyway, just for the money."

"And a few other things," I said, grinning. "Well, why don't you sleep on it and see what you think in the morning."

CHAPTER SEVEN

⫸

J inx was a good alarm clock. He seldom let me sleep past what he thought was time for breakfast, and since Handy joined he had been getting roused at the same time. We followed Jinx downstairs and into the dining room for the best breakfast I'd ever had, then sat on the porch to let it settle and wait for Bill, who was supposed to meet us at 10:00.

When we were both seated in rocking chairs, cat in my lap, he finally brought up the subject but in a roundabout way. "Are we leaving today?" he asked.

"So, you made up your mind?" I asked.

"Well, I look at it like this. This trip with you two is a once in a lifetime thing and I want to go along" he said. "As far as Mr. Cody, if his show is a success, when I come back, I'll maybe have grown up enough and learned enough that it won't be so scary to me and maybe then I can do it. But right now, I don't think I could if I tried."

"I'm glad to hear it," I said. "I like having you around and I know Jinx feels the same way."

A few minutes later Bill rode up to the hitching rail. He came up on the porch, leaned against the porch railing and said with a smile,

"I'd say from the look of you, you've made up your mind to go on with your trip."

Handy nodded. "Yes sir, I have," he said. "I can't leave Johnny with only Jinx to look out for him. When we get where we're going, I might just send you a wire applying for a job, but I want to get there first."

"Well I must say it doesn't surprise me," Cody said. "At your age I'd probably done the same. That's quite an adventure you boys have in front of you. When are you planning to leave?"

"I think I want one more breakfast at the hotel, and we'll pull out in the morning," I said with a glance at Handy. He nodded his agreement.

"My place, 'Scout's Rest', is out of town on the north road. If you're not in a hurry, stop out and we can have lunch and we can talk a bit about the trip," Cody said. "I've got to meet some people and I'll be tied up all day today, but I'd love to show you around the place and maybe tell you a few things that will help you on your journey. I have been over a lot of that country."

'Scout's Rest' was a half day's ride out of town and we got there just in time for lunch the next day with Cody and Frank North, his partner at the ranch.

They had established a partnership in 1878 and North found the land about twenty miles north of town. He had stocked it by buying Texas cattle in Ogallala and mixed them with some short-horned stock brought from the east. It had the beginnings of being something special.

The house sat back in a grove of trees. Cody and North met us on the porch, and we sat there to talk until lunch was ready. It was the first time in my life I was served by servants. Afterwards North departed on some ranch business. The three of us sat on the porch and watched Jinx explore the front yard and climb a few trees.

"Where do you go from here?" Cody asked. "The Pony trail crosses the river west of town and it goes over to Julesburg in Colorado. You plan on heading that way?

"That's what we planned," I said. "So far we've been able to keep to the trail, and if we can we want to take it all the way."

Cody lit a cigar and said, "Let me tell you about Julesburg." He sat for minute. "As a hunter for the railroad and a scout for the army, I've seen all the towns of western Nebraska, Wyoming and Colorado. The end-of-track towns were the worst, and the worst of those was Julesburg." He paused to let that sink in.

"Gamblers, thieves, murderers, conmen, common thugs and gunfighters, all trying to separate the railroad men from their money. Some of these towns have proved up and become nice places, like North Platte and Kearney, but Julesburg hasn't changed much." He blew out a cloud of smoke. "If you go in, be careful," he said. "There are people there who would steal your long johns while you slept and cut your throat if you objected."

Handy and I both chuckled at this, but we took the warning seriously. From what I'd read and seen on a map, there was a way around the town. The Pony ran south of Julesburg to a ford at Overland City on the South Platte, a few miles west of town.

"That seems to be the best way to avoid trouble," I said.

"I'd agree," said Cody. "You can stock up when you go back through North Platte. And something else to remember, there's not much between Julesburg and the Wyoming Territory. You've got an extra horse, so I'd think carefully about what you're going to need. Ammunition, food, water; make sure you got the essentials, but take a few things for comfort and enjoyment too."

When we were mounted, he stood between our horses and grasped my hand, then Handy's and finally Jinx's paw.

"One final piece of advice," he said. "If you must draw your gun on someone, shoot to kill because the other fellow will, I assure you. Firing a warning shot or shooting to wound could get you killed." He looked up at Handy and said, "When you get there, wire me and we can talk about that job."

When we turned on the crest of a small hill to look back, he was still standing on the porch smoking his cigar.

We stopped for the night early, and I got out pencil and paper to make a list of the things we wanted to buy on the way through town. We got back into North Platte just shy of noon the next day, and with everything packed, rode out of town about an hour later.

The trail now lay along the south bank of the South Platte, but to get to it we had to cross the North Platte and then the South Platte. Since both fords had been used by a lot of people and livestock since the 1840's they were well marked and firm. We had no trouble and were soon riding across some beautiful country in the afternoon of a beautiful day. We were in no hurry and it was a good time to talk, so we talked.

"So, what did you think about Mr. Cody?" asked Handy.

"I think I'm glad we met him," I said. "Before I left Junction City, people told me the world was a dangerous place and I've found that's true. But I've got a list in my mind of the good people I've met since I started this trip and Buffalo Bill Cody is on that list."

"Yeah," said Handy, "he's on my list too. What did you think of his advice?"

"I think if we make it to Sacramento, his advice will be one of the reasons," I said.

Cottonwoods lined the river along a stretch where we stopped to water the horses and let them crop some grass. Handy was sitting on a tree trunk petting Jinx when he looked up and asked, "Johnny, have you ever killed anybody?"

Considering the talk with Cody and our scrap back in Kearney, I had been thinking along the same lines. "No, never have," I answered. "Closest I've come is that time with the Gambler back in Marysville."

"That's something Pa and I talked about when we were shooting, and sometimes at night by the fire when we were camping," I said. "He said a gun is a tool, and unless you're practicing, don't draw it unless you need to use it."

Handy scratched his head and looked out across the river. "It seems to me," he said, "that since we're riding into country where men carry guns, we need to talk about how we're going to deal with them if we have to. I mean, it's a little late to think about whether or not you could kill a man when he's pulling a gun on you."

"I guess Pa killed his share of men during the war," I said, 'but he never liked it. He told me once to do what you have to when you have to, but it's ok to regret it; it's ok to wish you hadn't had to."

"But he also told me if you have to shoot a man, aim for the middle of the chest, that way if you miss, you'll still hit something vital."

"I imagine if you hit him anywhere in the chest with a .44 slug, he'd have real problems," Handy said with a chuckle. He stood up and stretched. "I guess what it amounts to is, men wear guns to protect themselves. If you need to and you don't, you'll likely be dead, and the right and wrong of it won't matter anymore."

That night we practiced with the guns.

It was two-day ride to Julesburg, and rather than get there at night, we camped early the next night. By mid-morning we were halfway around the town when Dusty began to limp. A quick look and we found a split shoe and, just like that, our plan to avoid Julesburg was gone.

The only place for a hundred miles to get a new shoe put on was, we hoped, in Julesburg. We might even have to get a shoe and do it ourselves. The livery stable was on the river side of main street when we rode into town, and we stopped there to see about solving our problem.

The proprietor was, like Pa, a jack of all trades and in the middle of replacing a wagon tire, so it would be a couple of hours before he could get to it. We left Jinx exploring the loft and walked two doors down to the local café to have a bite while we waited.

Within an hour the blacksmith came in. He had finished the tire quicker than he thought and after a cup of coffee, he told us he'd do the shoeing and have us on the road in a half an hour.

"You don't rent out that cat do you?" he asked with a grin. "He brought me a dead mouse a little while ago. I imagine he'd be right handy to have around." Jinx had come in with him and the owner of the café had immediately declared him to be 'precious' and given him a dish of chicken and gravy. No wonder he thought he was something.

I was tightening the girth on Black's saddle when a couple of cowboys came out of the saloon across the street. One of them was obviously drunk. He looked at Black, pushed his friend aside and came across the street, staggering a little, to where I was standing waiting for Handy.

He pushed me aside and said, "I'm going to take this horse for a ride."

He was halfway into the saddle when I grabbed his belt and pulled him backwards. Working in the blacksmith shop with Pa had given me strong hands and arms, and he staggered backwards and sat down in a fresh pile that some horse had just dropped.

His friend, coming across the street, let out a whoop of laughter and the cowboy reacted with fury. He staggered to his feet, and with a snarl, his hand dropped to his gun.

My bullet hit him in the middle of his chest.

CHAPTER EIGHT

Handy had just come out of the restaurant. He took in the scene at a glance, and in three long strides he was beside the other cowboy, holding his wrist so he couldn't draw his gun.

"Don't do anything you'll be sorry for," he said in a quiet voice. The cowboy looked up at him for a moment then let go of the gun. Handy quickly threw it into a water trough and let him go.

"Gawd amighty," he moaned, "what am I going to tell the boys?"

"Tell them he died of his own stupidity," said the owner of the general store who had come out to see what the fuss was. "He was going to shoot this boy because he fell in some horseshit. He's lucky someone hasn't done it before now."

I had turned toward them, gun in hand, and now turned back to the man I had shot. He was lying on his back, shoulders and neck up against the edge of the boardwalk. I stood looking at his face for a long moment and felt several people come up around me. When I looked up I saw one of them had a star on his shirt.

An hour later I was sitting in the café, Jinx in my lap, rubbing my forehead and thinking. Handy had taken over and done everything necessary to get us out of Julesburg and back on the trail.

The deputy had asked a few questions, listened to a few witnesses, and told us we could go. The cowboys worked at a local ranch, and while he didn't think it would be a problem, he thought it might be best if we got out of town as soon as possible.

While all this was swirling around me, I sat wondering about how much my life had changed in the last hour. How much of a line had I crossed? Was it one that separated me from what I had been? I guess I had known this moment would come but thought it would be later, when I was older and better able to handle it.

I knew it gave me something to talk to Handy about as we rode west and while we sat around the fire at night. Though I'd only known him for about a week, I knew they'd be good talks and would help me get a hold of what had just happened.

The first couple of hours back on the trail we were both quiet though. We left Julesburg around dinner time, but since we weren't hungry, we rode for a while. Near dark we found a nice bend in the river and a clearing in some cottonwoods. It was defensible and had a place to picket the horses close to a creek that ran down to the river. When we had coffee in our hands after dinner, I said, "We've had time to think about it, so talk to me."

He looked at me over the fire and shook his head. "It's as new and out of the blue to me as it is to you," he said. He had Jinx's rope in his hand and was playing with him kind of absent-mindedly.

"We tried to avoid the place and we sure weren't looking for trouble," he said. "Five people said you did what you had to, so maybe we can just put it behind us and move on." He and Jinx got into a tug of war for a minute and then he said, "It's either that or carry it with us and that kind of thing can get heavy after a while."

"Hmm," I leaned back against the tree behind me. "I don't know if I can just forget it like that. Killing a man ought to be more important, somehow."

"I can see that," he said. "But look at it like this. If thinkin' about it makes you not do it so good next time, it could get you killed. I believe we're going to run into a lot more of this kind of thing the farther west we go. If the next time someone draws a gun on you, you're slower because you're thinkin' about that cowboy back there," his voice trailed off. He shook his head, and sat looking at me.

"Have all the conscience you want, Johnny," he said after a minute, "but don't let it get you killed."

It was hard to argue with his logic. So, we didn't have to talk about it nearly as much as I thought we would. He was right. If I'd have let scruples about killing a man keep me from defending myself back there, then that drunken cowboy would have gone on living and I could have died. Where we were going, I might be forced to do it again and more than once. If I didn't do it right, the results could be painful, even fatal.

Nice thing about talking to Handy; he got to the heart of the matter real quick.

After the Pony crossed the South Platte at Overland City, just west of Julesburg, it bent west along Lodgepole Creek and for about forty miles we rode within sight of the creek, crossing it several times and camping beside it one night. The final time we crossed it, we rode past what was likely the sight of the Pole Creek Pony Station. Here the trail swung around to the north and headed back to the North Platte River, about a day's ride distant.

We were getting out of the farming country and into the grass-lands. A few years ago, there would have been a good chance to see millions of buffalo moving steadily across the landscape and likely many Indians. The Indians of the Plains had created a life woven into the movements and habits of the buffalo. With the great herds gone, they were gone too, mostly driven onto reservations by the US Army. This was becoming ranching country, with a few big ranches controlling large areas and a few small ranches living on the edges.

To see the grass out there was something you never forgot. The wind rippling through a field of grass in the moonlight, stretching out of sight in every direction, was a sight to behold.

Of course, railroads changed this country just like they changed the country in any place they ran. Right after the war, cattle came mostly from Texas. Thousands of them had been left to run wild when Texas men had gone off to war. When the railroads began building, these cattle were rounded up and driven north to the railheads in Kansas for sale or slaughter and shipment back east.

I'd read some about the men who had begun the great cattle drives. They were men who had resources and vision, but mainly they were leaders of men. These men talked young men and boys into work-ing for forty dollars a month and found, day and night, in all weather, for months at a time without a day off. While some of the leaders got rich in the process, most of the cowboys just got old; but along the way, they had changed the way people ate in this country.

After a few years of cattle drives, some people in western Kansas and Nebraska looked around and wondered why they should bring the cows all the way up from Texas when they could raise them around here and not walk the fat off them getting them to market. So, they brought in cattle from the east and from Oregon, mixed them with some bought from the Texas herds, and a new industry was born. The great cattle drives were suddenly a thing of the past.

First thing we noticed about the North Platte was that it was a different kind of river here than it was 150 miles east of here. No question it was clearer. I imagined it was a fact that the farther west we came the less sand and dirt there was to carry downstream. When I first saw the Platte, it was a creamy brown; here it was a clear, pretty mountain river that had found the plains.

Rain clouds were building the next morning when we came to Courthouse Rock and Jail Rock, and to a couple of flatlanders, the sight of those huge, gray and white buildings with dark grey clouds towering above them was enough to make a jaw drop. That's what they looked like, buildings.

We could see lightning flashes in the clouds and began to look around for a place to hole up. Unfortunately, we were a long way from any place that would keep us dry, so we set up a tarp among some trees that were on the side of a hill away from the coming storm and waited for it to hit.

We spent the next hour holding on to everything we didn't want to have blown away and getting soaked in the process. I'd seen a few like this in Kansas but it was new to Handy.

We spent another hour wringing things out and laying them out to dry in the sun. Jinx was the only one who didn't get wet. I had put him in his box and covered it before the storm hit.

I had seen a covey of prairie grouse within walking distance, so while Handy was laying in the sun drying out, I loaded the ten-gage with bird shot and went hunting. An hour later I came back with six of them. Firing one barrel after the other I got them all in one sweep.

That ten-gauge sure did give you an advantage, though it was hard on the shoulder.

It was such a beautiful afternoon that we decided to spend the rest of the day there and go on in the morning. We made this decision mainly because the idea of prairie grouse roasted over a nice fire made our mouths water. While Handy built up the fire and cut and cleaned several skewers, I cleaned the birds and then the two of us picked out what shot we could find. In a surprisingly short time, the birds were being turned over the fire and we were reduced to defending them from Jinx. Fire or no fire, he wanted some and patience was not his strong suit.

They were excellent, the best thing we'd eaten since we left North Platte. We each ate two, keeping the other two for breakfast and still had enough to keep Jinx busy eating while we finished ours.

Later that evening I stood staring at those huge rocks and thinking how many people had passed this way over the same trail we were riding. People going to Oregon and California, and The Dakotas; people going to find gold and build farms and raise families; and in the case of the Mormons, people going to their promised land. I wondered why so few of them chose to stay here instead. A land that would feed that many buffalo for that many years would have to be good for raising almost any kind of grazing animal. I guessed it just didn't fit their dreams.

CHAPTER NINE

The next morning, after a bird breakfast for all three of us, we packed up and headed west. Apparently, the storm had dumped a lot of water into the river west of us. In some places it was out of its banks and some of the creeks were running so high we had to work our way upstream to cross them.

About once a day we saw a train passing each way, but the tracks were usually so far away we couldn't see the people riding in the cars. When they built the railroad, they knew the river would flood in the spring and at other times, so they built it far enough away so that it would be safe.

Occasionally, we'd see a section gang working on a water tower or building a place to store wood or the coal they were burning now. They were never close enough to talk to, though.

We camped in sight of Chimney Rock that evening. It looked like a man's hand with the first finger pointed at God. When I mentioned this to Handy, he thought about it for a minute and then asked me, "Johnny do you believe in God?"

"I never have been able to figure that one out," I answered. "I've read some stuff about religion, but it didn't talk about God much. More about how we should treat each other."

I thought for a moment and then continued. "It seems to me there are an awful lot of churches and each one of them believes something different. And each one seems to believe their way is right and the others are wrong. I remember Pa and I talking about it and he said he didn't think God put much stock in religion. He believed religion should be about how people treat each other, and not so much about following rules that had been written down a couple thousand years ago and worrying about the people who didn't."

"Church back home was a lot like the Grange," Handy said. "A place where people got together and helped one another because when they needed help, people were there to help them. We had dances and weddings and suppers at the church, and a whole lot else, but I don't really believe people paid much attention to the rules and such. They just did what they believed was right."

Later that night, lying beside a dying fire, looking up and thinking, I could see how someone could believe in God. But whether he was there or not didn't really matter when you looked up at the night sky.

Looking up at the stars, I remembered some of the talks I'd had with Pa. He was almost driven to read, and many of our conversations round the stove, after work was finished for the day, began with "I'm reading this book…", and off we'd go into a discussion of whatever book, magazine or newspaper we happened to be involved in right then.

He would read most anything and by the time I was ten or eleven I was much the same way. He was a natural teacher and I could see how much he enjoyed helping me understand things that puzzled me at first look. We'd talked about the moon and the stars and other things, almost too many to count.

Lying there, Jinx purring on my chest, I could almost hear Pa's voice sharing with me all he had done and believed and felt so I wouldn't have to learn it the hard way.

Talking to the blacksmith at Julesburg, we had learned of a trading post at Scott's Bluff which was a bit more than a day's ride west, so we stopped for the night a little early. From what we knew, the place was about ten miles farther on, so we planned on a morning arrival.

Scott's Bluff began rising out of the prairie almost as soon as we hit the trail the next day. It was a huge, grey rock that looked a lot like what I'd think a castle would look, with towers on top and steep walls protecting the people inside. By the time the sun was well up we could see the trail turning to pass through the Bluff and as we came out of the pass, we saw the trading post in the distance.

We didn't have to get too close to realize it wasn't much; a low soddy, with a sod roof that had a couple of goats grazing on it. There were frames for windows but where glass would have been there was oiled paper.

Trash and manure were scattered across the front of the place, and even out here in the fresh air we could smell a rancid odor coming from inside.

"Just so's you'll know," said Handy as we dismounted at the only piece of wood in view and tied the horses, "I ain't interested in eating anything they got to sell."

When we followed Jinx into the place, the first thing we saw was a big piece of canvas lying on the floor beside the doorway. With no door in sight, this apparently was to keep the varmints out at night. Jinx hopped up on it and began to examine some of the fascinating odors, tail lashing.

"Get that damned cat out of here," growled a voice from behind a counter that stretched across one end of the place. I stood, a little startled by this, and as my eyes adjusted to the light, I could see the speaker, a tall lanky fellow with a long scraggly dirty looking beard. He came around the counter and advanced on us. "Did you hear me? I said out," he almost shouted and swung a foot at Jinx, who dodged and jumped on to my shoulder from the tarp.

"Mister, that cat ain't hurting you," Handy said mildly and he shifted the ten-gage from the crook of his arm to his hands. He had brought it into the store to see if they had any shells to fit it, but now he was ready to use it if necessary.

Apparently, the sight of a very large man holding a very large gun made the fellow pause and he stopped. "I hate cats," he said, a threat in his voice, "so if you want to keep him alive get him out of my reach."

I considered the situation, and while I was thinking about it, a man who had been sitting in a chair propped against the back wall brought it down with a crash and bolted out a back door behind the counter.

I nodded at the proprietor and said, "Ok," and began to back out of the door, my hand close to the Colt. I took it for granted Handy would cover me with the ten-gage, and when I got outside, I drew my Colt and faced the door to cover him while he mounted.

When he was up, facing the door, shotgun in hand, I holstered the Colt and started to mount when the proprietor came out the door followed by three other men, all wearing guns, including the man who'd been sitting in the chair.

As a kid I had learned that when someone pushes you, push back hard and it usually saved you a lot of trouble in the long run. Handy cocked both hammers on the ten-gage, and when they looked at him, I drew the Colt again so when they looked back at me, it was pointed right at the middle of the headman's chest.

We all stood looking at one another for a bit and then I said, "If anything starts, you die first, and I'll bet not one person within a hundred miles would give a damn if I pulled the trigger."

From three feet away he knew I couldn't miss, and suddenly he had a sickly smile on his face. "No reason to get upset, boys. Is there anything you need? We'd be glad to do business with you."

"I'd never do business with a man who's rude to my cat," said Handy. He was looking at the two men standing in front of him when he said, "You know, I'll bet this ten-gage would take a good bit of you fellows right through that wall behind you."

He let them think about that for a minute and continued, "It would be a big mistake to think of us as boys. That fellow right there has a seventeen shot Henry rifle and, as you might have noticed, he's pretty handy with that six-gun. I've got a Winchester and this here cannon. If we see you anywhere, anytime, were going to suspect you of being up to something and we're going to start shooting. Understand? Now take out your pistols and throw them on the ground."

When all four pistols were lying in the dirt he said, "now kick them away."

By that time, I was mounted and continuing to cover them, we carefully turned our horses and spurred them into a gallop. When I glanced back, they were all picking up the guns, but no one seemed inclined to use them.

From that day forward things were different. Before we had glanced over our shoulders, but we didn't worry too much about being followed. Now being able to defend our campsite was the first thing we thought about. One of us stood guard while the other did the unpacking and setting up camp, and one of us was watching our back trail and scanning the area while the other was fixing dinner or doing camp chores. The guard always had the Henry Rifle and the telescope, and we always arranged things so he would have a clear shot if someone approached.

We had no idea if we were being followed by the men from the trading post, but rather than take a chance and get caught unawares, we decided to be cautious. We talked a lot about tactics and defense and within a few days, had a regular routine in place to provide us cover if we needed it. Since we knew we'd be outnumbered, the plan was to get off the first shot and cut down the odds.

When we camped that first night after our faceoff at the trading post, I took the old holster Handy's Pa had given him with the pistol and, with some leather and tools I had brought with me, reworked it so it would work better for a cross draw.

Three days after the problem at the trading post, we camped on a rise about a hundred yards off the trail, and after dinner, moved out away from camp to practice with the Colts for a while.

Handy was improving rapidly but he still didn't like the .36 caliber pistol he had brought from home. He had been practicing drawing and shooting from the hip but seemed to have trouble getting the knack of it.

"It's like you're pointing your finger at something," I said. I had practiced with Pa so much it was just natural for the Colt to find its target.

When we got back to camp, he sank down cross-legged on the ground, took Jinx into his lap and sat stroking him and looking off into the dark. I walked to where the horses were picketed, opened my saddle bag and took out the Gambler's gun.

I hadn't paid much attention to it before. Looking at it with the eye of a gunsmith's son, I could see it was a beautiful piece. It was a Colt .45 caliber Peacemaker revolver with the seven-and-a-half-inch barrel of the original model. The medal was dark, almost black and that made the scrimshawed ivory grips standout like none I'd ever seen. It was amazingly balanced and fitted into the hand like it belonged. The sight was gone but where it had been there was no trace and the etching on the barrel and the frame was intricate and unlike any I'd ever seen.

He looked up at me when I walked back into the firelight. I handed him the gun. He took it, looked at it for a moment, then looked at me with his eyes wide and his mouth slightly open. With an almost bemused expression on his face he put Jinx down and slowly began to uncoil himself to his full height. The old gun was gone and the new one, in the old remade holster, looked like a jewel in the weeds. He stood for a second and suddenly the gun was in his hand.

He stood for a moment, the gun aimed at the dark like a finger pointing, then turned with the gun reversed in his hand.

"Johnny I can't take this," he said. "If you want to give me a gun, give me yours and you take this one."

I shook my head. "Pa gave me this gun when I was thirteen," I said. "He taught me how to shoot with it and how to take care of it. Whenever I fire it, or clean it or just look at it, I remember him."

"Look Handy, you need a gun, I have a gun I'm not using; it's as simple as that. But think about this. In Kearney, the day after I met you, you helped me out in a fight that could have meant the end of this trip if I had lost. In Julesburg I would have been shot, maybe killed, if you hadn't stepped in. That cowboy might have been sorry later, but he sure enough would have shot me if you hadn't stopped him," I said. "The other day at the trading post I didn't need to look. I knew you were there. You're the kind of friend most men will never have. Just take the damn gun."

He grinned, reversed the gun and slid it back into the holster. "Thanks," he said.

CHAPTER TEN

T he next morning, we rode through Fort Laramie. I say rode through
it because a quick glance helped us decide we didn't need anything they
had. Casper was our next stop, and unlike Fort Laramie, it was an actual
town. If we pushed it a bit, we could get there on the morning of the
fourth day, so we pushed it a bit.

The ride to Casper was amazing for two boys from the flat lands
who had never seen anything quite like the mountains rising before us
and running away to the north and south, or the hills and buttes we
rode around or through.

Topping a rise and stopping to let the horses take a breather and
take a quick meal, we sat there and took it all in.

"It feels like a cool drink of water for your soul," said Handy after
a minute.

Even though I wasn't really sure about the soul part of it, I had
to agree.

That night at the fire, I held out a handful of cartridges to Handy
and he went off to practice with a smile. Until we could be assured of
resupply, we had decided not to waste bullets. Tonight though, I thought

he might want to practice firing the gun, and we could spare a few shells. Rather than go with him I sat by the fire and counted the shots.

Pa had taught me dry firing a weapon is bad for it, and I had passed this on to Handy. When we practiced, we would draw and cock and then release the hammer gently and let it seat. After he ran through his allotment of shells, I heard the metallic clicking of him going through the drill. He kept at it as the evening darkened. When he finally came back, I judged he had been at it for an hour and a half.

"What do you think?" I asked when he finally sat down by the fire.

He sat for a minute, seemingly thinking and said, "I've never seen anything like it. It seems to jump into my hand, and I hit everything I aimed at." He paused for a moment then added, "It felt like the most natural thing I've ever done." He smiled and looked at me. "It was just like you said, 'like pointing a finger.'"

For the next three days we started early and rode until evening, usually setting up camp at dusk. We were both anxious to see people again. We'd had no one to talk to since we left Julesburg and seen only a couple of cowboys at a distance. Of course, we weren't counting the men at the trading post. You never really count that kind.

We rode into Casper late one afternoon, ten days after we left Julesburg. It was a small place but like most places we had passed through, people were building, and for the first time I realized the prairie was really behind us. Everything here was built out of wood and there was new lumber all around us. That wasn't the case back on the plains where most places were built of sod and trees were an occasional thing.

And then there were the mountains, Mount Casper the most immediate. We had been watching it get bigger every day but seeing it up close was almost hypnotizing. One of the deputies at the Sheriff's

Office told us it was over 8000 feet high and he knew people who had climbed it.

There was a message for us from Handy's Uncle Joe. The Gambler's friends had broken him out of jail. No one was injured and the culprits were seen but not stopped in North Platte. The message was ten days old.

There was no way to know if they were pursuing us, but it would hurt nothing to be alert and careful. When we left the Sheriff's Office, we led our horses across the street to where the town's only hotel was located. In addition to being a hotel it was a café, a saloon, a barber shop and, according to the deputy, the permanent home of the town's only doctor, who usually had office hours in the saloon. He advised us not to get sick or shot while we were in town.

The hotel room was small and crude, but dry, and the bed reasonably comfortable. Jinx climbed out the window and sat on the upper porch watching the town while Handy and I unpacked our duffel and tested the bed. Before dinner I went down to the café to see if they had a problem with Jinx eating under our table. They didn't and Jinx led the way an hour or so later.

The little place was crowded but we got the last table and ordered our dinner. While we were eating, an old black man came in the door and stood looking over the room. When he saw there was a seat at our table, he wove his way through the other tables and stopped in front of us.

"Do you gentlemen mind if I join you?" he asked in a deep, gravelly voice, with a friendly smile. He wasn't as old as he had looked across the room, maybe 45 or so. He was short and stocky with white hair and the most bowed legs I'd ever seen.

Handy looked at me and when I nodded my head said, "Sit you down, Sir. We're happy to have you, though we're just finishing up. We might have a cup of coffee with you, though."

He pulled out the chair and sat. "The name's George Washington Moore, "He paused and said with a big smile, "Call me Wash," he said.

'Johnny Fry," I said, and indicated Handy, "Handy Josephson." We held out our hands and he shook each in turn.

A chair scraped at the next table and a roughly dressed man stood and said in a loud voice. "Where I come from, we don't let niggers eat with white folks." Our guest hunched his shoulders forward. He wasn't smiling anymore.

I could see the owner coming out from behind the bar and could feel the tension rising in the room. Handy slipped his gun out and laid it on the table next to his plate.

The man at the next table looked startled, "What's that for?" he asked.

"Varmints," said Handy with a straight face.

"Are you calling me a varmint?" he asked with a threat in his voice.

"No sir, I'm not," said Handy, "You asked me why I put the gun on the table, and I told you. You never know when you're going to see a rat."

Even when Handy was sitting down it was easy to see he was a very large fellow and his hand was resting on the gun. I could almost see the fellow's horns pull in. He picked his hat up off the table and stalked out of the room.

The owner of the place got to our table as this scene was ending. He looked at Wash and said politely, "I'm sorry Sir, but we can't serve you in here. I have no problems with you eating here but I can't afford to lose my customers. You're probably leaving tomorrow but I've got to live here."

Wash bowed his head for a moment, then looked up and said, "I understand," he said.

The owner continued, "If you want to come around back, you can sit in the kitchen and eat."

Wash's face had an unreadable expression on it. "Thank you, sir," he said in that deep gravelly voice, "but no thanks. I'm not so hungry after all."

When we came out of the place there was no sign of him. He was a strange looking man and for some reason, I was fascinated by him. Though we were leaving in the morning I somehow knew I would see him again.

There was chill in the air when we walked out of the hotel the next morning. In late June it felt a little strange, but I knew it was the altitude. We were probably a mile above sea level, and we were getting up into the mountains.

We had a few things to do before we left so, we split up to save time. Handy walked down to the Sheriff's Office to send a telegram to his uncle, while I went into the general store.

A couple days before I'd torn one of my shirts on a low hanging branch and I wanted to see if they had any that would fit me. The lady behind the counter showed me what she had, but they all seemed a bit too big for me.

"Pick the one you want, and I'll run it up for you" she said.

I looked at her for a moment, trying to figure out what she meant. "I have a sewing machine in the back. For an extra quarter I'll make it fit," she said then added, "While I'm at it I'll fix the other one if you leave it. No charge."

She had me take my shirt off and put a string around my chest, then across my shoulders and finally, down my arm. She told me it would be ready in about an hour.

While I put my shirt back on, I watched her take each piece of string and lay it along a strip of wood. She wrote some numbers down and disappeared into a back room.

Instead of hanging around waiting, I decided to walk down to the livery stable to get the horses and bring them back to the hotel where we could load them. Handy joined me there and, after several trips to the room we were ready to go.

Thinking about her measuring me gave me an idea. When she came out of the back carrying my shirt, I asked her, "Would you let me use that string and your measuring stick for something?"

"Of course," she said, and opened the gate to let me behind the counter. I brought Handy over and measured him then he did the same for me. "I'm 5' 9" and it looks like you're 6' 8-1/2'," I told him.

He grinned. "Always wondered how tall I am," he said. We rode out of town a few minutes later.

We were among the evergreens now, riding south and a little west. Casper Mountain rose steeply on our right hand. We were leaving the North Platte for good now and rode across a meadow bordered by trees for several miles to strike a wooded trail that led to the Sweetwater River.

Jinx was riding in front of me on the saddle when we came out of the woods on a bend in the river and saw as pretty a mountain stream as you could imagine. I sat stroking him while Handy caught up. We both took a deep breath and looked around for a minute.

All day our way ran along the Sweetwater and late that afternoon we set up camp among some scattered trees along the river.

Later, by the fire, I was reading and Handy was playing with Jinx when we heard a voice from out of the dark beyond the circle of firelight.

"Hello the fire." And after a moment, "Can I ride in?" The deep, gravelly voice sounded familiar.

In that moment, Handy stood, picked up his Winchester and moved back into the dark a bit. I did the same with the ten-gage on the other side of the fire. "Come ahead," said Handy and we watched the black man from the café in Casper ride a tall dark mule to the edge of the firelight. We stepped out of the dark and lowered our weapons while he slid to the ground.

"Handy," he said, with his hand outstretched, then he turned to me. "Johnny," he said with a nod.

We sat by the fire and talked. "I heard last night in the Wagon Wheel that you boys are headed to Salt Lake; that right?" he asked.

"We plan to get there in a few weeks and stay through the winter, then on to Sacramento next spring," I said. "We're riding the Pony trail."

"Like your Pa," he said and smiled at me.

I must admit my mouth dropped open. "How do you know about my Pa," I said, wondering aloud.

He was still smiling. "I thought I recognized you last night and when I heard your name, I was sure," he said. "I was in the Tenth at Fort Riley. I remember you and your Pa from the livery stable in Junction City."

I know I was smiling broadly, "You were a Buffalo Soldier?" I said.

"Indeed, I was. For six years, till I got tired of it and left to see the mountains." His smile had broadened into a grin. "I left in 76, so you'd probably have been around ten or eleven. I remember you were wherever your Pa was, working right beside him, even at your age." He stirred the ashes with a stick, looked up at me and said, "If you're way out here on the Pony, I'd say he's probably dead."

"He died last month," I said. "Did you ever know my Uncle Bill?"

"Likely not," he said, "I didn't know the names of too many people in town back then."

"He settled in Sacramento and I set out to ride the Pony out there with Jinx here. We picked up Handy in Kearney," I said.

"We figure we've got about 700 miles behind us and about 400 more to Salt Lake. Is that about right?" asked Handy.

"I'd say that was pretty close" he said. "What do you figure to do when you get there,"

"We plan to find a place to spend the winter and look around some while we're there. We also need to find out as much as we can about the ride in front of us, so I imagine we'll talk to some people." Handy said.

"Well, that's one of the things I want to talk to you about. I'd like to ride along with you." I looked at him for a long moment, and then at Handy. He went on, "I know the country you'll be traveling through, and I've got grub and stuff to put in the pot, so I won't be a burden. And that mule of mine can walk down a horse any day."

"Why do you want to go to California?" I asked him, "And why with us?"

Handy echoed me, "Yeah, why us?"

"Because that's what I do," he said "When you like to travel you got to go somewhere. And besides, you two seem to be the kind of folks I'd like to ride with."

I grinned and looked at him. "You sure you're not just trying to steal my cat."

He laughed and said, "Never had much truck with cats. It'll be interesting to get to know him."

This whole time Jinx had been up in a tree that hung over the campsite. I called him and he came slowly down and sat next to me, looking intently at Wash. Handy and I looked at each other and nodded in mutual agreement.

"Unsaddle your mule and picket him out there with the horses," I said.

When he had unpacked and settled in and we were sitting by the fire again, I asked him, "You said going with us was one thing you wanted to talk about. What was the other?"

"The men I heard talking seemed to think you had something worth stealing. They were making plans to do it," he said.

CHAPTER ELEVEN

W e sat looking at him, waiting for him to go on. When he didn't, Handy asked, "How many and what'd they look like?"

"I saw four, but from what was said I think there might be another. From the way they talked he was probably the leader," said Wash. "They looked like men you see in any saloon in the country. Nothing special about them except they all had guns and looked ready to use them. One of them said something like, "He wants the gun and the horse, and we all split the rest."

Handy and I looked at each other. He had been in the scrap with the Gambler back in Kearney and heard him say in the jail he would see us again. "We got a telegram saying he was headed west. You reckon it's him?" he asked.

"Well, what they said about the gun and the horse makes it a pretty good bet," I replied.

I looked at Wash. "Why in the world would you want to hook up with us when you know they likely going to attack us?"

"Last night in the café, I had the feeling that if I had objected to either that southron or the manager, you two would have backed me," he said, looking straight into my eyes. "That's all the reason I need."

I scratched Jinx's ears for a minute and then said, "Let's sleep on it and see what we think in the morning."

Every time I thought I was going to have trouble sleeping, it ambushed me. When Jinx woke me in the morning, Wash already had a fire going and was just putting coffee in the pot. A couple of minutes later Handy stumbled in from watering the trees, stretched mightily and went to the horses to get the frying pan. We ate in silence and after, over coffee, Wash lit an old pipe and we sat round the fire.

"Let's do it this way," I said. "I'll start and then one of you pick it up and then the other. Let's all put our ideas into the middle and then we can decide which are the best."

They agreed and I began. "It seems to me we have four choices. One, we can go looking for them and force a showdown. Two, we can fort up and wait for them to find us. Three, we're ahead of them; we can try to stay ahead of them and get to Salt Lake as quickly as we can. And four, we can go about our business as usual while keeping an eye out for them and deal with the situation as it comes up."

We were all quiet for a minute. Then Handy said, "I'd say that covers the possibilities. So, which one do we choose?" he asked.

I looked at Wash. "I'm the new one here," he said. "I'll listen for a while."

"It seems like you have much more experience with this kind of thing, so I'd like to hear what you have to say," I said, looking at Handy, who nodded.

He seemed to think for a minute and said, "I'd say you got the choices right, so the question is, given how we are, which is the best one for us? I'd say the last one." His pipe had gone out, so we sat for a minute while he got it going again. "I don't like the idea of forting up and waiting for them to come to us. That way the only thing we choose is where to fight. They make all the other choices."

"As far as looking for them, I don't know we could find them," he said. "This is a pretty big country with lots of places to hide. And when it comes to it, I don't like running. It just puts it off to another day. From the way it sounds, this fellow has followed you halfway across the country. Don't seem like he's going to give up too easy."

"That sounds like pretty good thinking," said Handy. "What do you think Johnny?"

"I agree. So now we've got to figure how we go about it," I said. "Here's what I think; Handy and I move on pretty much at the speed we have planned, and along the trail we want to ride. We've already had a couple of scrapes since we started and have learned a bit about watching our back trail and being careful where we camp to have a good position for fighting if we have to." I stopped and looked at Wash who was sitting, listening, calmly smoking his pipe. "The question is how do you fit into this?"

Again, the pause before he spoke. "I'd say I could use my experience and ride a kind of screen between you and them while you move on down the trail," he said. "These fellows likely don't know the country around here as well as I do. They have to get ahead of you if their plan is to set an ambush for you, and I think it is." He knocked his pipe out on a rock by the fire and continued. "If we can figure where they plan on making the try, we can beat them to the punch." He looked back and forth at us and said, "It likely means fightin' and probably killin'. You boys ready for that?" he asked.

"We've talked about it a bit since we started," I said, "and we're both ready to do what we have to keep ourselves and Jinx here safe. As far as killing, we aren't the ones looking for trouble, but if they come looking, then they got to pay the bill."

Wash chewed on his pipe stem a bit and said, "If I put on my dark suit and find them, I could, maybe, whittle down the odds a bit. Might be that would help them change their minds about the whole thing."

I thought I knew what he meant and when he patted the haft of the big Bowie on his belt, I was sure of it. "What's your 'dark suit'?" I asked.

He grinned. "I've got pretty dark skin. When I put on an all-black outfit, cover my hair with a black hat and don't smile, I'm pretty much invisible in the dark. Maybe tonight I go out and see what I can find." The idea of him moving around in the dark with that Bowie gave me a chill.

Watching him walk around camp in the daytime I could see he walked with a different gait and his spine seemed a little crooked. He had a powerful looking chest and shoulders and seemed agile despite his spine problem. He was a couple inches shorter than me, but heavier, and had a scar that ran across his face from below his left eye across his mouth to his chin on the right side of his face. All in all, I decided I wouldn't want to pick a fight with him.

Given his age there was a good chance he had been born a slave. Buffalo Soldiers had the reputation of being tough men. I had seen some of them from the fort with their shirts off when they were helping Pa around the livery or when they were having a wash at the pump before going into town and remembered the scars some of them bore. It wouldn't have surprised me to see the same kind of scars on Wash's back.

We'd probably be riding together for the next couple of weeks, so I'd likely find out as much about him as he wanted to tell. With those men coming for us, I was glad to have him around regardless of who he was or where he came from.

Later that day, while Handy and I were riding near the river, Wash came out of the trees ahead of us and dismounted along the trail.

"Let's sit over here and talk a bit," he said, gesturing to a clearing with a couple of logs conveniently positioned for us to sit and talk.

When the horses had been watered and we were sitting chewing some jerky, he leaned over and drew a rough map with his finger. "I found them right here," he said pointing to a spot in the dust. "Right now, I'd say they're about eight to ten miles behind us and they're moving on a trail that runs along with ours about three miles east of here."

I looked at Handy. He shook his head and said, "It looks like they plan to lap us real soon and then lay the trap. When you figure they'll hit us? And where?" he asked Wash.

"It looks like someone is with them who knows the country," he said. "The trail they're on is the kind of thing not many people know about. This fellow knows as well as I do that Three Crossings is the best place on this trail for an ambush, though he might pick Split Rock."

"What's at Three Crossings?" I asked.

"It's where the river runs into a gorge. The sides of the gorge are too narrow for riders in places, so you got to cross the river three times real quick. A couple of rifles on top of the gorge could make a lot of trouble. Besides, there are several more crossings, and someone on top could move faster than we could." He looked at me.

I understood what he was saying. We could be under their guns for miles while we were crossing the river time and again. We were all quiet for a minute, thinking.

Handy spoke first, "So, what choices do we have? Doesn't seem like trying to bull our way through is a good idea. What else can we do?"

I looked at Wash, "Is there any way around the Crossings? Do we have to go that way?" I asked.

"Yes, there is a way; it's difficult for wagons, not so bad for horses," he said. "I don't know the name of it. I just call it the 'sand'. It's a twenty mile stretch of deep sand we'd have to go through to get back to the river. For a rider it's a hard day."

"That sounds like the way to go, hard day or not," Handy said.

"The only trouble is, it's not going to solve your problem." He looked at Handy and then at me. "This fellow, he's followed you 700 miles across the country. He ain't gonna stop. I've heard these men talk. They don't care if you live or die. They just want something you got." His gaze had locked on to my eyes.

"What you're saying is, we've got to kill them to keep them from killing us," I said. He nodded slowly.

I looked away from him and took a deep breath. After a moment, I stood, walked across the clearing and sat down on a fallen tree. Jinx followed me and jumped into my lap. Somehow, I always thought better when I was petting him.

My mind went back to Julesburg; how I felt when I saw the look on that cowboy's face or when he fell, blood on his shirt. I shook my head. This was different. That man had drawn a gun and without thinking, I had defended myself, done what had to be done to stay alive.

How was this different? These men wanted to rob us and kill us if we resisted. But to ambush them was something else again. Could I look down the sights of the Henry at a man I didn't know, had never even seen before, and pull the trigger? With my emotions pulling me one way, logic, I reckon it was, pulled me back.

We had come into an uncivilized land. There was no law to protect us here, so we had to protect ourselves. These were bad men and if we didn't fight back, they would win and that was not right.

Suddenly I knew I wouldn't have a problem. When I looked down the sights of the Henry, I'd see what was there; a vicious, dangerous animal stalking me, not a man. When we came to civilization again, he could be a man, not before.

I looked at Handy. He answered my thought. "We don't have a choice, Johnny."

"Well," I said to Wash. "We think we can do what we have to. I guess all we can do is see what happens when the time comes. Is that answer enough for you?"

He looked at me for a long moment, then at Handy. "I think I can take that to the bank," he said, nodding his head.

We set up the camp, and while Handy was cooking dinner, Wash took me on a sweep through the country between us and the trail they were on. "They might want to press their luck," he said. "You never know." We saw no sign of them but got close enough to smell wood smoke from their cookfire. On the way back we swung west and came into our camp from the west.

Dinner was ready and Handy was glad to see us. "It's a little nervous, being here by myself, knowing they're out there." Though we had left Jinx with him, I could see his point. During a gunfight, Jinx would be up the closest tree.

Around the fire that night we talked strategy and tactics. It seemed important to keep them away from Three Crossings. If they got into those rocks it would be tough getting them out. And we didn't want them behind us again, so we needed to finish it now or at least put a crimp in their plans.

Wash talked about the kind of country we were going into and the landmarks we would see. We had to decide how and where to confront them and to make sure we knew where they were so we wouldn't be surprised.

"It seems like we're one up on 'em, cause we know they're here and they don't know we know," said Handy.

"I'd say that's right," said Wash. "We need to decide how, when and where. We also need to whittle down the odds a bit, so I'd like to go out tonight and pay them a visit. What do you think, Johnny?"

I nodded. "I'd like to go with you," I said, "but I'd just be in the way. How will you go about it?"

"Lay out and wait till one of them answers the call, I reckon," he said. "That's as good a time as any to meet your maker."

"That will take it down a bit, but still leaves it at four against three," said Handy. "Of course, it might make some of them remember something they left in Kansas City, which would be a good thing." He gave a short laugh. "Probably make the rest of them damn sure not to take a leak by themselves ever again."

"That kind of thing makes men nervous," said Wash, "and nervous men don't think too good. Could make 'em see shadows and things that aren't there."

"We do have some advantages. One is surprise and another is firepower," he went on. "I saw what a Henry can do at Nashville and a few other places, and that ten-gage is a cannon. You boys look like you can handle a pistol too if it come to that. I got a Sharps .50 and an eight shot Remington pistol, and we got plenty of shells."

"Another is their state of mind," he said, and took a puff on his pipe. "Men like those have no respect for a good man. Think they're soft and afraid. They won't hesitate to kill but think you will."

"Looks like we'll just have to prove them wrong," I said, looking up from cleaning the Colt.

That night Wash went out in his dark suit. I was standing at the fire playing with Jinx when he suddenly re-appeared.

"Now the odds are better," he said, and took off the suit, replacing it with his regular clothes.

"One?" I asked. He nodded. "I tried to leave as little sign as I could, other than the body. Maybe they'll think it was a ghost."

Wash started the fire and made coffee next morning while I cleaned up and packed up, getting ready to leave. Handy got the horses ready. When we were packed and ready to ride, we sat down with a cup of coffee to plan the day.

That morning, for the first time, I began to think of this as a battle. That's what it came down to. Since we knew we would have to fight these men one day, we needed to put everything into winning or our adventure was over. It seemed to me that Wash was already thinking that way when he joined us.

What he brought to our little army was hard to add up. From the first he looked at it as war, but he let us get around to thinking that way by ourselves. Handy seemed to see it the same way, though not in so much detail. To him, it was not something to be upset over. We decided what we needed to do, and we did it. Thinking about it too much got confusing.

Something puzzled me. Why were these two men looking to me so much? Why was I the leader? So, I asked them.

Handy pulled at the fresh growth on his chin and looked thoughtful. "Couple of reasons, I guess," he said. "First off, it's your trip. I just joined up because it sounded like something I wanted to do. Second, I've never met anyone that's read as much as you have, not even my brother, and he went to a college in Indiana. It just seems like you've got a lot in your head and I like the way it comes out."

"I'm just a tool here," said Wash when I looked at him. "I'm here to do what has to be done, but I figure you can think about the whole thing better. In the army I learned the difference between strategy and tactics. I'm tactics. You're strategy."

"Ok," I said, nodding to myself. "It seems to me if we plan to ambush these men, we need to stay in front of them and the farther out we are, the more time we have to get set. So, I'd like to increase our speed, find the place we're going to use and hit 'em hard when we hit 'em. When we do hit 'em, we need to make sure we have plenty of ammunition, some food and water handy in case it turns into a long fight, and a line of retreat in case we need it."

"We also need to make sure the horses are safe and ready to ride if need be." I stood to stretch and asked, "What do you think Wash?"

He puffed on his pipe a bit before he answered. "Sounds right, but we got to think about the country we're coming to," he said. "Yesterday we began to come out of the trees and the sides began opening up. Come tomorrow afternoon you'll be in some dry country. Gonna see more and more sage brush and some cactus, and the mountains will get farther away."

"Independence Rock we should see in an hour or so and then the Devil's Gate," he said, "and then, a little farther on, Split Rock. There a place at Split Rock leading up to the actual cut where we could settle in and hit 'em. We could probably leave the stock on the other side of the split. That way they'd be safe, but we could get to them quick."

"How long will it take to get there?" Handy asked.

Wash took a while to answer. "Maybe three hours, if we push it."

Handy stood up, "Let's push it. If we got to do this thing, let's get it over with. I don't like carrying it around."

We agreed and within five minutes we'd put out the fire and were riding out.

CHAPTER TWELVE

J inx liked to ride fast. When we were ambling along at a walk, he would usually be sleeping behind the saddle or just lying back there watching out the back door. But get up a little speed and he would be sitting in front of me, paws on the saddle horn, ears almost flat to his head. He was there most of the day that day. We rode hard for a half an hour, slowed to a walk to give the horses a breather, then rode hard again.

A little less than three hours after we left camp, we were approaching Split Rock. We passed Independence Rock at a lope and decided not to stop.

At Devil's Gate, the Sweetwater plunged through a steep, narrow notch. The only way to get beyond it was to go around it, so we did. At the bottom of the canyon, where the river came crashing down to the plain below, we stood for a moment and let the scene sink in. The narrow canyon walls with the water spilling over the rim and falling to hit the bottom with a continuous roar could put you in a daze until you shook it off.

After that the land flattened out almost like the plains, but not so green. We had set a steady pace, and now sat looking at the switchback trail that ran up the steep rocky hillside to the notch.

Handy and I sat quiet, while Wash looked it over. Finally, he pointed up the hill at the notch and said, "Here's my idea. One of us takes the horses through the notch and hikes back. The others stay here and look over the ground and decide what to do and where to do it. Then we all get into position and wait."

Handy volunteered to lead the horses to safety and join us after. Wash and I looked over the land we'd chosen for our fight. I trusted him totally to make good choices that would get us ready. The plan was to get in position and wait until dark. If they hadn't come by then, two of us would fall back to the horses, feed and water them, and set up a camp of sorts, leaving the other to keep watch on the trail.

We'd talked about it and decided that the odds against them coming that night were pretty long. They didn't know we were aware of them, and while they wanted to get in front of us, they didn't seem to be in a hurry yet.

It wouldn't be smart to sit in the dark all night and go into a fight tired and jumpy, so we decided to play the odds.

One man would watch the trail and signal us if the light from the full moon showed him anything coming. We would rotate every three hours. If they did come, we didn't want to alert them with a gunshot, so the signal would be lighting a small, pre-laid fire that we could see back at our camp, but they couldn't.

When Handy got back we showed him the positions and Wash put us in place. Each of us had a spot with some shade because we had no idea how long we'd have to wait. The plan was to let them get to a certain point on the switchback and then open up. If we could empty three saddles right off, that would likely end the battle before it started.

I'd been around long enough to realize that life doesn't always go as planned, so while we sat waiting for them, I thought about what could happen instead of what we thought would happen. Even if we missed some of the first shots and they got into the rocks below us, we had shade, water and plenty of ammunition, so the odds were in our favor. Of course, there are such things as stray bullets, so I planned to keep my head down.

Wash had given me the first man in line, Handy the second and he, the third. The signal to fire would be his shot.

We sat in our places waiting, sweating, looking through the telescope, and occasionally taking a drink of water. The early summer sun was reflected off the rocky soil. It was hot, and it got hotter as the day went slowly by. With the horizon as far away as it was, we could see them coming for quite a distance, so we decided to sit together under a tree with Jinx roaming around the rocks and investigating the tree above us. To keep us alert we talked about our lives, so by the time it began to get dark, we were well acquainted.

As I suspected, Wash had been born into slavery on a South Carolina rice plantation. He wasn't sure about when but had worked it out that he was about forty-five. He was in New Orleans with his master expecting to be sold at auction when the war broke out.

Business kept them there until the US Navy came along, and shortly after he left his owner and found the Union Army. He worked first as a teamster and later joined a new black regiment and put his hand on a musket for the first time.

When Grant put Vicksburg under the gun, he became a scout and that's when he first used the 'dark suit'. When it was over, he came west as a Buffalo Soldier, served six years, got his discharge and headed west to be really free for the first time. Since then he had roamed through the mountains, from Colorado to the Oregon Territory, all through California, and most of the rest of the West.

He had come to Casper as part of a small group that broke up and was thus at loose ends when he ran into us.

By the time we had shared our lives with him it was getting dark and we put the plan into place.

Handy and Wash went back to set up the camp and I took the first watch.

Pa had told me once of a night when he had to sit waiting for a battle to begin the next morning. He never forgot it. At night, with no one to talk to and nothing to do but watch, your thoughts are your only companions.

Jinx was with me and that helped a lot. I talked to him in a low voice and petted him while he sat in my lap purring, but the thoughts were still there. I also watched him because his senses could tell me more than my eyes could see in the dark. His alertness had kept me out of trouble a few times already on this trip.

Thinking about the Gambler, I remembered he wore a vest; at least he had both times I had seen him. Tomorrow when I saw him ride up the trail before me, I would aim the Henry right at the V where the vest buttons ended and pull the trigger. I didn't want to do it, but there was a good possibility that the rocky hillside leading up the slope to Split Rock would be the last thing he'd ever see.

But what if they figured out what we were doing, foiled our ambush and attacked us instead, using the rocks below as cover? Bullets would be flying and the rocky hillside leading up the slope to Split Rock might be the last thing I would ever see. Was I afraid? I didn't think I was, but I guessed I'd find that out the next day.

When I thought of my two companions, I felt reassured. I couldn't think of anyone I'd rather have with me in a fight. Though I'd known them for only a short time, I felt they were, as Handy put it, 'men to ride the river with'. Again, tomorrow we would see.

When Handy relieved me, I walked back to the fire, Jinx riding on my shoulder, and with Wash watching for the signal fire, I lay down to try to rest for a bit.

Usually having Jinx lying on my chest purring was a good way of getting to sleep, but that night it didn't help. After lying there for a few minutes, I sat up and looked at Wash sitting across the fire.

He was gazing out to where the signal fire could be seen when lit. Every once in a while, he'd turn his head, make a sweep around the area and then go back to watching for the fire.

When I sat down beside him, he glanced at me and nodded. "Can't sleep?" he asked. He was speaking in a low voice. "A voice sometimes carries a long way on a night like this," he said by way of explanation.

"There's something that's been bothering me about this man who's so bent on finding you and killing you," he said. "Why?" He sucked on his dry pipe and was quiet for a while. "What's so important to a man like that, that he'll chase a fellow halfway across the country to get it and likely kill people in the bargain?" He stopped for a minute to let me think about that and then went on.

"Revenge?" He paused. "Because you made him walk ten miles barefoot in his long johns? Could be, but I don't think so". Again, the pause. "What do you have that's worth that much?"

I was still thinking about that when Wash went out to relieve Handy a couple of hours later.

It took about fifteen minutes for Handy to walk from the forward position back to the camp. When he got there, he threw his hat on his bedroll, ran both hands through his hair, then thrust both arms in the air in a mighty stretch.

"Three hours sitting on a rock in the dark waiting for someone to kill is not fun," he said. "I've got muscles hurting I didn't even know I had."

While he was getting a drink of water from a canteen hanging from Rusty's saddle, I told him what Wash had asked me.

"What do we have that's worth that much?" I asked. "What is there about a gun and horse that would make a man do what he's doing?" While I was talking, I was looking for the signal fire and, following Wash's lead, once in a while swept my eyes around the area.

Handy sat down across the fire from me and looked thoughtful for a couple of minutes. Finally, he looked up and said, "I'll be damned if I know, Johnny, but I'll tell you this. Whether or not I have the answer to that question tomorrow won't help me a damn bit when the shooting starts, so if you don't mind, I'm not going to worry about it right now". He scooted over to his bed roll, stretched out with a sigh and put his hat over his eyes.

He had a point, but my mind wouldn't let the question be. While I sat there looking out at the dark, I tried to organize my thoughts so I could at least try to figure the answer to that question, but at that point it was hopeless. Too many other things crowded it out.

The fire was burning low when I woke Handy after a couple of hours.

"It's just before daybreak," he said. "Let's see what's up front."

He stood, stretched, and slung his gun belt around his hips. I picked up the Henry and the ten-gage and followed him through the cut, with Jinx running ahead of us.

I was a little nervous about Jinx being in the middle of a gunfight. He hated the sound of gunfire and I could only hope that a prolonged fight wouldn't goad him into doing something that might get him hurt or killed. On the other hand, this was a situation where we all had to share the danger. He was a part of what we were doing, and my focus had to be on this fight so, until it was over, he was on his own, just like the rest of us.

Sitting under the tree we could see a good distance out into the prairie, so as long as it was a clear day, we shouldn't have to worry about them sneaking up on us. We were looking north and east so Wash was reluctant to use the telescope for fear it would reflect sunlight and give us away.

I think maybe time is a little different when you're waiting like that. Minutes sure did seem to take forever to go by. Then suddenly we saw dust, and shortly there they were. Soon they were at the bottom of the hill where the trail began, and then they were coming zigzag up the rocky path.

The V on his shirt was lined up in my sights when I heard the Sharp's boom. As I took up slack on the trigger, his horse seemed to stumble and then fell away from me toward the rocks. I shifted my aim and pulled the trigger, then cocked the Henry and shot again, and then again. What, if anything, I hit I couldn't tell.

The third man in line had flown backwards from the saddle when the fifty caliber Sharp's bullet hit him. All we could see of him were his legs sprawled in the rocks. They weren't moving.

Handy's man was down, wounded, in some of the rocks and firing back, though without much effect.

I had no idea what had happened to the Gambler. When I pulled the trigger, he was close enough for me to recognize him and see that he hadn't shaved for a while, but when he fell, he disappeared behind a large boulder and I didn't know if he was alive or dead or even if he was still where he had fallen.

His horse was down, apparently with a broken leg, and its struggles and shrill cries caused Handy to put a bullet into its brain.

Jinx had surprised me by staying with me inside my position during the fight and about an hour after the last shots were fired, he suddenly began to lash his tail and meow quietly. I turned in the direction he was looking and heard Wash's deep, gravelly voice. "Hello Johnny," he said, "We're comin' in."

They both crouched low as they came into my little bowl and took positions on either side of me, guns pointed into the rocks below us.

"Where is he?" asked Handy.

"He went down in that nest of rocks," I said. I pointed with the Henry. "His horse stepped in a hole or something and when he fell, I lost my sight. I tried to pick it up again, but I don't know if I hit him or not." I paused. "I haven't seen or heard anything, but that horse looks different than it did a while ago. I think the saddle bags are gone."

We sat for a minute and thought about that. "It could mean a couple of things," I said. "It could well be that he's alive and alert enough to get those bags while I was watching, or it could be that I didn't really see the bags in the first place and he's lying behind that rock bleeding to death."

"No matter what," said Wash, "don't go thinking you need to know one way or another, cause ya don't. Going down there would be like hunting a rattlesnake in tall grass. Very dangerous".

None of us took our eyes off the rocks in front of us.

After a minute Handy said, "There's that one fellow laying down there and I think I got two bullets in the second man. Even if it didn't kill him, he'd likely bleed to death, so that's two down for sure. The Gambler is without a horse 150 miles from the closest town. The only one left is the one we didn't get a shot at. I'd say this is a good time to count our blessing and get the hell out of here".

I looked at Wash. "Makes sense to me," he said, and I agreed with him.

It didn't make any sense to stop being careful, so we came up with a plan where one man would cover the other two and we sort of leap-frogged up the slope to the notch, with Jinx running before us. Once on the other side we moved quickly; we all felt a great desire to put this place behind us.

We had packed the horses that morning, so when we strode up to the lip of the little hollow where we had picketed them, we were ready to ride.

The horses were gone.

CHAPTER THIRTEEN

W ash was the first to recover from the shock.

"Stay here for a bit and let me look around," he said. He trotted down the hill and began to look over the ground. After a couple of minutes, he waved us in.

"This fellow wasn't a part of that bunch," he said. "I think he just happened onto the horses and figured it was too good to pass up. And," he paused and looked at us in turn, "I think I know who he is".

I gaped at him.

"He's a fellow I ran with for a while up in Oregon. I haven't seen him in a few years, but when you travel with someone for six months you learn to recognize his track and some of his habits."

"What do we do?" asked Handy. He shook his head ruefully. "Looks like that gambler fellow isn't the only one without a horse, 150 miles from town."

"I'd guess he left here less than half an hour ago and he's pulling three horses, so he won't be riding fast." He'd seen me whistle for Rusty before and he said, "Call him and see what happens."

I put my fingers to my lips and gave out with a shrill whistle and then another but heard nothing in response. With nothing else to do, we tagged along behind Wash, following the tracks of our horses and all our worldly goods.

It wasn't long before we heard hoofbeats and suddenly Rusty, rope dangling from his neck, came over a rise in the trail and stopped to wait for us to come up to him. He was saddled and loaded just as he had been that morning and seemed as happy to see us as we were to see him.

We quickly decided that Wash could best handle things from that point. We watched him mount up and as he took up the reins, I slid the ten-gage into the saddle holster under his leg.

"In case your friend needs a little extra persuadin," I said looking up at him, feeling glad he was on our side. I'd hate to have him coming after me.

Since we really didn't know what to look for from the Gambler and his friends it just made sense to fort up. We didn't have the horses, so it was easy to find a good spot. We settled on some rocky ground on a hillside just above the trail, about 200 feet to the north. A few trees gave us some shadow to hide in and the full moon on the slope below us meant we could see any movement along the trail.

It was a strange night, sitting up in turns, listening and watching, trying to stay awake and trying to catch some sleep.

"I'm just curious about something," Handy said. "Have you thought about whether or not he'll come back?"

I couldn't see his face when he said this. He was sitting in a little hollow with his Winchester out in front of him, looking out toward the trail.

"I must admit it went through my mind," I replied. "I mean, how long have we known him, and we just put our whole future in his hands." I shook my head. "For some reason I trust him."

"Me too," said Handy, and again, "Me too."

I could tell he was grinning at me. "If he takes off with his partner, it sure will make the rest of the trip interesting with no food and no horses."

"It will be a great story to tell our grandchildren," I said. "How long you reckon it would take us to hike all the way to Salt Lake, or near it, at any rate?

"Probably a couple of weeks if we're lucky," he replied. Maybe a week to Ft. Bridger. And there's another thing to think about. If it happens, we'd come into Salt Lake as a couple of beggars, at least in the beginning, instead of travelers who can pay their way."

We thought about that in silence for a bit then he asked, "Do you know anything about the Mormons?"

I nodded, though he couldn't see me in the dark, and said, "When I decided to try this trip, which was before Pa died, by the way, I wrote away for a book and I've read several articles about them in magazines and newspapers, a lot of it not good. I'll bet Wash knows a bit about them. He's passed through Salt Lake a few times, from what he said."

"I believe he's coming back," said Handy. "For some reason I trust him."

"As do I," I said.

The sound of a shot in the distance startled both of us alert and we stared out through the darkness as though we could see something from a shot that far away. How far, we couldn't tell, but there were no more shots and a couple hours later we heard Wash's deep gravelly voice, "Johnny, I'm coming in," and he rode his mule into the hollow, leading the horses.

A quick look showed us most everything was where it was supposed to be.

With the horses back as sentinels we could relax a little, with a fire, some hot food and hot coffee so we did. The hollow was big enough, and we picketed the horses not far from the fire. Jinx had greeted the horses when they returned, and after dinner, he jumped onto Rusty's back, took a bath, then lay down watching us.

One thing we'd already learned about Wash was that when he had a story to tell he told it when he was ready to and that was usually after a meal with his pipe in his hand.

"It was like I thought," he said. "Fellow's name is Jed Hubbard, but everybody calls him Doc. I traveled with him and a few others out in California for about six months some years ago. We called him Doc because he took care of the wounded for a while during the war and whenever someone got hurt or sick he'd doctor them.

He saw his chance and figured it was worth a try. Of course, he knew my rig and that he'd be leaving us a foot in the middle of nowhere, but he figured 'what the hell'. Probably his idea of a joke."

"Did you fire that shot we heard?" Handy asked.

"Fired a shot a couple of hours ago but it was a good fifteen miles from here. If you heard it, it must have been an echo," he replied.

"Is he dead?" I asked.

Wash shook his head, "Didn't see no reason to kill him. Once he knew I had the horse he knew I'd come up with him, sooner or later. I put a bullet into a tree right next to where he was standing, and he decided it wasn't worth it after all. He took off, leaving the horses and all our stuff, which is all I wanted anyway. He's sort of a friend. We pulled each other out of a scrape or two a few years back. Got into a tussle with some Modocs up near the Oregon border. I owed him one. Now we're even."

He looked at me, his face twisted into a half grin. "You boys wonder if I was coming back?"

"Well, we talked about it and decided we trusted you," Handy replied with a broad smile. "Sure did make for an interesting conversation, though."

The next morning Jinx woke me by sitting on my chest and meowing loudly. He was hungry and I was sleeping instead of fixing breakfast. Looking around I could see Handy getting the horses ready for the day and no sign of Wash.

For a few minutes I lay there petting the purring Jinx and thinking about the day and what had happened the last couple of days. I had lived a lot of my life in the last two days.

By the time breakfast was ready he was back, and after we had finished eating, he loaded his pipe, lit it and we sat and talked a while before hitting the trail.

"I went back to see what had happened on the battlefield," he said. "Kind of interesting."

He took a long pull on the pipe, "Looks like your gambler friend got away, least I didn't see any blood where he fell and sometime, probably later that night, his friend showed up and so he's got a horse now and they've got all the tucker and such they brought with them. Even stripped the horse Handy shot. Sooo," he dragged the word out, "what now?"

I sat and thought about that for a while. Handy got up from the log he'd been sitting on and stretched mightily. "Seems like the odds have shifted in our favor a bit," he said. "That's going to change things."

I agreed. "They know we're here now. They're going to act differently because of that, and we out-number them now, so we've got to make sure they don't catch us in an ambush and turn the tables on us."

I looked at Wash. He liked to have his pipe in hand when we were talking. Now he fiddled with it a bit and finally said, "There are things we don't know. We don't know if they're coming after us or going off with their tails between their legs. But we have to think like they're after us and be careful. I think they'll go back to their original plan. Try to catch us in an ambush, but they might be in more of a hurry than they were before."

He got up, poured the remains of the coffee on the fire and began to scatter it. "Men in a hurry might make some mistakes," he said. "We need to make sure they pay for those mistakes."

Wash had an interesting way of pausing to let you think about things he said. "Why don't I do this; I'll still act as a screen between you and them. That will protect us from surprise as much as anything could, and at the same time give us information so we can decide how to deal with them."

"That's the question isn't it?" I asked. "How do we deal with 'em? Go after them and force a fight? Stay ahead of them until we get to Salt Lake, or maybe Fort Bridger, and deal with it there? Stay put and let them come to us?"

"I'd say head for Salt Lake and deal with it when we have to," said Handy. "We don't have to run, but if we ride steady, long days we could be there in a week or so. They're behind us so we make it difficult for them to catch up, and if they get too close, we hit them. With Wash doing the screen, we should be able to pull that off."

"That sounds like a good plan," said Wash. "There's a couple of places between here and Salt Lake where we can stop and let people know what's happening behind us. Don't know that they can do anything, but it might be best to get it out in the open." He turned to mount his mule, and when he was up, he looked down at me and said, "Have you been thinking about that question I asked you last night?"

"Yes, I have," I replied. "A lot. But I don't have any answers yet. I have been a bit busy since yesterday, you know. Believe me, when I figure it out, you'll be the first to know."

"Don't forget; three men have already died over this, so I'd say it's as important to you as it is to him. Trouble is you don't know what it is, and he does." He turned the mule and rode off down the trail.

Handy watched hm go. "He sure is a handy fellow to have around. Without him, I'd say we'd be dead or pretty shot up by now."

Black wanted to run so we let the horses out for a while and then settled into a fast walk, breaking out into a lope at times. Like Handy had said, we weren't running from them, but if they were still after us, it just made sense to stay ahead of them.

Our next passage was through the gorge at Three Crossings and I wasn't really looking forward to that, but if the choice was between seven river crossing and riding twenty miles in sand, I thought I'd take the river. Of course, any planning about that would have to wait for Wash to come in and let us know what was out there.

Beyond Three Crossings was the South Pass. From what I read and heard, it was not the usual pass, not really what you'd expect for a pass through the Rockies. For some reason the idea that at that point all the water we'd see would be running to the Pacific Ocean amazed me.

It wasn't long until we began to see the hills rising on either side of the river and decided to stop and wait for Wash to join us. We got a fire going on the slope of a hill facing away from the trail and then climbed to the top to look back at the way we had come.

Considering we were surrounded by mountains, it was amazingly flat country, though I thought it was rising so gradually it was hard to notice. It looked like mostly sagebrush and sand with a few pinyons here and there. The river was flowing fast, and we could hear it running noisily over rocks even up on the hill where we were. It was still early summer, and the snow melt was likely making it run a little higher than normal.

Of all the country I'd seen since Kansas, this was the most barren. Except in a few places, it was surrounded by distant mountains and hills, but though it was flat, it had none of the beauty and majesty of the Great Plains, none of the miles and miles of grass rippling in the wind.

Even the river was different. All the rivers I had ever seen were bordered with trees to some extent, but not here. I think if you rode here on a moonless night you could ride right into the river without noticing it until you got wet.

Wash rode in about an hour before dark. We had the coffee ready for him. He filled his pipe and we talked.

"No trace of them anywhere so far," he said. He lit his pipe and we waited while he took a long pull and blew out a cloud of smoke. "I think we will be OK in the gorge tomorrow and should be able to cross the river without too much problem. It's mostly shallow at the fords now and the bottom is rocky."

"If memory serves, the last ford, about the eighth or ninth, is sometimes deep enough that the horses might have to swim. I think the best thing for me to do is to get above the crossings and make sure no one else is up there." He gestured toward the hills and cliffs rising above the river. We couldn't see them in the dark, but we all knew they were there.

"Up at daybreak and on the way, how long do you figure to make it out of the hills?" I asked.

"You'll have to cross the river seven times in about twelve miles, so I'd say four or five hours ought to do it," he replied. "Once you finish with these crossings, there are a couple more before we get into South Pass. It's about 35 miles to Pacific Springs on the other side so we could get close to it by quittin' time tomorrow."

Just as I crawled into my blanket Wash said, "I been thinking how to stay in touch tomorrow, and I thought I'd use a looking glass to reflect the sun. You'll see the flash and know where I am and that everything's alright."

With him on top of the cliffs looking down, he could likely see anyone coming up behind us.

"It's likely I'll join up with you from the west tomorrow, "he said. "If we don't see any sign tomorrow, I think we might be free of 'em. And besides, there's someone who lives along the river I'd like to see.

"Why the west?" asked Handy.

"Because I'll be covering ground faster than you, so I'll probably beat you to where the trails meet. I can help you get through the last couple of fords," said Wash.

"If it's faster, how come we're going along the river?" asked Handy.

"Because it's a lot harder on horses than it is down below. Up and down those ridges and then about four miles of deep sand. Master don't mind that as much as a horse."

"Who's Master?" I asked.

He nodded toward the mule. He winked at me and said, "Bottom rail on top, now."

I burst out laughing.

The next morning as the sun was coming up behind us, Handy, Jinx and I sat looking at the first of the initial three crossings that had given this stretch of the trail its name. I was riding Black. It seemed logical that the bigger horse would handle the fords better and, from what Wash had said, the Sweetwater could be a little rowdy along this stretch.

Suddenly there was a flash from on top of one of the hills in the gorge and we knew Wash was in place, so we began the first crossing. Jinx was riding in front of me and I put my hand on him when we first hit the water. Handy was leading Rusty and he moved away from me a bit so we wouldn't get tangled up in the middle of the river.

The water, cold and shallow, was moving swiftly over a gravel bar under our feet, but the horses had good footing and, in a minute or two, we were climbing a low bank on the north side of the river.

We turned on to a narrow path that ran beneath a sheer rock wall. Ahead of us was the second ford, less than a half mile farther on. On the wall above us countless names were carved into the stone, some weathered and some fresh and new looking.

People had first used this trail going to Oregon as early as the 1830's and in the last fifty years, thousands and thousands of wagons had tracked over this spot. I had read of long lines of wagons moving a few yards at a time along this stretch of the trail and while they were waiting it would seem natural to leave a memorial of some kind.

At the next ford we dismounted and checked out equipment before riding into the river again. With the same kind of firm bottom, we had no problems and were soon across for the second time. The third was much the same. Handy was riding upstream from me and a little ahead so I could see if anything carried away, but everything stayed in place.

The next two crossings were about three miles along and the trail on this side was wide enough for the two of us to ride abreast, though without much to spare. Another flash from atop a cliff a bit farther on and we could see Wash waving his hat, letting us know all was clear.

Truth be told, I was so involved with the crossings and the beauty of the river in this narrow gorge, I had forgotten to be worried, which was probably not a good idea. The fourth and fifth crossings were like the first and second, close together; when we were across them, we would probably meet Wash. I was interested to see who he knew that lived along the river this far out in the wilderness.

CHAPTER FOURTEEN

Wash was waiting for us at the entrance to a lane that led through a grove of trees, the first we had seen for a few days. At the end of the lane we could see what looked like a low house with a sod roof. From a hundred yards away, we could see goats grazing on the roof. The house itself was built of logs, lumber and sod in a strange mix, but it looked cozy and clean.

Wash indicated a sign nailed on a tree behind him. "Welcome to Sarah's Store," he said with a grin. "Biggest store between Casper and Fort Bridger. Of course, as far as I know it's the only one."

"So, you knew this was here and didn't tell us." I said.

"No reason to," he said. "Besides, I wasn't sure it was still open. This isn't the safest place in the world for a woman alone to raise a family. No telling what might have happened."

Handy gaped at him. "There's really a woman running a store and raising a family here, in the middle of nowhere?

"Well, she was the last time I was by here. That was about a year and a half ago, and it looks like she's still open. "Let's go see." He turned his mule and led us to the tie rail by the front porch where we were greeted by barking dogs; rather large dogs at that. When dogs are around, Jinx usually stayed on my shoulders, but this time he was on Handy's. I guess he felt safer up there.

Standing in the doorway was a woman, and as we rode up, she stepped forward and came slowly down the steps.

"George Washington Moore!" she said, reaching up to take his hands. "Welcome back." She looked over her shoulder. "Jed," she cried, "go get your sister. Tell her Wash is back."

After introducing us Wash said, "I'm not going to tell you her story, cause she tells it so much better than me."

When we shook hands, I could feel the strength and roughness there, but her smile was pure friendship. "Well, come on in and we can catch up." She led the way into a big open room that was clearly the store, and then through a back door into a kitchen where a pot of coffee sat on the stove.

By the time the children came in, we were all seated with coffee and some bread and cheese. Jed looked to be about 14, was red headed and freckled much like his mother. His sister, Rebecca, a couple of years older, was clearly an Indian. She had coal black hair and dark skin. Despite the baggy shirt and pants she wore, and the closely cropped hair, she was clearly a young woman.

"It's just less trouble with the men that come in here if they don't notice she's a girl," said Sarah. "So far, it's worked, because she tries to stay out of sight. But, if she keeps growing, I guess it's just a matter of time until it's a problem."

Her daughter stuck out her tongue at her and she grinned. They both gave Wash a hug and sat with us while Sarah told us her story.

She had been fifteen when she was kidnaped from her village in Wisconsin by Indians. She was carried a long way away, and even if she escaped, she didn't know how to get home.

She was given to an older warrior as a second wife. She bore his daughter and, as time passed, came to respect him for his dignity and fairness. When he was killed by other Indians who raided their village, she grieved for him.

The raid gave her an opportunity to escape, and with her daughter she fled into the forest. Several nights later, lost, cold and hungry, she stumbled on the campfire of a group of hunters from her home village.

Three days later she was home with her mother again, but with a difference. She had Rebecca, and in that town, at that time, the general feeling was that she should have killed herself or the baby or both rather than bring a savage into their midst.

After a few weeks of this she had decided she must leave the town to have any future. Jed had been one of the rescue party and was a child-hood friend. When he saw what was happening, he came forward, offered to help her get away, and told her he would care for her and treat Rebecca as though she were his own. It seemed he had always loved her but had been too shy to speak up.

With help from her mother and his parents they were able to put together an outfit, and within a month they were part of a wagon train rolling slowly up the Platte Valley toward somewhere.

When they came to the store in the canyon the proprietor was ill, and his wife was in desperate need of help to keep the store operating. They pulled their wagon out of line and went to work. Within a week the old man had died, and not a month had passed before his wife followed him.

They knew nothing of any heirs, so just like that, they had a store and a place to live in a beautiful spot. For the first couple of years there was enough travel on the road that they were able to make many improvements, but when the telegraph was followed swiftly by the railroad to the north of them, suddenly it slowed to a trickle.

They had planted a big kitchen garden, and both hunted. As a family they loved the way things were and all worked together to keep them that way.

In 1870 a gold strike at nearby South Pass had brought miners streaming into the area and things were better for a while, but after that petered out, travel slowed on the trail again. It had pretty much remained the same since.

Besides the few mountain men in the area, most of the business at the store came from Mormons passing on the way to and from Salt Lake City, teamsters hauling goods to and from Salt Lake, or roving Indians.

Seven years before, Jed had gone hunting and never returned. In the intervening time she had never found or heard a clue about what happened to him.

Handy looked at her with a puzzled expression on his face. "How have you managed to stay out here all these years without harm? I'll bet you sometimes in the winter it will be two or three months without seeing anyone. And on this trip, we've sure seen some of the quality of people you've had to run up against."

"It's probably always in the back of my mind, but we've got a few things going for us." She pointed to the shotgun leaning against the doorjamb. "I keep two pistols under the counter too and had to use them more than once. Another thing - I don't sell alcohol of any kind, which has likely saved me a lot of grief over the years."

"But the biggest thing is sitting right there," she said, pointing at Wash. She burst out laughing at the looks on our faces.

"I've probably got two dozen like him, men I've done favors for or helped out with a hot meal and a warm place to sleep when needed." She smiled. "They've all let me, and the rest of the world know, that if anyone hurts me or mine, they'll be here to help, and someone will pay. Not too many people want enemies like that."

"That's for sure," I said, and Handy echoed the sentiment.

"What she says is gospel," said Wash. "I know most of those fellows and they would not be forgiving of such."

"And we've got the dogs. They can make a fierce racket and several times have chased drunks off." She had exiled the dogs outside because of Jinx, and he was sitting in the window aggravating them."

The four of us slept in one room, but it was warm and comfortable. When I woke up Wash was gone, which was normal, and so was Jinx, which wasn't. A few minutes later I found him in the kitchen talking up a storm to Sarah and Rebecca ("don't call me Becky"). He usually sings for his meals, but they were determinedly ignoring him. He was my cat and I would feed him.

One of the reasons I love him is because he makes me laugh or smile a dozen times a day. The ladies were smiling now at the way he was cozying up to me now that they hadn't fallen for his song. Anything for a good breakfast.

Later that morning, with Sarah's OK, Handy and I did our practice routines with the Colts. Handy had improved greatly since he had gotten the new gun, and we were having a little contest when Jed came sidling up to me.

"Can you teach me to shoot like that?" he asked. "I can do ok with a rifle and even the shotgun, but I've never fired a pistol much."

"I'll be glad to teach you what I can," I said, "and, if your mother approves, you can practice with us while we're here. But I'm not sure how much you can do right now. The Colt is a heavy gun and I don't know if you're stout enough to handle one quite yet."

"Momma bought me a .25 caliber pistol and I can use that until I get bigger," he said excitedly. He showed me the gun and it seemed like it would help him get the basics without too much trouble.

"Let me talk to her and see what she thinks," I said.

The next morning while I was watching her prepare our breakfast, I asked her about teaching Jed, and she agreed it would be a good idea for him to learn from someone who would teach him how to handle it properly.

"As a matter of fact, how did you learn to handle a gun so well at your age?" she asked while she was pouring me a cup of coffee.

By the time Handy and Rebecca came in for breakfast I had told her my story and put in a little about Handy while I was at it.

"Wash told me a little about the adventures and how you've had to deal with them," she said. "And now," she said to Handy with a serious expression on her face, "exactly what are your intentions as regards to my daughter and her future?"

Rebecca let out an exasperated, "Mother!" and Handy's face turned bright red and he stuttered, not really saying anything.

"Every time I turn around you two are off doing something together or talking in a corner or laughing at something none of the rest of us know anything about." She grinned at Handy's discomfort. "Relax, boy," she said. "I'm just pulling your leg. I haven't even loaded my shotgun, so don't worry, although you two are spending a lot of time together without a chaperone."

She looked at Wash. "You reckon you could keep an eye on them to make sure there's no hanky-panky?"

Wash held up his hands. "Don't you get me involved in this. I've got enough things to worry about without that."

Handy finally got his words straightened out and blurted, "I'd like to marry her, but I've been too afraid to ask, afraid she think maybe I was acting a fool or something."

Rebecca looked across the table at him and gave him a radiant smile. "Yes," she said. "Yes! Yes! Yes! Yes, I'll marry you."

"Slow down, you two," her mother said, "In case you hadn't noticed, he's got some other plans, so it may have to wait till after they come back from this jaunt they're on."

Handy was looking at Rebecca. "Really?" he asked with a huge grin on his face. "You'd really marry me?"

She came around the table and gave him a kiss on his lips. "In a minute," she said.

"How long have you known each other?" Sarah asked. "Two days! Don't you think you're rushing thing a mite?"

She turned to Handy and asked, "What are you going to do about your trip with Johnny and Wash?"

Handy just sat for a minute getting his thoughts under control. Finally, he shook his head and said, "I've got to finish what I started with Johnny, but if you'll wait for me, I'll be back as soon as I can." He looked at Rebecca, "Would you wait for me to come back?"

"Of course, she would," Sarah said looking at her daughter's face. "We could spend the time making her wedding dress and getting her ready for you."

"Oh, Mother," said Rebecca. "Really, is it alright with you?"

"At your age and with your looks, it's just a matter of time until someone grabs you," Sarah replied, "and at least he's someone I like. Most of the men who come around here I have to chase off with the dogs."

Later in the room while he undressed, Handy told me about how he felt and how dumbstruck he was when she said yes. "I never thought to have a girl like that, never in a hundred years," he said. "She's so beautiful and so smart and she makes me laugh all the time."

"She's a saucy little thing, although come to think of it she's not really that little," I said. "She's quite the young lady and are you sure you want to wait and maybe miss the chance?"

"I'm sure," he said. "I believe her and like her mother says, if not me then someone else will want her pretty soon. I think Sarah is glad it won't be some mountain man who'll put her in a tepee in the backcountry and leave her to rot. I think she likes me."

"Have you told her about Mr. Cody and his offer?" I asked.

"We talked about it," he replied. "But not a lot." I guess that's just one of the things we'll have to find out about each other. Ought to be fun learning at that."

He looked at me as though he'd just been struck with a thought. "How long do you reckon it will take us to get to Sacramento?" he asked, "And how long before we get started back on the trail again?"

"Well, we've still got about eight or nine hundred miles to go and we won't even be ready to start until early spring," I replied, "so I'd say the answer to the first question is we will likely get there about this time next year." As far as the second one, I'm not in a hurry, so we can stay here for a while if you like, but I'd like to get settled in Salt Lake by the middle of September or so. We're about ten days from there, so if we left, say, in a couple of weeks that would work."

I turned to where Wash was sitting on his bed listening. "We haven't asked you what your plans are," I said. "Are you still planning on making the whole trip with us?

"That's my plan if it works out with you two," he replied. "I must say a marriage might put a kink or two in things, but I don't think it will be a problem from where I stand. I personally think it's a great idea and that you both would be getting someone special." He held out his hand to Handy who took it with a big smile on his face.

"I can't seem to stop smiling since she said yes," he said.

"I think that's how it's supposed to be," I said with a laugh.

For the next couple of days, we enjoyed ourselves. Wash spent time at the river fishing and replaced a couple of posts in the corral.

I spent an hour or so each day working with Jed and his .25 caliber revolver. After handling the Colt and nothing else for a while, it felt very light, but seemed just right for him. I let him shoot at some targets the first day, then taught him how to clean and oil it. After that I taught him a drill where he would draw and cock the pistol, pointing it at a target, then ease the hammer forward and holster the gun and then again.

Since we would be leaving soon, I let him know that this was the drill he would have to practice every day until he did it without thinking. That's the way Pa had taught me, and it was a big part of the drill that Handy and I used when we practiced. Drill first and marksmanship later.

Most of the rest of my time I spent sitting in a big leather chair reading. Sarah had a nice collection of books, some for sale and some for her own shelf, and there were several about the Mormons and about travel over the country from Salt Lake to California which I wanted to read. One in particular I wanted to have with me the rest of the way was City of the Saints by a fellow named Richard Burton. He was an English writer who spent time in Salt Lake and had some interesting talks with Brigham Young. He also traveled on to California over the same route we planned to take.

I was reading a week-old newspaper from Salt Lake when Handy and Rebecca came in with Wash in tow and sat down.

Handy had a silly grin on his face, which was not unusual lately, and sat with Rebecca very close beside him. Jinx, who had been spending most of his time with the two of them, hopped into my lap and settle down to be petted.

"We've been talking," Handy said, nodding at her, "and we think maybe it would be best if we leave in the morning."

Trying to keep a straight face I asked, "Why's that?"

He blushed a deep red and mumbled something.

With a mischievous look on her face Rebecca answered. "He seems utterly unable to keep his hands to himself and he's making suggestions altogether improper for a young woman of my age and virtue."

For a moment Wash and I looked at each other in astonishment and then burst out laughing. She continued, "I read that in one of Mama's books."

About this time Sarah appeared in the doorway with a 'what's going on' look on her face.

When it was explained to her, she said, "I'm glad someone else has come to that conclusion. It's been plenty obvious it's not safe to leave them alone. What time are you leaving? I'll have breakfast ready."

We spent the evening packing our gear and the next morning, just after sunup, all stood on the front porch to say goodbye.

"The last few years we usually close up the store around the end of October and come into the city for the winter," Sarah said as she

took my hand, "so we'll probably see you then. We usually stay with
the Crawfords. He's a doctor who lives on the outskirts of town. Poor
fellow has three wives and four daughters. Wash knows them, so make
sure you stop by. I'll send you a note when we get there."

"Thanks for your hospitality, Sarah," I said, "but, you know, I don't
know your last name."

She gave me a hug. "It's usually just 'Sarah who has the store at the
fifth crossing,'" she said, "but it's Travers."

Wash and I sat on our mounts waiting for Handy and Rebecca to
finish saying goodbye. Finally, he pushed her away and said, "Git, you,
or I'll never get on my horse."

He mounted, sat looking at her for a moment, then turned his
horse and led us out of the yard. He didn't look back.

CHAPTER FIFTEEN

A couple of hours later we sat looking at the ninth and final crossing of the Sweetwater. We had crossed it three times since we left Sarah's and, according to Wash, we would probably have to swim the horses across this one. Beyond the river the steep climb of Rocky Ridge reared its broken head into the sky. Most accounts of this trail told us this was the most difficult climb we would face on this stretch, and the way it looked from this distance, we could see the problems.

Of course, we had one advantage over the pioneers that went before us; we didn't have wagons, and that would likely make the climb much easier.

"Well, we won't get across sitting here looking at it," said Handy. "So, lead on," he said to Wash, "and we'll follow."

Wash put the mule into the river and within a few feet from the bank he was swimming. We followed, putting some space between each of us so we wouldn't get tangled up with one another.

The Sweetwater was deep here, and swift. Wash led us at an angle to strike the opposite bank downstream from where we went in. All three of us slid off our mounts and hung onto our saddle horns during the crossing. Jinx stayed in the saddle. I could tell he was nervous, and his claws were out. He got a little wet but hung on without a problem

Since I wasn't the best swimmer, and neither was Handy, there were a few moments of anxiety, but the horses handled it well, and shortly we were climbing out on the far side.

We dismounted to check our gear and dry out what needed it, then re-mounted and began our trek over the ridge before us. There were places where the horses had to scramble among boulders and loose rocks, but before long, we were cresting the hill. We stopped for a minute to let the horses catch their breath and gazed out at what was known as South Pass.

"Well fellows," said Wash, "believe it or not that's the pass across the Rocky Mountains."

It was what looked like a large flat plain, much like some of what we had passed over before we got to the Three Crossings; sage brush prairie with a few stunted pines scattered here and there.

"It don't look like any pass I've ever seen," said Handy. "Of course, I haven't seen many passes, but it sure is easier to get across the Rockies than I thought it'd be."

Wash got down to check his cinch. "I really believe if this pass wasn't here, the Oregon Country would never have been settled, at least not from the east anyway. There's no other pass where wagons could have made it unless you go a far piece to the south, probably as far as New Mexico."

We camped near Pacific Springs in a drizzling rain. For the first time since Wash had joined us, we wanted to set up a tarp to help keep us and our equipment dry, but with no trees and no poles we had to settle for pulling it over us. The sagebrush prairie stretched in every direction, so we settled in to stay dry through the night and hope for better tomorrow.

For the next three days we rode steadily south and west, which was more difficult in this part of the territory. Where the Sweetwater had run north-east to south-west, which was the way we were traveling, the rivers hereabouts ran across that line, and some of them were big. Fortunately, at the Green there was a ferry operating to get us across or we would have had to swim, and it was a quarter mile wide and running fast.

When we got to the ferry it was moored on the far side. We could see what looked like a homestead of sorts just beyond it. On Wash's hail, a woman came out of the house and called to someone in one of the outbuildings. Soon a man was cranking the raft across. When he landed, we led our horses on and pulled up the gate.

When we came into the mooring there was another woman and several children standing watching us. These were the first Mormons we had seen. The man, his two wives and four children lived at the ferry on a commission from the church to operate it and help Mormons cross the river at need. He took us across for the money but the fare was reasonable. They also served as an overnight, so if we wanted to, we could sleep there and rest the horses before we went on.

We'd been told of their probable existence by Sarah, but she hadn't been sure they were still operating. On her trips to Salt Lake she would carry messages and cart supplies back for them, which put her on the good side of the Mormons and gave her allies in the area if she should need them. The woman was a born politician.

Thirty miles south of the ferry the town of Green River had grown up along the right of way for the Union Pacific, and as we sat at a fork in the road the next morning, we needed to decide whether to stay on the Pony or spend a day riding south to town and then another day riding back.

Handy wanted to mail a letter to Rebecca, no surprise, and I wanted to send a wire to Sheriff Bob back in Marysville to let hm know we were alive and well. Wash just believed you had to go somewhere, so he reckoned he'd come along. Besides, there were a few things we needed, especially since we were adding two days to the trip.

The trail didn't just run along the river, but even though we were forced away from it several times, we finally came back to it at Green River.

Sarah had told me a bit about the town, and I'd read a little. When the Union Pacific tracklayers got to this point in 1868, they found a town of about 2000 people here anticipating their arrival. This created a problem because the approaches to the bridge they planned to build, and the land around the town, were in the hands of people who wanted to make a profit by selling the land to the railroad.

Rather than be robbed by the local speculators, the UP moved the bridge twelve miles up the river and began a new town. Green River rapidly became a ghost town, as all the people moved to the new town.

The problem came a year later when the tributary of the Green they were using dried up and they suddenly had no water for the steam locomotives. They went back to Green River and built another bridge there. When we rode into town there were probably three or four hundred people living on both sides of the river.

Much like North Platte, the railroad had put up buildings for various things while they built the bridge, and we settled into to a much nicer hotel than we could have expected.

The next morning, we each went about our business and met afterwards for breakfast in the hotel dining room. Just as we finished a voice from behind me said, "Hello Wash."

Wash looked up and his face split into a bright grin, all teeth showing. He got up slowly and the man walked around the table to shake hands.

His friend was a rough around the edge's kind of fellow. Heavy beard, long tangled hair that hadn't seen a comb in a while, tooth missing in the front, wearing buckskin leggings and shirt that needed a wash. Wash turned to us still holding his friend's hand and said, "Handy, Johnny, I want you to meet Jed Hubbard, the man who stole your horses."

"Call me Doc," he said, extending his hand.

For the next hour we talked to the man who stole our horses and found out it was a prank he pulled on his old friend.

"I figured when that bullet hit the tree, it was probably not a good time to explain," he said, "so I left, actually in rather a hurry." His accent sounded English and so it was. He was born in Surry, just south of London, and came to America to join in our Civil War as a soldier of fortune. He ventured into the mountains in the early seventies and hadn't been out much since.

"Doc and I spent a year or so running around Oregon and California together with some other fellows a few years ago," Wash said. "Good times, mostly." He looked at Jed for a minute. "Bill and Wiley Joe had a run-in with some Blackfeet last year up in Dakota and didn't make it out, or so I heard."

"I heard that too. Last I heard Blue was still wearing his hair, and I saw Andy in Casper," said Doc. "He's settled down with a squaw and has a couple kids. He's a guide for hunters and trappers now."

"Why did that bunch break up anyway?" asked Wash. "I disremember."

"Guess we had different things we wanted to do, maybe different places to go," Doc replied.

"Speakin' of that," he continued, "what are you into now? I been following you for a few days and you seem to be heading somewhere."

'Well, that's a story," said Wash. He finished loading his pipe, lit it and blew out a cloud. "Johnny's Pa died a few weeks ago and Johnny's headed out to Sacramento to live and work with his uncle. His Pa rode for the Pony and he listened to stories about it all his life. So, he decided to ride the Pony Trail to get there. Handy joined up with him in Kearney and I hooked on at Casper. We've had to shoo off a few varmints on the way, but it's been interesting, and I'm planning on going on to Sacramento with them."

About that time Jinx came out from under the table and jumped up into my lap.

"So that's Jinx, is it?" said Doc. He reached out and took Jinx's paw and shook it. "Sarah told me about him when I stopped by. She and Rebecca were busy working on a trousseau and Jed was practicing with a pistol fiercely. He's not planning to shoot the groom, is he?"

We all laughed. "Gosh, I hope not," said Handy. "How did she look?"

"You know Sarah, she don't change much," replied Doc with a mischievous look.

"I didn't mean Sarah," Handy sputtered.

"I kinda figured that," said Doc dryly, and we all laughed again.

"So, your plan is to spend the winter in Salt Lake with Brigham and the Saints?" he asked me.

"Well, I don't really feel it's a good idea to tackle the country west of there in the summer," I said, "and since I'm not in a hurry, it seemed like the natural place to rest and get ready for the finish. I figure we can learn a lot from them about where we're headed."

"If it's all right with you, I'd like to tag along, at least to Salt Lake." He glanced around at all of us. "I promise I'm reformed. I won't try to steal your horses again, or your cat for that matter. If things work out, and we fit together, I might like to join you in going further."

I looked at Handy and then at Wash, and seeing no problems, welcomed him to the bunch.

That night I was lying by the campfire with Jinx sitting between my legs giving himself a bath for what seemed like the twentieth time that day. In the shadows by the river I could hear Wash and Doc yarning about old friends and old adventures.

While we had been finishing up our packing getting ready to leave the next morning, Doc had gone to the barber for a bath and shave, disposed of his old clothes and replaced them with some from the general store so he looked and smelled somewhat better. Handy was writing another letter to Rebecca which he planned to mail the next day at Ft. Bridger. The horses and Master were cropping grass just out of the light and I was thinking about the people I was traveling with.

After Ma died it seemed like Pa was my only real friend. He included me in all parts of his life and taught me the things that would help make me a good man. I guess Jinx was my next real friend. And now I had two more and maybe a new one.

Of course, Doc was an unknown, at least to Handy and me. We had accepted him strictly on Wash's word and I'd already decided I'd take Wash's word on anything. If we became friends, what with it all beginning with his theft of our horses, it would be the strangest beginning for a friendship I'd ever heard.

Wash was an unusual man. He had been made in ways I couldn't even imagine. He was quiet and slow to speak, but when he did, it was always worth listening to. I had no doubt about his honesty and loyalty, but we really didn't know much about him. And I'd say there was a good chance we never would.

Handy was one of a kind. I guess because of his growing up the youngest in his family and surrounded by so many kinfolks, he seemed to feel very secure. He was able to trust first but could deal with things if it turned out he was mistaken. I had never seen someone who could cut down to the root of a problem like he could and some of the things he said made my jaw drop.

Somehow these two people were friends I could count on, for God knows what reason, but with them around I felt protected, the same way I felt with Pa.

CHAPTER SIXTEEN

꧁ ꧂

Fort Bridger was built and opened on Black's Fork of the Green as a trading post by Jim Bridger and his partner in 1843. It didn't look much like a fort, just a collection of buildings around a big open grassy area with a flagpole in the center. It was located where the Oregon Trail turned sharply northwest toward Fort Hall, Idaho, while the Pony continued toward Salt Lake City, 125 miles south and west. The California and Mormon Trails had also passed that way, as had the Union Pacific in 1868

The place had been the center of a dispute since shortly after its founding. With the Mormons passing through on the way to Salt Lake came problems of one sort or another. In 1853 Mormon settlers in the area complained Bridger was selling whiskey and ammunition to the Indians, and Brigham Young, the federal Indian agent, sent the Mormon militia to deal with the problem. Bridger left the scene in a hurry ahead of them.

For the next few years, Mormons controlled the area and they built Fort Supply, twelve miles south, with much more reasonable prices for the faithful.

In 1857 President Buchanan sent federal troops into the area to get control of things for the US Government, but Mormons burned both forts ahead of the troops, leaving them to spend a miserable winter at high altitude with little shelter and few supplies.

The commander of that expedition was a man I'd heard Pa speak of. Albert Sidney Johnson had been commander of the Confederate forces at Shiloh in 1862. He was killed the first day of the battle.

That was the first battle Pa was ever a part of, and he had told me about it. He and his squad were just cleaning up from breakfast when the Rebels came out of the woods, screaming like banshees. Over 23,000 men were killed or wounded in two beautiful April days. Sometimes he woke up sweating, having dreamed of it.

The Fort was manned by federal troops during the War and until 1878, when it was closed. When we got there, it had been reoccupied only a couple of years and was operated by William A. Carter. He had come out as a sutler with the army in 1862 and stayed to run the place.

He was rumored to have business interests back east, but loved the country hereabouts, so he married a Ute Indian woman, had three children, and settled down to become a prominent man in the territory.

We met Mr. Carter when he welcomed Wash and Doc with warm words, a hearty handshake, and some spiced cider he had made himself. He was a small man, bearded, with no hair at all on his head, but there was something about him that said he was in charge.

It was a beautiful evening, so we sat in front of the store and Rain Cloud, his wife who was a head taller than him, brought us bread and cheese with the cider. We talked a little about our trip and mentioned our problem with the gambler and his friends.

"You don't have any idea why he's after you?" Mr. Carter asked.

"Wash has me thinking about that and for the life of me I can't figure it out," I answered. I shook my head and continued. "Whatever it is it must be small, and we don't carry much, so where would we hide whatever it was? It's a puzzle."

After dinner Handy and I sat up-wind as Wash, Doc and Mr. Carter all smoked their pipes, which seemed to keep the mosquitoes off.

"Wash tells me you boys are planning to spend the winter in Salt Lake amongst the Saints," Mr. Carter said. He sat and pulled at his beard, and when I nodded, continued, "Know much about them?"

"No," I admitted, "but I'm reading Mr. Burton's book about his trip and the time he spent among them. So far, it seems like they are just people, though they do seem suspicious of gentiles, as they call us."

"There was some trouble between them and the Army back in '57 and '58," he said, "but things have been peaceable since I came out in '62. I get along with them fine, most times. Of course, with that many people you're bound to find an occasional bad actor, but nothing else."

"But, they think a little differently from most folks. It's like they drink from a different well, so things taste a little different to them. Things we think are normal, they don't, and things they think are normal, we don't; not a lot of things, but it's noticeable."

"They run a pretty tight ship, so I think this fellow that's after you will probably steer clear of Salt Lake. If he's still after you there's plenty of places west of there, and the cars can get him ahead of you pretty easy." He looked at Wash. "What do you think, Wash? Maybe Carson City?"

"I'd say it's a probable," answered Wash. "For some reason I think someone's going to have to kill him to make him quit."

"Well, from the looks of your horses when you rode in, I'd say you got enough firepower to take care of him," said Mr. Carter. He stood and put his hand on Wash's shoulder. "I'll see you boys in the morning."

Every couple of days, Handy and I like to practice with our Colts, so after breakfast the next morning we saddled the horses, rode a little way from the fort to a bank we could use to catch the slugs, and set up some targets. Wash had seen us practice before and chose to stay and visit with the Carters, but he recommended Doc go along just to watch.

Our usual routine was to toss something into the air, and when it hit the ground, we would draw and fire at targets about fifty feet away. We had gotten some bottles from Mr. Carter and we spent the next half hour breaking them. Afterwards we sat in a clearing to clean the pistols and talk for a while.

"Where'd you boys learned to shoot like that?" Doc asked. He had been sitting leaning against a log watching us without a word.

"Johnny taught me in the last couple of weeks," replied Handy. "I left home with an old Navy Colt but after we had that kerfuffle at Scott's Bluff and began to start thinking more about what was behind us, Johnny gave me this." He held up the Gambler's gun. "I never saw anything like it. It just felt like I'd been drawing and shooting it every day of my life."

Doc looked at me. "My Pa was a gunsmith, among other things, and I been handling all kinds of guns since I was a boy," I said. "He taught me how to draw and shoot from the hip and it's been like a game with me ever since. And since Handy joined me, we like to see who's best."

"I hope you understand he also taught me to respect a gun and that it was a tool to be used only as needed when the situation called for it," I continued. "And of course, that's the problem, isn't it? How do you decide when it's what the situation calls for?"

Doc scratched his head and replied, "I don't know about that, but I'd say if I had to bet on which of you was best, I'd say it was a toss-up."

"Handy seems to have a knack for it," I said, "and he's so strong that the weight of the gun is not a problem. The first time I fired a Colt I had to hold it up with both hands. Pa started me out with smaller pistols so I guess I was probably about fourteen before I could draw and fire a Colt. I can do it left-handed now but not nearly so well."

Wash was sitting on the porch with Mr. Carter when we rode up. "What do you think?" he asked Doc.

Doc shook his head and said, "Never seen anything like it. Remind me not to steal their horses again."

Reading Sir Richard's book was making the trip more interesting. He gave many details of the surrounding country and pointed out many things I'd probably have missed without it. The trail running west and south from Fort Bridger seemed to really excite him, and as we rode, I could understand why.

Everything I'd read and heard led me to believe the country between Fort Bridger and Salt Lake would be the roughest, most difficult country we would face since we left the plains. It wasn't long before I had to agree, though in places it was breathtaking. Time and time again Handy and I drew up to sit and stare in wonder at the vistas around us.

Jinx usually rode with Handy or me, sitting in front with paws on the saddle horn, though occasionally he slept on the saddle we used to carry supplies and equipment on the spare horse. When we camped, he never strayed far from sight, as though he realized there might be danger around him. He seemed to look around just like we did but I know he didn't see the same things.

Our path led us into deep, narrow canyons where we sometimes had to dismount and lead the horses in rocky defiles and over rock strewn cliffs and mountains. We crossed what seemed like a hundred streams, each one clear and rushing down to a bigger stream somewhere ahead, and we could always see the pebbles on their bottoms. There were grassy meadows and towering buttes along the trail, and the nights were cool as we climbed to almost 9000 feet above sea level.

Again and again, Wash and Doc kept us from problems with their knowledge of the country and the little things their travels had taught them. Doc had first seen the Great Salt Lake in the Fall of 1867, Wash a few years later, but between them had been there half a dozen times. By the time we passed through, all the early mountain men and trappers were dead, many of them killed by the Indians or the mountains they loved.

Salt Lake City was a thriving place by this time, and we begin to see signs of settlers and businesses spreading out toward us almost immediately after we left Fort Bridger.

With the coming of the railroad the population had exploded. Salt Lake City was almost as big as Kansas City now and there were several other good-sized towns in the Valley of the Great Salt Lake.

Early in the evening of the third day after we left the fort, we rode up to Echo Station. Most of the old Pony stations we had passed since we left Nebraska were either gone or beyond human habitation, but now we found many had been turned into ranch buildings or stores or businesses of one kind or another. Echo Station was clean and looked well maintained with several fenced areas for livestock and white painted stones along the road leading to the front of the station.

"Bet you there's a lady around somewhere," said Handy as we swung down at the hitching rail. "Place wouldn't look this nice if it was just men."

"No bet," said Doc. "The last time I was here the fellow running the place had three wives and six kids, three of them girls. From the looks of things, he's still here."

Several women had come out on the stoop to welcome us, and since food was still hot from supper we soon sat down to a nice meal with good talk for dessert. Jinx met one of the resident cats with no problems and was soon sharing a plate of beef with him.

Handy had been pretty poor company since we left Sarah's place, but the landlord brewed some good beer and after we sat and talked with a couple of mugs, he began to be himself again.

The daughters of the house knew Rebecca and were thrilled to hear of the impending nuptials. Of course, the things they wanted to hear about were a little out of his line of thought, but he tried his best to tell them how excited he was.

We talked about our trip and the landlord, whose name was Rose, joined Wash and Doc in a pipe and told us what we would see the next day.

"It's the prettiest country under God's heaven," he said, leaning back in his chair and sending a large smoke cloud to the ceiling. "At least I've never seen anything prettier, and I was with the Mormon Battalion back in the Mexican War and traveled a far piece in the country south and west of here." He looked to be in his sixties, so he was a young man at the time of his trek around the country.

I had read of the Mormon Battalion. In 1846, President Polk asked the Mormons to volunteer men for service and march as a Battalion from Council Bluffs, Iowa to south California to control the area if we went to war with Mexico, which we did while they were on the march. It took them six months to cover the 2000 miles, and their route covered the same kind of country as our trip, the Great Plains and the mountains and deserts of what became the Arizona Territory when the war was over.

Listening to him talk and answer our questions made me think of Pa. Once, when he had taken me to Kansas City with him, we had gone to a museum. The thing that had fascinated me the most was a mural of the history of Missouri painted on an entire wall in a large room. From then on, I looked at history like it was a mural. New things I learned about my country went in the mural, and the more I learned, the more detailed it got. Sitting listening to Mr. Rose, I added more than a few new things to my mural.

He talked about the dust and the thirst of the prairie, and of the heat crossing the deserts, and the cold in the mountains; about the women along as cooks and laundresses, and about the children who played around the campfires and somehow made things a little better.

A group of sick men, many of the thirty or so women, and most of the children left the train at Santa Fe for Pueblo, Colorado, and most of them ended up in Salt Lake. Most of the rest of the men made it to California and, after the war was won, traveled either to Salt Lake or back to Iowa, some completing a round trip of over 5000 miles, though some settled in the west.

There were members of the Battalion at Sutter's Mill in 1848 when gold was discovered on the American River. That began the Gold Rush and brought California into the Union as a free state in time for the Civil War. Many of these men came eventually to Salt Lake and tried to persuade Brigham Young to relocate the Saints to gold country. He decided instead to keep his people in the isolation of Utah rather than live again among the gentiles who had persecuted them so many times in the past.

Young had died five years before, but his vision for the future of the Saints was still the driving force behind the Mormon presence in the West, and as he'd planned, the Mormon Battalion had broadcast the seeds of the faith throughout the land west of the Rocky Mountains.

They had also helped pay for much of the supplies and equipment that had carried the migration of the Saints across Nebraska and Wyoming into the Valley of the Great Salt Lake.

Before the Battalion left Council Bluffs, the departing men had given a large part of their future Army pay to Young, who had used the money to buy goods at wholesale prices in St. Louis. These goods were, in turn, used to outfit the wagon trains carrying his people west to their promised land. That Brigham always seemed to be two jumps ahead of everyone else.

The station had no extra beds, but since the weather was nice, we unrolled our beds near a stream and settled in. Before long Jinx was on my chest purring, and I was thinking about the Mormons and how much a part of my life they were going to be for the next little while.

Funny thing was the decision to winter in Salt Lake had been taken without much thought. On the map it looked like the halfway point and with a desert beyond, and us arriving there in summertime, it made sense to break the trip there.

Besides, Salt Lake was a good-sized city and I'd always lived in a small place. I was curious about what it would be like to live with that many people. Although I knew some Mormon history, I hadn't really thought much about what they believed.

I knew they were a stick-together kind of people. The picture of them in my mind was like the barn raising times back home where everyone came out to help. Everyone had a job to do, and they did it, and suddenly you had a barn.

They had built Salt Lake like that and were a long way toward having their own state because they all worked together in an organized fashion to do the things that needed doing.

From what I'd heard, they were fair and honest and good businesspeople who happened to have extra wives and lots of kids. Since marriage wasn't high on my list of things to worry about, I wasn't sure how many wives a man needed and didn't really care. Given all the work a woman had to do at home it really made sense to have someone to share it with.

I'd read somewhere that polygamy was the main issue keeping Utah out of the Union. If that were so, and if they really wanted to get into the Union, I didn't understand why they wouldn't give it up. I was hoping Burton's book would help me figure them out.

According to Sir Richard, "Echo Kanyon has but one fault: it's sublimity will make all similar features look tame." By the time we had camped for the night I had to agree with him.

The canyon is about 30 miles long, dropping steadily to the Weber River. That's usually an easy day's ride for us, but we crossed the stream running down the canyon so many times that by nightfall we were still five miles short of Weber Station.

We rode into the station about midmorning, the next day, and after a short stop to water the stock, turned to follow the river a little north of west and toward Emigration Canyon, the final stage to Salt Lake and considered the roughest part of the long trip from Kansas by Wash and most others who passed through it.

We camped at the head of the canyon that night. Early the next morning, with Wash in the lead and Doc bringing up the rear, we started the rugged decent.

I had heard the sound of a rattler a few times back home, usually from far enough away to be avoided, but this one seemed to be right under Rusty's forelegs. He reared, and when he came down, the crust under his hooves gave way and we were falling over the edge and down a steep slope toward the creek.

I felt Jinx jump and I managed to get my feet out of the stirrups and push free of the saddle while Rusty fell beneath me. I must have hit a tree or something else solid because everything went suddenly black and I felt myself falling into a pit.

Book Two

CHAPTER SEVENTEEN

I woke up in a strange place. Bright sunlight was streaming in large windows on either side of the large, comfortable bed I was lying in. The ceiling was white and had a plastered look. I turned my head to see the rest of the room and pain struck and took my breath away. When the room stopped swirling around me, I opened my eyes again to see a woman looking down at me.

"Welcome back," she said, giving me a big smile. I closed my eyes again and took a deep breath, trying to figure how I'd gotten to this place from where I was the last time I remembered anything. I tried to say something, but my mouth and lips were dry, so it came out as a croak. "Where's Jinx?" I asked.

She burst out laughing and answered. "He just went out to do his business. He's been on the foot of your bed or on the pillow next to your head for three days now except for answering the call and eating of course." She ran a cool cloth across my lips and then wiped the rest of my face. "He wouldn't let anyone near you when you first came in, but we finally convinced him we were here to help, and he relented."

I closed my eyes again. "I have some questions," I said after a minute. I felt weak and hurt all over.

"I'd be amazed if you didn't," she said. "But I'll save you time by telling what has happened these last three days. Your horse spooked at a rattlesnake and fell off the side of a rather steep hill. You managed to get off when he fell, but probably broke your right arm, left ankle, at least two ribs, and got a concussion and many cuts and bruises when you hit the ground or while you rolled about twenty feet down the hill and ended up against a tree beside the creek."

"Apparently Jinx was able to jump clear and is fine. Your friend Wash rode down here - here being Salt Lake City - to my father's house, and we brought a wagon up to the scene and here you are."

"My father, the doctor, has set your broken bones, wrapped your ribs, put casts on your arm and ankle and prescribed bed rest for the concussion." My father's name is William Crawford. Mine is Annaliese and I'm taking care of you, which is what I'm going to do now."

She raised my left arm and thrust her hand into my armpit, then dropped the arm leaving her hand in place. When she moved it a minute later, she murmured, "No fever, that's good." Then she took a long tube and, with one end on my chest and the other in her ear, she listened for a minute or so. "Sounds a little rough in there," she said. "We worry about pneumonia when someone is in bed for a while. It's going to hurt to cough until your ribs get healed a little, but we need for you to cough as much as you can stand. The more you cough up the better." She held up three fingers. "How many do you see?" she asked.

"Three," I answered. "Where are my friends?" I asked quickly before she could say something else.

"They're on the front porch, last I saw," she returned. "I'm going to give you a sponge bath and then I'll get them."

"Why am I getting a bath?" I asked. "I had one last week."

In a tone that suggested she was explaining something to a dim-witted child she said. "When a man lies in bed for three days, unconscious, he gets dirty. Take my word for it. I've been a nurse for a while."

I thought about that a bit and I couldn't resist. "How do I know you don't just like giving baths to young men?" I said.

She looked at me, startled, and then slapped me playfully on the arm. "Hush," she said and continued what she was doing.

She pulled the sheet down and began looking at various parts of me, occasionally touching a bandage or bending to sniff at something. There were apparently many cuts and places where the skin had been scraped off. As much as I wanted to look I couldn't. It hurt too much.

She was gentle but took her time, and by the time she'd finished I'd forgotten to be embarrassed. Again, she was gentle when she gave me the bath, but still it hurt in many places, although, by the time she finished, I had to admit I felt better, regardless of the pain.

"I'm going to give you some laudanum, so you'll probably be drowsy after a bit. You can visit with your friends for a few minutes, but the doctor wants to see you and tell you what he did and what you're going to have to do to get better. If you want to finish up this trip I hear you're on, I suggest you pay attention. After that I'll give you your medicine for pain." She said this last part as she opened the door and left.

Jinx hopped up on the bed, purring loudly and rubbing against my chin. "Hey, Little Buddy," I murmured. "Thanks for taking care of me." I tried to stroke his head, but it hurt too much. He seemed to understand and finally, after rubbing against my face and head, curled up at the foot of the bed.

Annalise had left the door open and I could hear her talking to someone. "Not too long this first time. I've already told him about what happened so don't get too much into that because he's still woozy. You can fill him in on the details when he's feeling better."

The door opened and Handy came in, ducking his head as usual. He stopped and grinned at me.

"Wow," he said. "You look like hell."

I tried to smile but that hurt too. "Bet I don't look as bad as I feel," I said. "Don't be funny. It hurts to laugh."

He moved into the room, and Wash and Doc came in behind him. Behind them came a short stocky man, balding with a white fringe of a beard around his jaw, and after him, my nurse with the laudanum. My friends stood against the walls and we all listened to what the doctor had to say.

He took my left hand and smiled down at me. "Son, you gave me more work in one day than I've had to do in the last month. But I'd say we got things patched up well enough and now it's up to you to let it all get better."

He pulled the sheet down and gave my various wounds a glance. "Annaliese says your skin hurts are all doing fine." He walked around the bed and began to look at the cast on my right arm. "This might be a problem." I had noticed my hand seemed to be turned at a little different angle.

"Apparently the damage was bad enough that when I splinted and then set it, it wouldn't assume the normal position compared to the arm. It's twisted a bit, so you probably won't be able to use it quite as well, at least for a while. It's hard to figure how it will work. We'll just have to wait and see."

He moved to the foot of the bed and bent over to look closely at the cast on it. "I'm using a new type of casting material and I think it is an improvement." He seemed to be looking for cracks in the cast.

He straightened up and looked at his daughter. "Can you get him his medicine?" he said. She stepped forward with a spoon and a bottle and I experienced the bitter taste of laudanum for the first time but not the last.

Dr. Crawford spoke again. "We need to make sure you cough when you need to. With you lying in this bed for a while and not being able to cough very well because of the pain and the laudanum, you could get pneumonia and we'd rather you didn't."

He stood regarding me in silence for a minute and then said, "As far as the pain goes, we can give you laudanum for it, but that keeps you from coughing, so we can't give you too much. Can you handle the pain?"

I thought about that for a bit and nodded.

"Good boy," he said and smiled at me. "We'll just take it a day at a time and see."

He left and Annaliese followed him out but was back in a minute. Handy pulled a chair up to one side of the bed and Wash and Doc arranged a bench so we could all talk.

"How's Rusty after that fall?" I asked Handy.

He shook his head. "I'm sorry Johnny," he said, "he broke both his forelegs and we had to put him down."

I closed my eyes. I had raised him from a colt and ridden him almost every day for the last six years. To lose him was a wrench. I seemed to open my eyes right away, but by the time I did they were gone, and then I drifted off into sleep.

Over the next few days I slept a lot and each time I woke up Annaliese was in the room, usually sitting by the window reading or standing by my bed washing me or doing some nursing thing. At the edges of my mind she was always there, doing things to me and for me.

There was a time when I began to feel strange, and after thinking about it realized this must be fever. After that things just sort of drifted in and out of my mind. I remembered some but forgot most.

My spells of consciousness usually came when pain from one place or another on my body made me realize I was alive. Other than that, I just felt like I was drifting around between heaven and hell, waiting for someone to make up their mind.

The next time I woke up it was dark. I lay for a few minutes staring into the darkness and letting my mind get hold of where I was and what was going on. I felt soreness with a deep breath but the sharp, stabbing pain I had felt before was mostly gone. I could feel the casts on my foot and arm but no pain there or anywhere else for that matter. My mind felt clear for the first time in a while.

I turned my head slowly, leery of the pain and saw Annaliese sitting by a lamp reading a book. As I watched she lifted her right hand slowly to her breast, pressed against it and moaned quietly. I knew enough about women that I thought I understood what she was doing. I couldn't take my eyes off her but didn't want her to know I had seen her at what I thought was a very private moment.

Maybe I gasped or something, but she looked up suddenly, caught my eye and the moment was over. She looked startled, then she smiled and then grinned.

"Looks like you caught me," she said. She didn't seem embarrassed, but I was. I closed my eyes for a moment and when I opened them she was standing by the bed, looking down at me.

"It looks like you're feeling better," she said and patted the growing bulge in the blanket.

I just lay there and looked at her. I couldn't think of anything to say. When I opened my eyes again the light was dim, and I heard the door close. I lay there trying to figure out what had just happened and what it meant. I guess I drifted off to sleep before I puzzled it out because I was thinking about it when I woke up the next morning.

I don't really know what I expected she'd say or do in the morning, but she behaved as though it never happened, and I began to question whether it was a dream or not. About the time I had decided I'd imagined the whole thing, she winked at me and suddenly I felt like laughing. It was a relief to know I wasn't going crazy.

There was a rap at the door and Dr. Crawford came in.

"Well, it looks like we're past the worst of it," he said as he pulled a chair up to my bed and sat down. "Your fever has broken, and your lungs sound almost normal. I think you may still be a little nervous about taking a deep breath, but you need to. Got to keep junk from building up in there. Your cuts and scrapes are healing fine and there doesn't seem to be a problem with your foot and arm." He made a note on a tablet he was carrying.

"We need to make a plan for helping you get back on your feet," he continued. "The one thing that could beat us is for you to lie in that bed for a couple more weeks and get pneumonia again. I don't know if we could pull you through again."

"So, here's what I'd like to do. The cast can come off your arm in about two more weeks. The foot or ankle will need a bit longer, so I'm going to fix a piece of wood to the bottom of the cast and that will allow you to get up and move around."

You're going to be weak and wobbly for a while, but with a little practice, you should be able to get around pretty good, though it will be tiring. Anna will help you until you get your balance and get used to it. It shouldn't take long for you to get your strength back." He looked up at her and she gave him a little salute.

"I can handle it, sir," she said. "I will keep him on his feet and off his backside, I promise." She looked like she would enjoy the job.

CHAPTER EIGHTEEN

"Annaliese has told me pretty much what happened that day, but I'll bet you three can fill in a lot of details," I said. "So, get started."

It was later that day and Handy was sitting at my bedside. Wash and Doc were on a bench at the foot of the bed.

"What's the last thing you remember?" asked Handy.

"I remember the sound of a rattlesnake and then the world sort of exploded," I said, and after I thought for a while I continued. "I remember falling but I don't remember hitting the ground. After that, nothing till I woke up here."

"Well, I guess I'll start, and you fellows can jump in when I get to where you fit," said Handy, looking around at the others. They nodded and he began.

"I was a couple of yards behind you when we heard the rattler," he said. "Rusty reared, and when he came down, apparently his left forehoof came down on some loose ground and he fell. You pushed off and away, so he didn't roll on you. I watched you roll down the hill and was off my horse by the time you fetched up against a tree near the bottom. When I got down there you were awake but groggy. You asked for a drink of water and by the time I got to the creek and back, Wash and Doc were there, and you had passed out." He stopped and looked at Doc who nodded and picked up the narrative.

"It was easy to see where you had broken bones and I splinted the arm with a couple of saplings. The ankle break was something I'd never handled before, so I just tried to keep you from moving it any more than necessary. Since Wash knew Doctor Crawford, we decided he should ride down to Salt Lake, get the doctor, and bring a wagon up the canyon to carry you into town. Handy built a fire and with some hot water, I cleaned and bandaged you as best I could. Since we couldn't figure how to get you back up the hill, we got you onto Handy's back and he carried you down to a place where the trail ran close to the creek. It was three hours before Wash got back with the doctor and Annaliese and then another two hours to get you down here and into that bed."

"You say you knew the doctor?" I asked Wash.

He nodded, "Sarah and the kids spend the winter with the Crawfords sometimes. I rode down here with them one winter and stayed to help out around the place."

"I knew I'd heard that name before but couldn't remember where," I said. "Sarah mentioned him before we left there, didn't she?"

He nodded. "Handy got a letter from them the other day and they're planning to come down around October first or so," said Wash. "I think he's been writing to Rebecca every day since we got here, encouraging them to come early this year. Just so they could see you, of course."

I glanced at Handy and could see the imp in his eyes. "I guess no one here had ever been in love," he said to the room in general, and we all laughed.

"How are you feeling?" asked Doc. "You still having pain in the lungs?"

"No, but I still get tired easy," I said, and as though she'd been listening at the door, Annaliese swept into the room.

"He needs to rest," she announced. "He'll still be here tomorrow."

Handy stood and said, "We've got a place in someone's house around the corner from here. If you need anything just let us know."

I think I was asleep before they were out the door.

For the next two weeks I fell into a routine of doing things to help me get better and was able to do a little more every day. My scrapes and skins healed up with no problems and my ribs, though still tender when I coughed, no longer interfered with my breathing. Annaliese had me on a routine to keep my lungs working and using what muscles that were not in a cast on a regular basis.

I was anxious to see how much my gun hand would be affected by the break in my arm. Though it was hard to tell in the cast, my thumb seemed to be twisted slightly away from my body and I wondered whether I'd even be able to use the Henry, not to mention the Colt. I needed to ask Handy where it was. I hadn't seen it and was anxious to see how it felt in my hand when the cast was off.

Of course, the main thing on my mind everyday was Annaliese. I had replayed what had happened that night again and again and gotten no closer to understanding what it meant. Now that I was awake and recovered enough to notice, I began to pay attention to her for the first time. She was almost as tall as me and her dark red hair was shoulder length when she didn't have it braided and wrapped around her head.

Her eyes were green, and she had a thick spray of freckles across her nose and on her cheeks and probably everywhere else. All in all, I'd call her pleasant looking with a generous figure, round hips and a large bust and she fascinated me. Although I had no idea how much I weighed, I'd guess she was about the same as me, and I knew she was stout because of the way she handled me when she had to move me or when she helped me out of bed to answer the call.

But the thing that fascinated me the most were her lips. They were full and moist looking, and I had a hard time keeping my eyes off them.

The night before I was supposed to have the cast on my arm removed, I was laying in the dark when I heard the door open and close. I could see a dark shadow looming above me, and then she leaned down and kissed me full on the lips.

Her mouth was open, and her tongue worked between my lips and opened my mouth. Suddenly we were exploring each other's mouths and it was the warmest, wettest, most wonderful thing I had ever felt. Her hand grasped the swelling through the blanket, and I could feel her smile against my mouth.

When she broke the kiss she whispered, "It won't be long now." Then she was gone, and I heard the door open and close.

It was a good thing I didn't have a cast on both my arms that night.

A couple of nights later I was sitting up reading to Jinx and trying to stay awake when I was startled by a light knock on my door. It was late for a visitor, and I was a little puzzled when Handy stuck his head around the door.

"Can I come in?" he asked and came in anyway.

"What are you doing tomcatting around this late?" I asked motioning for him to sit.

"How are you doing?" he asked. "Looks like you got your cast off. Have you been moving around more?" One thing about Handy, he could carry on both sides of a conversation sometimes.

I hadn't seen him for a couple of days. They had ridden up to Ogden and Brigham City to scout for a place to spend the winter and had just gotten back. Tomorrow or the next day they were planning to ride south of the city to Camp Floyd with some soldier friends of Wash's to show Handy the beginning of the trail we would take come spring. From there they planned to swing north to see the Great Salt Lake and then back to town.

I filled him in on my progress. A couple of day before, the doctor had taken the cast off my arm and Annaliese was nagging me to do the exercises he wanted me to do to get it back to full use. The same day a fellow had brought in a thin wooden shoe-like piece of wood and using plaster, the doctor had attached it to the bottom of my foot cast so I could get up and move around.

Jinx hopped from the bed into his lap, said hello, and Handy petted him and scratched under his chin while we talked.

After a few minutes he leaned back in his chair and stretched his long arms. "Ran into a friend of yours yesterday."

I looked a question at him.

"Fellow come up to our table at dinner, and without so much as a by your leave, pulled out a chair and sat. At first I didn't recognize him, beard, long hair and a new bullet scar on the right side of his face. Kinda scruffy looking. When Wash pulled his chair out some so he could get at his gun, it dawned on me who it was."

My mouth must have fallen open. "The Gambler," I said.

"Sure enough." He paused for a moment, then continued. "I stood and put my hand on my gun, but he just sat there and smiled at me."

"You don't want to do that in a place like this," he said smooth as silk. I looked around at the citizens of Salt Lake, enjoying dinner with their families, and could see his point.

When I was back in my chair I asked, "What can we do for you?"

He looked around the table and smiled. "Since you all seem to know who I am, I won't bother to introduce myself." He looked at me and said, "Aren't you fellows one short? Where's your friend?"

Wash answered, "I can't think of a good reason to tell you that, but I would like to know why you're chasing us."

"I'm not chasing you, so if you don't get in the way you won't get hurt."

"If you're chasing Johnny, you're chasing us," I said. "So why don't you answer the man."

"He thought about that for a minute and said, 'All right, he's got some things of mine and I want them back.' He nodded at my holster and said, 'As a matter of fact, there's one right there.'"

"I stood up again, and Wash and Doc stood up with me. "Johnny Fry gave me this gun and I don't believe he stole it from you or anybody, so that means it's mine. If you want to argue about that let's step outside."

"He looked at us, one after another and said, "No, I don't think so. Not now. But I believe you boys are headed for Sacramento, and there's a lot of places between here and there, so I'll wait."

"I knew both Doc and Wash wanted to put a bullet into him then and there, but we knew it wouldn't sit right at that time and place, so we left him sitting there."

Handy looked at me and pursed his lips. "So, what do you think?"

"I think I want my gun. Where is it?" I said.

He shook his head. "By the time we got you loaded up that night up in the canyon and thought to look, it was dark, and we never found it. I'm sorry Johnny, your holster was all tore up and it must have come out when you fell." He stood and unwrapped a package he'd been carrying when he came in and handed me the Gambler's gun. I looked at his holster and saw a new Colt 44.

"I bought a new one today." He slid a new Colt out of his holster and showed it to me. "No arguments," he said. "That's your gun. This one's fine for me."

I took it in my left hand. It was loaded and the weight of it dragged my hand down onto the bed. My right hand, fresh out of the cast, couldn't even wrap around the butt. It was going to take a while.

After he'd gone, I couldn't sleep. I tossed and turned, thinking about what he had told me. Was I going to have to spend my life looking over my shoulder? I didn't like the idea of that man being so important to me.

I awoke to the sound of my door opening and Annaliese came into the room. She slowly pulled back the blanket and lay down beside me, then pulled the blanket over both of us. I could feel her nakedness and a warm flush seemed to rush across my body and into my crotch. When she kissed me, my heart tried to leap out of my chest, and suddenly I didn't care if there was someone trying to kill me or anything else, for that matter. The only important thing in the world was that warm, firm, exciting body beside me, then on top of me.

After, I lay beside her staring at nothing on the ceiling, wondering at how good I felt.

"Does this mean I've been seduced?" I whispered.

She had to hide her face in the pillow so her laughter wouldn't wake up the house.

"Yes," she whispered, her lips against my ear and her voice so low I could just hear her. "Would you like me to do it again?"

Before we did, I lifted her gown and pulled it over her head. I very much wanted to feel all of her body against mine.

It felt as wonderful as I thought it would.

CHAPTER NINETEEN

I woke up the next morning in love, though I had to admit I didn't really have any idea what it was or what happened next. When she came in in her uniform and helped me into my chair, it didn't take me long to realize she was my nurse again and not the woman who'd come to me the night before.

She did have a sneaky smile for me when she brought me my breakfast though.

This was all new to me, so I had to let her lead me until I learned a little more, but one thing I couldn't control, and it popped up regularly whenever she was around. Or when she wasn't for that matter. She grinned at me the first time she saw it, then ignored it. Maybe that's what love is, wanting to do it all the time. If that was the case, you'd think it would be all that ever got done.

I was still thinking about it after lunch when Handy, Wash, and Doc came in. Jinx had been on the porch when they rode up and led them into the room. He hopped up in the chair and curled up in my lap. This was the first time they'd seen me out of bed for almost a month, and all sat down with big smiles on their faces.

Since I couldn't talk to them about what was on my mind, I waited to hear what they had on theirs.

"No sense in retelling what Handy told you," said Wash. "I'm sure you been thinking about it."

I felt a little sheepish. I hadn't thought about it at all since she walked into the room last night.

"Doc and I went around to most places in town we could think where he might be staying or hanging out," he continued, "but no sign of him."

I held up my finger. "Give me a minute to get my thoughts together," I said. I sat petting Jinx and thinking of some of the questions I wanted answered.

"Do you think he'll try anything in Salt Lake?" I asked. "He did say he'd see us down the road, didn't he?"

Handy put in, "I'd not put too much faith in that. He's probably a liar as well as a thief."

"Doc and I have talked about it some, and we feel he won't try anything in the city," said Wash. "There are half dozen towns within a day or two where he can hide out and spend the winter. He probably can figure pretty close when we'll pull out in the spring, and he can get out ahead of us.

"He likely don't want to stick his head in a noose around here," said Doc. "These people don't have much patience with the kind of thing he's plannin' and the courts around here have a reputation for being hasty with a rope."

"Of course, the biggest problem we got," said Handy, "is he not only knows where were going, he knows how we plan to get there and pretty much when we're leaving. Probably plenty of places between here and Sacramento where he could make it unpleasant for us."

"One thing to remember," said Doc, "if we were to find him, we have to be careful of those same people who are quick with a rope." He paused and nodded at Wash. "It ain't like some places we've been where they didn't care who shot who, just so it wasn't them. Port Rockwell and Bill Hickman might be dead but there are others like them around."

"You fellows sure you want to hang around with me anymore?" I asked. "If I keep on the Pony it will be like being ducks in a shooting gallery."

I looked at Handy. "If that's what you want to do then I reckon I'm with you," he said.

"I signed up for the duration," said Wash, the old soldier. "But we need to do some serious thinking this winter and come up with a plan to get us through in one piece."

I looked at Doc. "I'll let you know in the spring," he said with a grin. "Don't know what will come up between now and then."

"I guess the first thing I got to do is get better," I said. "I'm a little worried about this hand. When I stand up it won't lay flat against my leg the way it should. It's really weak right now and I can't use my thumb right. When I get this cast off my foot, I want to start working the Colt with my left hand just in case it doesn't get right by spring."

"I've seen you shoot lefty before," said Handy. You did alright. Of course, you might not be as fast." His voice trailed off; then, "I finally might be able to beat you," he said with a grin.

We all laughed, but my laugh wasn't as long as theirs.

That night Annaliese came to me again, and it was better than the first time. She took the time to teach me some little things she liked, and I tried to be a good pupil. After, we talked in low tones.

Since she spent so much time with patients in this part of the house, she had made up a small room with all she needed to stay overnight when she had one. No one ever came into this area at night unless there was a patient who needed the doctor, or she needed help with someone. Even so, she didn't want to take a chance and be overheard.

She leaned over me and kissed me. There was enough moonlight in the room that I could see her silhouette but not her face.

"Do you know how old I am, Johnny?" she whispered.

I had to admit I'd wondered.

"I'll be twenty-eight in January." She paused. "You're eighteen."

I pulled her into a strong embrace and whispered in her ear. "Good."

She was smiling when I kissed her with as much passion as I knew how. Later she helped me position my bulky cast, and I mounted her for the first time. She held me back and we made love slowly for a long time, finally finishing exhausted in each other's arms.

After, I lay looking up at nothing on the ceiling again. She kissed me on the cheek and said, "I don't want to fall asleep so I'm going to leave now." With that she stood and pulled her gown on over her head. The moonlight was behind her, and I could see the shape of her body through the gown.

"I'm not sure this is a good idea," she said. "I'm not sure how it will end." After a moment she continued, "but I don't care." She kissed me on the forehead. "Let's take a night off so you can get some rest and then we can do it again." She paused and kissed me on the nose. "And again." She paused and kissed me on the lips. "And again." A third pause. "OK?"

Before I could think of an answer she was gone, closing the door behind her.

The following week was nice. Except for my left foot, all my hurts were better, and I was able to get up without help and move around enough to get used to the wooden foot on my cast. One of the boys always seemed to be around. We sat on the porch, talked, and watched people go by.

The Crawford's house was on the east side of Salt Lake, close to Emigration Canyon and on a main road leading to the Temple in the center of town, so there were people passing by all day, especially on Sunday.

Actually, it wasn't really a house. It was much larger than any of the other houses I could see from the front porch and seemed to function as a small hospital as well as the home of the doctor and his family, which was substantial. He had three wives and five daughters living at the house. The only son was away doing something for the church.

Annaliese was the third oldest child and her father's right hand with patients. She had applied herself by reading, and learned much from her father, so that she was almost as trusted as he was when someone sick needed help.

I was sitting on the porch one rainy Sunday morning. The boys had ridden north to Ogden the day before and were not due back till the next day. The doctor and the family had gone to the Temple. My cast was to come off the next day and I would be able to begin living my life again, though I must admit, I didn't like the idea of leaving the hospital. While here Annaliese came to me almost every night, and when I left I would leave that too.

It was really a strange routine we had fallen into. In the daytime she was my nurse and she smiled at me and treated me like I was any other patient.

At night she was different. She could be gentle and patient, teaching me new ways to please her. She could also be passionate and demanding and I carried the image in my mind of her riding me like she was on a galloping horse.

We always needed to be quiet and it was always dark, so I never really saw her body or face when we were making love or heard her cry out from the pleasure and passion I could tell she felt. We loved lying in each other's arms, feeling the nakedness, in a daze, afterward.

One night I felt a thump when Jinx leaped onto the bed and crawled up to lay down between us. He meowed and there was definitely a question in it. Annaliese and I looked at each other and then grabbed a pillow to muffle our laughter. He had never seen such a commotion and wondered what was going on. I was sure he'd get used to it.

I was doing a drill, cocking and leveling the Colt, trying to get used to the feel of it in my left hand when she came out on the porch and sat in a chair beside me.

Ever the nurse she asked, "Are you warm enough?" I had a blanket wrapped around my legs, my cast up on a stool and was plenty warm, probably from what I was thinking.

"We're all alone," she said with a smile of mischief on her face. "What shall we do?"

"Do we have time?" I asked, and she laughed and leaned over and kissed me on the cheek.

"What are you reading?" she asked. She picked up the book I had beside me and looked at the binding.

"It's a book I got from Sarah. It's about the Mormons and Salt Lake City," I replied. "I had it in my duffel and Handy brought it over yesterday. Englishman named Burton wrote it back in '62. Since I hope to spend the winter here, I figure it would be a good idea to read up on the people hereabouts. He also talks about the trip west from here, and that will come in handy in the spring."

She nodded and said, "I met him when he was here. He spent some weeks here and I remember him sitting in the Doctor's office and them talking all day. I couldn't have been more than five, but I remember he gave me an English coin and I kept it for a long time. It had the Queen's picture on it."

She cocked her head and looked thoughtful. "I wonder what happened to that thing? I'll bet Tommy stole it. We lived in the same room for years and she was always taking my stuff." Her sister's name was Thomasina, hence Tommy.

"Considering how much time we spend together in bed, I really don't know much about you," I said. "So why don't we tell each other all our secrets while we can?"

She looked at me, then turned her head and stared out at the rain, apparently thinking. I had enough sense to sit quiet, and after a minute she finally asked, "Have you ever heard of the Mountain Meadows Massacre?" I had.

CHAPTER TWENTY

In 1857, a wagon train made up of people from Missouri and Arkansas headed for California was attacked 300 miles southwest of Salt Lake by Mormons dressed as Indians. After a siege of five days and under a flag of truce, Mormon militia had murdered every man, woman and child over the age of six.

I was sure there were two sides to that story, but the things I had read and heard about Mormons had made me realize that one of the problems in finding out much about them was that everyone was either for or against them. Trying to find out what really happened was hard because everyone seemed to have a dog in the fight.

That's what I liked about Burton's book. He took no sides. He was from England and he had written about traveling all over. When he left here, he probably went to someplace in Africa to write another book. I trusted him to tell me what he found out, good and bad. Nothing I had seen or heard had made me come down on one side or another.

Annaliese was still looking out at the rain. She smiled a little. "I was a babe in arms," she almost whispered. She paused, probably remembering, and then continued. "I was born before we left Missouri;

I was maybe 6 months old. I had two sisters, one twelve and one five, and two brothers, one ten and one eight. That was Ben. He was small for his age, so they let him live. "

"They killed everyone over seven, so that left the three of us alive. The rest of the kids who lived through it were adopted by Mormons in the area and after a while, all the rest were taken back to their relatives in Arkansas but for some reason we weren't. I guess they couldn't find any of our relatives."

"Ben remembered most of it and he told me. He and his sister saw their mother and father and brother and sister led away and heard the gunshots that killed them. They had seen the bodies the next day when they were taken to live with strangers who had been a part of it."

She stood up, perched herself on the porch rail and looked down at me, sitting with Jinx in my lap. I had put the gun down, so he reclaimed his spot.

"Later Dr. Crawford came to town. When he left, he took Ben and me with him, and I've been here ever since."

"Did you ever see your sister again?" I asked.

"She comes to town now and again. I'm not close with her," she replied. "She's become a regular Mormon. Her husband is a local elder in Cedar City and has three other wives."

"So how about you?" I asked. "I have the feeling you're not a 'regular Mormon."

She sat next to me again and took my hand. "Do you think I'm terrible?" she said, "seducing a child and leading him into sin?"

"Actually, I kind of like it," I replied, "and I can't think of one thing about you that's terrible unless it would be that freckle right there." I kissed her on the nose.

I sat holding her hand and looking at her for a while, then asked, "How about Ben? Is he a good Mormon?"

"He is," she replied, "strangely enough, although I think it's more the social part of it that's important to him. He grew up in it and all his friends and neighbors are involved much like he is. He has two wives and is very active at the Temple. I don't believe he takes the spiritual side of it too seriously."

"It sounds like you don't take it too seriously either," I said.

"Let me tell you about my life. One of these days I'll let you read my diary, but until then I'll just talk about it."

"I guess the first really important thing happened when I was eight and Ben sat me down and told me everything about that day. He did it gently and fairly, but from then on, I looked at everyone a little differently."

"I don't want you to think my life has been hard or I have been ill-treated. I have always been one of the family and been taken care of, but my 'mothers' never loved me. They had their own children and I grew up different. Ben and the Doctor loved me, though, and I always knew that."

"I call him the Doctor, but he's always been a loving and wonderful father to me. He raised me as a daughter and a friend, and now a colleague.

"I began to help him in the hospital when I was eleven, and by the time you came along I had been doing it for sixteen years. Nursing that is," she said, responding to my leer."

"He taught me how to care for people, to care what happens to them, and always treated me as an equal, which is why I could never marry a Mormon. I won't allow anyone to treat me as less than an equal.

The Doctor gave me my life's work and straight and true answers to any question I ever asked him, no matter what it was about."

"He also gave me his library and always had ideas about what I might like to read. Whether I wanted to talk about a book or an idea or a heartache, he was always willing to listen. He always encouraged me to do what I felt I could and helped me to do what I felt was right."

"He's strange about Mormons and their beliefs. He loves the strong sense of community and the bonds of friendship and responsibility that bind Mormons together, but he never really enjoyed having three wives and couldn't bring himself to believe Brigham Young talked to God whenever either of them had a problem.

"Both he and Ben had always given me the space I needed to find faith or not. It was always my choice. So far, Mormonism hasn't stuck with me. I've read a lot about the faith and the history, but it's never appealed to me as a way to think or to live my life. Even though I'm part of a Mormon family I'm allowed to live here as a gentile if I choose to.

"Ben and I have been as close as two kids can be, separated by eight years, but he loves the Doctor and has grown up to be a lot like him. He treats me much the same as the Doctor does.

"Other than those two the person I love most is your friend, Sarah. She's like a sister to me. She and the children have spent winters here at the hospital for the last eight years. She lent me a copy of Burton's book and has recommended many that have helped me get a pretty good grip on Mormons and their secrets and the Mountain Meadows Massacre."

She was quiet for a minute and stood looking down the road at the rain, then turned to me and said, "So does that answer your questions, little boy?" and kissed me on the lips.

I grinned beneath her kiss and replied, "No. I want to know where you learned all the things you teach me in bed. How do you know what feels good to you and to me too?"

She looked at me with a big grin on her face. "Are you the jealous type?"

"I don't really know," I said. "I never had anything to be jealous about before now."

"Well, you're not the first patient I've fallen for, Johnny." She sat next to me and took my hand again. "I was seventeen and had read many novels and he was so handsome. He was a Frenchman named Jean Pierre Moreau. I've always thought that was a very romantic name."

"He was twenty-six and a trapper. He had been wounded in a fight with the Ute Indians, and by the time he got to us, his arm was badly infected. We managed to save his arm, but he was here for a month and I fell in love."

"I came to his bed every night for the last week he was here, and we didn't get much sleep. I think the Doctor kept him longer than necessary because he could see what was happening and had no objection. After he got better and left the hospital, he stayed in town for a while and we spent time together at a place he'd found up in the Canyon."

She picked Jinx up, moved him off my lap and lay with her head on my chest so I could put my arms around her. "I was heartbroken when he left," she said. "About the time I began to get over it, he showed up again and stayed a month. He came back again the following year and then I heard he drowned at a place called Klamath Falls up in Oregon. That was eight years ago."

I kissed her on the top of her head. "Do you make a habit of seducing your patients?" I asked.

"You're the first since Jean Pierre," she said. She raised her head so that her nose was almost touching mine and looked directly into my eyes. "Do you believe me?"

I kissed her on the lips and let it linger for a bit. "I'd believe you if you told me the moon was purple," I said. "Besides, from the way you Seem to want it all the time, I thought it must have been a while."

She gave me a friendly swat and stood. Down the street we could hear people returning from Temple. "Not enough time for you to tell your story," she said. "But I think Handy has told me most of it. You can fill in the details next time."

"I get the feeling I'm going to be able to leave here before long," I said. "Do you remember where that place in the woods is?"

She laughed and said, "It's coming on to fall and winter soon. We'd freeze. Besides, I think we can find someplace better than that. Give me a kiss before they get here."

About mid-morning the next day, she came into my room following the Doctor. He was carrying a long, curved blade that looked like a saw. He sat by my bed and showed it to me.

"This is what I'm going to use to take the cast off," he said, "so I need for you to be as still as you can. It shouldn't take long. Once it's off we can talk about the next step."

He was right. Ten minutes of careful cutting and sawing and it was gone, and Annaliese was washing my foot in warm water.

After it was all cleaned up, he sat and patted me on the arm. "It looks like we've pulled you through. Everything looks fine, although I think you may have lost some of the use of your right hand. I've got a crutch for you and I want you to use it for a couple of days."

Actually, you should use it in your right hand but since that's still a little weak, you can use your left. Then you can go to a cane for a couple of days. Put more and more weight on it every day and I believe by the end of the week you should be ready to leave us."

He stood, and with my left arm I reached to take his hand. "Thank you for everything Doctor," I said.

"I won't see you much this week," he said, "but Anna will be here if you need anything. She'll support you till you get strong enough to feel comfortable again. Come Saturday, unless there's a problem, I'll try to be here to see you off."

When he had gone, Annaliese helped me up and stood back and let me try the crutch to see how I handled it. The fifty feet to the front porch wore me out and I was relieved to collapse into my chair.

I looked up at her, a little breathless. She had let me struggle with the crutch and now sat on the edge of the chair and asked, "Does your foot feel really light?"

I nodded. "It makes me feel clumsy and off balance. I don't think I could have made it without the crutch."

"It won't take long for you to get used to it. You'll be surprised at how quick you'll be back to normal."

She was right. By the second day I got rid of the crutch and picked up the cane.

A couple of days later she came into the room with a basket on her arm. "It's a great fall day out there, so let's go for a ride in the buggy," she said.

This was my first time out of the house since the day I fell, and I was excited just thinking about it. The look in her eyes made me excited about what we would do when we got to where we were going.

When we were out of sight in the canyon, I asked her to stop, then sat looking into her bright, blue eyes and kissed her. "Is there someplace near here we can lie down?" I mumbled through the kiss.

She laughed her pretty laugh. "Aren't you the impatient one? Don't worry. I have a place in mind a few minutes from here. We can hide the buggy and walk a little way to a beautiful little clearing where you can have your way with me."

She said this last with a straight face and we both laughed. She chirped to the horse and we were soon turning off the road, hiding the buggy and walking, hand in hand, up a path in the woods, thinking about what we would do when we got to where we were going.

The clearing was about fifteen feet across and open to the sky. We spread the blanket and stood looking at each other.

"I want to see you," I said breathlessly; "all of you."

The whole time she was shedding her clothes she was watching me doing the same. When we were naked, I fell to my knees in front of her and pressed my mouth to her pubic hair, the same dark red as her beautiful curls. She had freckles here, as everywhere, and I began to kiss them one by one. "Will you kiss me down there?" she breathed. And I did.

When I mounted her I was able to see, for the first time, her eyes widen, then close when I entered her; see for the first time her large, pink tipped breasts and feel them against my chest; feel her need and hear her voice, not caring who heard, telling me of her need for more... and more.

Afterward we lay looking up into a pure blue sky, holding hands and smiling at nothing.

After a while, I began to count her freckles, one by one, with my tongue. I didn't get very far before she straddled me, guided me in and rode me slowly for a very long time, all the while swinging her breasts before my eyes and guiding them to my mouth. Near the end she was almost violent, and we finished in a frenzy.

Afterward we talked.

"What do we do now?" I asked her. We had dressed and she was laying our lunch out on the blanket.

"What do you mean?" she answered with a question.

"Well, I'm probably leaving in a few days and I don't want to lose what we have had. So how will we see each other again and what about when I leave in the spring?" I paused. "I can't think of anything I'd want in a wife that I haven't found in you. I'd ask you to marry me, but I don't know how you feel about that. We've never talked about the future, so I don't know how you feel or what you want."

She sat quiet, hugging her knees and rocking for a while. "I don't want you to think I haven't thought about it," she finally said, "because I haven't thought about much else for a while. None of the men around here pay me much attention, so getting married has never been part of my plans. In addition to being opinionated, stubborn, outspoken, headstrong and a gentile, I'm not a beauty and I'm getting old."

She held up her hand when I started to protest. "Not everyone loves freckles like you do and I'm a big girl; hefty is the word I've heard used. I hadn't thought about marriage since Jean Pierre was killed. I didn't expect to fall in love again, and yet here I am. There's one problem." She paused. "I'm almost ten years older than you and I haven't figured out how to think about that yet." She paused again and looked at me for a long moment.

"But I do have a suggestion. The Doctor has to go to Carson City and Sacramento in the spring to help set up a clinic in Carson City and another one in a Mormon community near Sacramento. I'm going with him, so let's do this. Whenever we can arrange it, we can see each other until you leave. When you get to Sacramento, if you still want to marry me, and if I still want to marry you, we will."

I sat still for a minute thinking that over. "I'm not going to change my mind," I protested.

"Well maybe you won't and maybe you will, but either way it's not going to be a hardship to wait a while. We can spend enough time together to keep us happy, and by then we should be able to figure out what's best; for both of us."

After we ate, we lay on the blanket and she fed me grapes one by one, like I was some oriental prince, and we made love again, this time with our clothes on, moving them aside just enough. It was late afternoon when we got back, and I was exhausted, so Jinx and I curled up on the bed and took a nap. When we woke it was dark. I was surprised to feel Annaliese sliding under the covers.

"Didn't you get enough today?" I whispered and she giggled.

"Let's just lie here and talk for a while." I put my arm around her, and she snuggled against me and sighed deeply.

"What do you want to do with your life, Johnny?" she asked, and while I was thinking about that, I fell asleep.

CHAPTER TWENTY-ONE

W hen I awoke, she was gone, but I was thinking about the question when she brought my breakfast. Right behind her came Handy and Wash.

We sat and talked for a while and I asked if they could take me to the closest general store so I could get out again. I was feeling stronger each day and wanted to get a new left-handed holster so I could work with the Colt some more.

The trip to the store was a revelation. Salt Lake City was a nice place. The streets were broad and well maintained, the houses spaced in an orderly manner, and the businesses appeared to be well cared for. Even the saloons looked nice. We stopped at a café, and with coffee in hand, sat at the front window for a bit and watched the people of the town pass by. It was an easy place to like.

At the general store I bought a new holster, and Handy bought a new one set up for the cross draw he preferred. I also bought some pieces of leather to modify them, so they fitted our needs. Pa had taught me enough leatherwork to add a few things that I wanted, and I had an idea for a new type of holster that I thought would bring the butt of the Colt a little closer to my hand and maybe make it a little quicker.

Handy took a different route home so I got to see even more of the town, but by this time I was tired and glad to sink into my chair again.

Annaliese gave me an occasional night off and I slept right through till breakfast. Wash showed up with my leatherworking tools, and he and Annaliese found a piece of board to lay across the chair. Once I was settled, they left me, and I got down to business.

I enjoy leatherwork and I was soon happily working away. I planned some bullet loops to go most of the way round, and after I cut the pattern in the belt, I was weaving a long leather strip through it when a thought struck me.

The saddle that came with Black, the Gambler's saddle, had some leather stitching woven around the cantle that was unlike any I'd ever seen, and now that I thought about it, the cantle was larger, that is thicker, than normal in a saddle. Was it possible that something was put into that space and that the leather stitches were that way because of what had been done?

Because it was the nicest saddle I'd ever seen, I had always kept it where I slept. I could see it sitting across the room, under a shelf of books. I couldn't imagine what could be hidden in it, but I was almost sure there was something.

About that time, Annaliese walked in the room.

"Can you help me, please?" I asked. "I think I may have solved a mystery."

She stared at me for a moment and then lifted the board off my lap and helped haul me out of the chair. I took a knife off the board, cut the center stitch on the back of the saddle, and drew the leather laces back on either side. I used the knife to carefully separate the leather pieces that had been glued together to form the cantle. From the space between I drew out a leather pouch that was tied with a thong.

I looked at Annaliese and held the pouch up. "I think this is the reason that man has followed me across the country." I put my hand on her shoulder. "I think I need to sit down. I don't know why, but my knees suddenly feel weak." When I was back in the chair I said, "Can you get a message to my friends? I want them here when I open this."

Within an hour they were seated around me. I untied the thong, opened the pouch, and pulled out two folded pieces of paper. The first was a letter of credit from a bank in St. Louis made out to Rene Paul in the amount of ten thousand dollars. The second was the deed to a silver mine in Carson City, Nevada.

I turned it over. "It's signed by someone to Mr. Rene Paul in payment of a debt and signed by two witnesses."

I looked at Wash. "Now I can answer your question. It seems this is the reason the Gambler has chased me all the way from Kansas."

"And," he said, "it probably means that the mine is worth some money, or he wouldn't have kept comin' like he has."

I handed the papers to Annaliese and she looked a question at me. When I nodded, she read them and passed them round the circle. When he handed them back to me, Doc asked, "Are these any use to you?" He paused and looked at the others, "To any of us?"

"Tell you the truth," I said. "I hadn't got around to asking that question yet."

Handy scratched his head like he did when he was thinking and said, "It looks to me like, unless you're willing and able to pass yourself off as Rene Paul to some bankers and mine owners, you might just as well use them in the outhouse."

I tended to agree, though I probably wouldn't have put it that way. "What do you think, Wash?

As usual he sat thinking a minute before he answered. "I don't know much about that kind of thing, but it looks to me like the only one it's any good to is this Rene Paul fellow, and we don't even know if he's the man we call the Gambler." He thought again. "And we don't even know where he is if we wanted to give it him. The next time we run in to him he's liable to be looking at us over the sights of a rifle."

I put my hands over my eyes, sat quiet for a moment and said, "Okay, what you're telling me is a man's trying to kill me to get something I'd give him willingly, but I can't because I don't know where he is and if I do find him he'll probably try to shoot me?"

"Yup, that's pretty much it." said Wash.

The situation was so ridiculous I burst out laughing.

Handy looked at me and shook his head. "That's one thing I love about you, Johnny; your sense of humor." But by that time Doc and Wash were laughing too and he couldn't help himself.

Annaliese looked at us like we were crazy, and while she was smiling, I pulled her down to where I could whisper. "Is it all right to tell them?"

She straightened up, looked at me for a second, nodded and mouthed, "Go ahead."

When everyone was looking at me with smiles still in place I said, "I think there has to be a change in plans. When I left Junction City I was sure the thing I wanted to do most was to ride the Pony Express Trail all the way to Sacramento."

"But now something's become more important than that. I can't see risking my life when I'm planning to get married, so let's find another way to get to Sacramento." While they were all gapping at me I put my finger to my lips, said, "Shhhh," and pulled Annaliese down for a kiss. It wasn't much of a kiss because she was smiling at their reactions.

Handy was the first to recover and swept Annaliese into a bear hug, and then shook my left hand in congratulations. He helped me to my feet, and while I was shaking hands with Doc and Wash, he blurted, "Me too Johnny, me too," as if I didn't know.

We sat by a stove at the kitchen table, ate biscuits with honey and drank hot tea in recognition of Doc's English heritage. While the others were talking, he leaned over and spoke in a low tone. "Some friends of mine are here and are leaving this week for South California. There's a nice little town near the border, San Diego, where they plan to spend the winter and they invited me along. I've been thinking about it and now that you boys are going to change your route you won't need me so much, so I think I might take them up on it."

"I owe you for being there when I needed you. If you ever need me just call and I'll do my best." I squeezed his shoulder. "Won't you miss old Wash?" I asked. "He talks to you a lot more than he ever does to us."

"Nah," he said with a grin. "We'll run into each other again and it'll be just like I never left."

After they left, Annaliese sat with me and we talked.

"I'm going to tell the Doctor in the morning," she said.

I nodded but didn't say anything for a bit. "You know, I've never thought much about being married, and Pa raised me after Ma died, so I've never known what a proper home and marriage is supposed to be."

I stood, pulled her into a hug, and we stood like that for a while, feeling each other's heartbeat. "I promise I'll always treat you as an equal and we'll make our decisions together."

She pulled away and stood with my hands in hers. "Let's get you to bed. By next spring we will probably have made and changed a dozen plans, but we'll do it together." She gave me a long slow kiss and slipped out the door.

It took me a while to get to sleep. Jinx lay on the pillow beside my ear and his purring was soothing, but thoughts kept whirling around in my brain. It seemed like tomorrow I would begin to make plans for the rest of my life but as I lay there thinking about Annaliese, I had trouble picking one thought out and staying with it.

Jinx moved to the foot of the bed and stretched between my legs. In the quiet, I must have drifted off to sleep.

In the morning I woke to the feel of him tapping me on the nose. I was glad to be back in the old routine where he never let me sleep when he wanted breakfast.

I had been thinking about the new holster and was anxious to see if I could make it work the way I thought. The idea was to attach the holster to the belt at an angle so that instead of hanging down the leg, the barrel would be forward, and the butt moved back. I was thinking this might make it easier to get the gun out quickly, and since I had to teach myself to use my left hand now, it seemed like a good time to make the change.

That morning was the first time I ate in the dining room with Annaliese, the Doctor and some of the family. He greeted me with a firm handshake and a big smile.

"Congratulations and welcome to the family," he said, and the rest of the family followed, although I could tell some of them wondered about Annaliese marrying outside the faith. I had met some of them, but Annaliese was the only one other than the Doctor who came into the hospital wing of the house, so I didn't know any of them very well.

After breakfast I sat on the porch with Jinx, surrounded by my duffel and waited for Handy and Wash to show up and take me to the place we hoped to spend the winter. Wash had found a job helping a farmer who lived a little north of town. His farmhand had been sent on a mission for the church and he needed help. We arranged to share the chores and he gave us room and board and some extra when there was extra work. The room was plenty big and had its own entrance.

Although I didn't need the money, Wash and Handy could both use it, so I pitched in when I could. With harvest coming on we stayed busy for a while. The farmer got his money's worth and I got some needed exercise.

On the second Monday after we began at the farm, Handy got a letter from Rebecca. Sarah had sold the store to a Mormon couple and they were coming to live in Salt Lake. He was beside himself, and for the next couple of days wasn't much use to anyone.

The plan was for them to stay with the Crawfords while they got their house ready to move in. Sarah had bought the place the year before so she must have been planning the move for a while. It was about halfway between the farm and the hospital. I imagined the impending nuptials might have made her decide to move a bit sooner than she might have.

According to Handy, Sarah's good relations with the Mormons helped her to get a good price and helped her get the loan she secured for the house when she bought it. Women couldn't usually borrow money without a husband, but one of the elders spoke to the bank and she got what she needed.

In fact, Annaliese believed the Saints helped the couple who bought the store find the money. Rebecca had included the address of the place and we went by to see it the next day. It was plenty big enough and it had a small cottage in the back yard where Rebecca and Handy could live.

CHAPTER TWENTY-TWO

For the next week we were kept busy around the farm. We were stacking hay for the winter, and the first couple of days I was stiff and sore, but as my muscles got more used to it, the aches and pains disappeared, and I could feel myself getting stronger every day. It felt good to work alongside my friends and feel we had accomplished something by the end of the day.

Our farmer friend was named Ephraim and he worked alongside of us and shared our food and drink. When I asked, he allowed us to use some haybales to set up a shooting range in one of his fallow fields.

I spent a couple of hours a day drilling with the Colt, sometimes with Handy, but most times by myself. Whenever he was there we usually had a contest, and I could see I was catching up. Of course, with him practicing again he was getting better too, so I was chasing a moving target.

My new holster was working out fine, although the movement to draw and level felt awkward and strange. The practice was building up the strength in my left hand and Handy said he could see me improving.

I liked the idea of the butt being closer to my hand and felt I could draw faster from that position than reaching across my front. I had worked from the left side occasionally for a few years and Pa had taught me enough good drill so that before long I was feeling comfortable with it.

My right hand I used as prop more than anything else. My thumb and forefinger didn't bend much and not with any strength, though the other fingers worked ok. My wrist was stiff and not too flexible, so I had to learn what I could do and not do from the right side.

Jinx spent the days hunting mice in the loft, sharing our lunch, and sleeping in the hayloft. He seemed to be glad to be riding on my shoulders again and was with me most of the time.

One day at noon we were sitting on in the grass in front of the barn with Wash while he had his lunchtime smoke when suddenly everyone burst out laughing. When I looked up to see why, Handy pointed at the corral where Black's head was leaning across the rails. Jinx was lying between his ears, fore legs hanging down the horse's forehead. It seemed like they were becoming as close as Jinx and Rusty.

"Have you thought any about how we get to Sacramento?" Wash asked when we had all sobered up.

"To be perfectly honest, I haven't been thinking much about it," I answered. "I've had a few other things on my mind."

"Boy do I know that feeling," chimed in Handy, and we all laughed.

"What do you think about it?" I asked Wash.

"Is there a way to get there without running into those fellows?"

He sat puffing on his pipe, blew out a cloud of smoke, and nodded. "Yeh, there's a couple of ways to do it, but before we talk about that, let me ask you a few questions."

"First, are you sure you still want to go to Sacramento?" He paused and let that hang in the air for a moment. "You're going to be marrying that lady, and this is where she lives. This is a nice place; why not stay here and set up housekeeping like Sarah? You've got enough money to buy a place, don't you?"

I had to admit I hadn't thought about it and Annaliese had never mentioned it.

"I'd like to hear your answer on that one," said Handy. "Don't get me wrong; if you want to go, then I'm with you, but if you don't, I think I could live with it."

"We're supposed to meet at Sarah's new place this evening," I said. "When we first talked about getting married, I promised her we would always make decisions together, so let me talk to her and then I can answer your question."

One thing about stacking hay bales, you can do it without thinking much, so I thought about Wash's question and what I believed Annaliese would say about it. I knew she felt like an outsider at home and being married to me would probably make that worse.

On the other hand, would she not rather stay here with the Doctor and her work and everything she has always known? And how would I feel about living in a place where almost everything was run by the Saints and most of the people had beliefs I didn't share?

The territory of Utah had been a part of the United States since the end of the Mexican War, but relations between Mormons and the U.S. government had never been particularly good. In 1857, Brigham Young's Mormon Militia had burned Ft. Bridger and Fort Supply before the advance of a thousand U.S. Cavalry, forcing the troops to spend a cold and miserable winter, under canvas, in the Wyoming wilderness.

Though there was no open combat, and no one was killed, feeling was running high in Salt Lake when a new governor replaced Young in 1860.

Since then the Saints, under Young's leadership, had tried many times to join the Union as a new state, but although it had more than enough people to qualify, there were two issues that neither side would compromise on: polygamy and the church's domination of Utah politics. Since the Civil War, Utah residents had seen five neighboring territories enter the Union as new states while they tried to decide if the changes demanded of them were worth it.

Most of the time that Annaliese and I were together we had other things to talk about besides Utah politics and the Mormon faith, but I could see we might have to begin.

Later that evening I was on the porch roof of Sarah's new place washing windows. Annaliese was washing the inside and we were making faces and kissing through the glass. Handy and I had come over to help get Sarah's house and the cottage ready for them.

A nice thing about Mormon houses, they were built for big families. She had bought the place from a family of eleven, three wives and seven kids, who had moved to Cedar City in the southwest corner of the territory.

They had decided to join others in a place of conservative sentiment and practice that harked back to the beginnings of the faith. Though fractious, the people there still accepted the leadership of the Elders in Salt Lake. However, based on experience, they rightly feared persecution by gentiles, and advocated another move into isolation rather than engaging them by joining the Union.

Brigham had realized they would soon run out of places to run and chose to pursue co-existence, believing that would eventually lead to acceptance. That area, around Cedar City, was the site of the Mountain Meadows Massacre, and there were people down there who had participated in and benefited from the killings.

When I climbed through the window, Annaliese was sitting on the bed. It had been ten days since we had made love and it was hard for me to resist grabbing her and laying her down, then and there. Instead I closed the door and sat next to her on the bed.

We sat for a minute just looking at each other and smiling, but when I moved to embrace her, she slipped sideways and stood.

"Too much work to do for that," she said. "Sarah and them will be here in a few days and we need to make sure this place is ready. It will be less of a problem and a lot less work if they can move right in instead of unloading at our place and then packing up again to move over here." Today her long, beautiful dark red hair was pulled back under a scarf and the dust on the end of her nose was just begging for a kiss.

"Of course, I do have a motive behind all this work," she said.

I reached out to flick the dust off her nose. "Tell me."

"When she's here and Rebecca and Handy are out back, we can send Jed out for something or other and have this room all to ourselves."

"What about Sarah?" I asked.

"She's in on the plot," she said. "She'll be in the den reading a book. She's our chaperone, so no one can complain about me being unaccompanied." She had a sly look on her face when she said this.

"Does this mean you're planning some more shenanigans in the bed?" I asked.

She bent over and gave me a long, searching kiss. "What do you think?" she asked. When I went to put my arms around her she danced away and opened the door.

"Bea, can you come up here for a minute?" she called to her sister, then stuck out her tongue at me.

Getting the house ready amounted to sweeping and dusting, washing down the kitchen and stove, and washing all the windows, which was a first for me. The closest glazier to Junction City was Kansas City and the cost meant there weren't many windows in town.

There had been a glazier among the original settlers of the valley and as a result, the houses and businesses here had many more windows and glass inset doors. This meant more light and better views which, with the mountains that towered above the city, was nice.

Bill, one of the family's hired men, was with Annaliese and her sisters, and he helped me clean and oil the pump and make sure there was firewood in the house and the barn ready for stock. The plan was to come back the next day, clean all the fireplaces and stoves, and give the cottage out back a good going over.

It was dusk when we took a lamp and went to see the cottage. It was just a couple of rooms, but it was bright and cheery even by lamp light. I could see that Handy was happy and excited about moving in.

Annaliese was unusual in her hometown. She was the only woman who could be seen driving herself somewhere at any time, day or night. People just assumed someone needed a doctor and her father was probably out of town.

On this cool evening she met me at Sarah's house, and before long we were naked and snuggled under a feather bed. We needed to talk but there were other things more important. It had been a while, and things were urgent and exciting.

Afterwards she lay close against me, head on my shoulder, with my arm around her. "Remember that time you asked me what I wanted to do with my life?" I asked.

"I remember I didn't get an answer because you fell asleep," she replied. "Have you decided yet?"

"Not so much, but Wash asked me something that's made me think."

She chuckled, "He's good at that, isn't he?"

"Yes, he is." I nuzzled her hair, inhaled its sweet fragrance. "He asked me if I'd thought about not going on to Sacramento in the spring."

She suddenly raised herself on her elbow and looked down into my face.

"How would you feel if I decided not to go on and instead, we got married and settled somewhere around here?"

She scrambled to her knees pulling the featherbed off me. Since it was cold I reacted by pulling her down against me. She struggled against me playfully for a minute and then relaxed, head on my shoulder again.

"Johnny, I was planning to go to Sacramento before you ever showed up." She was quiet for a while, then continued. "I'm tired of living where I'm judged on how I think and live differently than folks around me. Because the Doctor and I provided a needed service to the Saints, I'm tolerated, but never accepted. The Doctor thinks I've learned enough here and should go to medical school and set up my own practice."

"Some of the states in the east have begun to require licenses to open a practice, but California doesn't, so my plan was to go with him, set things up in the clinics, then stay when he comes home. The Elders want him to stay for a month or two, and by then they hope to have someone ready to step in and take over. Which means I'll be free to leave once he's gone, and the place is working."

She raised herself on elbow again and looked down at me. "How would you feel about being married to a doctor?"

"I'd love being married to you anytime, anywhere." We kissed and I held her. "Are there any woman doctors in the country? I've never heard of any."

"As far as I've been able to find out, two or three in California, a couple in Oregon and several in Colorado." She sat up and took the covers again and sat cross legged on the bed. Since she had taken most of the featherbed, I began to get dressed.

"I wrote to Dr. Hopkins in Colorado Springs and we've kept in touch. Her letters are full of the problems she faced and advice for how to deal with them," she said. "I keep them in my diary and read them often."

"Well if I could read them, maybe I could help," I said. "In fact, I really am looking forward to reading that diary and talking to you about it."

She was on her knees and she wriggled over and hugged me. "I love you for saying that. Of course, I'd love you even if you didn't." She kissed me, for a long time.

"I tell you what let's do. I'll bring it over after Sarah gets settled, when we can plan some time alone, and I'll read it to you." She kissed me again. "No making love that time."

"Really?" I asked

"Probably," she said with a shrug and grinned at me. "Rules are for breaking, you know."

I bowed at the waist. "My dear, I can think of no one I'd rather break rules with."

CHAPTER TWENTY-THREE

Now that I knew she didn't want to stay in Salt Lake, I had to think about how to get to Sacramento and, for the first time, what I would do when I got there. For the first of those I'd talk to Handy and Wash; the second I'd spend a lot of time thinking about.

The next morning, I awoke early and lay for a while petting Jinx and thinking. With all I had on my mind the one thing I kept coming back to was that I hadn't been on a horse since I went flying through the air in Emigration Canyon a couple of months before. For the last few days, I felt like I was strong enough, that both arm and leg could probably handle it as long as I took it slow and easy. But for some reason I still put it off.

The truth was Black scared me a little. He was the biggest horse I'd ever seen, and whenever I sat on him, I felt his energy like I was sitting on a bomb ready to explode. Only once had I let him run as fast as he could, and the memory of that was not reassuring at present. When I rode him, I always felt he had plenty more in reserve. To mount when I first got him I had to improvise a strap to allow me to pull up and grasp the horn.

That was when I was healthy. Now I had a recently healed left ankle and a right hand that wouldn't hold a grip. To mount I always put my left foot in the stirrup and pull myself up. Of course, I could try it on another horse before Black, but I felt like he was my horse now that Rusty was gone, and I might as well find out if I could ride him.

Just before lunch, with Wash and Handy watching and cheering me on, I led him out of his stall. If I was going to bust my butt, I'd probably be better off with an empty stomach.

"Do you want me to saddle him for you?" asked Handy. More than a few times on the trail I found him saddled in the morning and believed it was because Handy knew it was a bit of a stretch for me to get the saddle over.

"No thanks," I replied. "I need to find out what I can do."

I had worked and fussed over him since I got to the farm and had even put a blanket on him and put Jinx up so they could get used to one another again.

Now I threw on the blanket, put on his bridle, and led him outside for a short walk. I'm sure he could feel my nervousness, but he stood solid when I lifted the saddle and sort of threw it on to his back. I must have been clumsy about it because he turned his head and looked at me for a moment.

When he was ready and I couldn't put it off any longer, I took the strap in the last three fingers of my right hand, lifted my foot into the stirrup and pulled myself up so that my left hand could grasp the saddle horn.

Once settled in the saddle, I took a deep breath and with a nod to my friends, guided him out of the barn, stopped to let Jinx hop on from a fence post, and turned him through the gate into the lane beyond. We started at a walk, then a trot and finally I lifted him into a canter. We left a gallop for another time.

By the time I rode back into the farmyard I was grinning ear to ear. Sitting on the back of that big, beautiful black horse I felt like I was back to normal.

Over the next few days, we talked a lot about the trip. Handy pointed out that until we could figure a way to let the Gambler know he could have the papers I had found, we had to worry about him whether we took one trail or another.

After a while we came up with a plan and a route. We would leave Salt Lake City by way of Camp Floyd to the south, then cut north to the Overland route and head due west. We would cross into Nevada at Wendover, Utah, but instead of a swing north to Wells and back south to Reno and then Carson City, we planned to go straight cross country to the Carson River, then west to Carson City where we planned to stay until the passes opened, then on to Sacramento.

"Of course, the chances are he'll have someone keeping an eye on us," said Wash, "and who ever that is will probably follow us out of town. When we take off north to the Overland he'll be in a spot. Does he keep following us or take off to find his boss to tell him? If he chooses the second, then we can probably look for the Gambler to show up in Carson City, maybe before we get there."

We sat for a moment thinking about that and Handy asked, "So, how do we handle that?"

"I'd say we hang together pretty much and deal with it when it comes up. Carson City is a different kind of town than Salt Lake. A lot rougher, and people pretty much handle their own problems when necessary." He looked at me solemnly and continued. "Say your prayers and keep your powder dry, as we used to say with Grant and Sherman."

Given all our choices it seemed like a reasonable plan, so we put it aside until we knew more and went to sleep.

We were all working in the barn the next day when Sarah and Annaliese drove up in a surrey. Of course, the first question Handy asked was, "Where's Rebecca?" and when he learned she was at the Crawford's, he mounted and rode off, leaving us all standing there talking. Ain't love grand?

They had arrived the night before and had already moved some of their duffel into the new house. The ladies left shortly after. We arranged to meet them at Sarah's place when we had finished our work for the day.

It was late afternoon when we rode into the yard and tied our mounts at the hitch rail in front of the house. There was a wagon backed up to the front steps and another unloading into the kitchen from the back porch.

Two of Annaliese's sisters had come with her to help and with Bill, Handy, Wash, myself, and Sarah, Rebecca and Jed, we were a large party. By dark there were lamps in every room and people acting like it was a celebration.

One thing I had already learned about the Saints, they loved celebrations. And dancing. Annaliese and others had told me about this, but this was the first time I had seen it for myself.

Several of Sarah's friends had brought their families to welcome her and help with doing things. Since every visitor had brought some food there was no lack, and we ate and talked while we worked to settle Sarah and her children into their new home. Among the crowd were a fiddler and a lady who played a guitar, and between the two, we danced a little and accomplished a lot.

After most everyone had left, we sat on the porch drinking lemonade and talking.

"It's really good to see you up and around so well," said Sarah. "From what I heard, I thought you'd still be recovering, but you look like you're pretty much back to normal."

"I feel good, and the work I've been doing has gotten my muscles past the sore stage. My biggest problem has been learning how to use my hand again." I held up my right hand. "I can't grip anything with my thumb and first finger and sometimes the others aren't strong enough for what I'm trying to do."

Jed was sitting next to me and he looked at my hand. "How can you hold a gun with your hand like that?" he asked. I had noticed he had his gun belted on, and I liked that while we worked in the house, he unloaded it and hung the belt in the kitchen.

I held up my left hand and everyone laughed. "I've working on drawing and handling it from the left side for a couple of hours most days and I'm getting more comfortable with it."

"Can I come to the farm and work out with you?" he asked eagerly. I looked at Sarah and she nodded.

"Anytime you want," I answered. "It would probably be best to arrange it beforehand cause somedays I'm doing other things." I sneaked a look at Annaliese when I said this and could see her face working to hide a smile.

Handy and Rebecca had been sitting in the swing talking together and holding hands while the rest of us visited, and now I asked Handy, "So, have you settled on a date for the wedding?"

Rebecca answered, looking at Handy. "We would like to make it this Saturday if we could. Is that all right with you, Mama?"

"The sooner the better," Sarah answered with a smile, "We can't keep trusting to restraint forever." She sat for a moment and continued. "It won't take long to put together. If we tell Jane Summers in the morning, the whole town will know about it by suppertime. We can talk about it in the morning." She stood, signaling the end of the evening.

"Thank you, gentlemen, for your help. We'd never have gotten it done without you. And now I want to get to bed. We still have a lot to do tomorrow."

They stood on the porch and watched us mount. Sarah handed Jinx up to me and said, "Oh, I forgot to mention it. There will be a friend of mine here in the morning. He'll be staying with us for a while. His name is Lemuel Waters. He's a bookseller."

Lying in bed that night, for some reason I was thinking about Lemuel, the bookseller.

CHAPTER TWENTY-FOUR

W hen we rode into the yard the next morning there was a strange looking wagon backed up to the porch and Bill was helping a fellow unload it into the house.

Tied to the porch railing was what appeared to be a bulldog pup who looked to be about a year old. He was determined to say hello to everyone and was so enthusiastic about it that he almost knocked me down trying to see what was on my shoulder.

Jinx stayed where he was and after a while, when the puppy had calmed down a bit, I introduced them with no real hope for a pleasant friendship.

They fooled me. Jinx was cautious at first and popped him on the snout a couple of quick ones, but the puppy wanted to play, and Jinx was still enough of a kitten to enjoy that himself. So, they played, and soon were chasing each through the house and around the yard, eventually getting into a tug-o-war with Jinx's rope toy which ended up with the bulldog dragging Jinx around the house like he was a toy himself.

Brutus didn't look like a Brutus quite yet, but I could see he'd probably grow into the name quite well. Lemuel had gotten him from a fellow in Casper and they had become fast friends. Wherever Lemuel or Greta were the pup wanted to be.

Lemuel Waters looked to be around fifty, with long white hair, and seemed to walk with a bit of a stoop. He was about my height if he stood up straight, but looked a bit frail, as though a good strong wind might blow him over. It didn't take me long to realize that wasn't so. He worked alongside us all day and then fed the horses while the rest of us were taking a break under a tree.

We got to know each other some while we were unloading and placing things around the house as directed by Sarah or Rebecca. Since the only way to get any work out of Handy and Rebecca was to separate them, Sarah took her daughter and Wash out to the cottage to get it ready while the rest of us finished up in the house.

Later, sitting on the porch talking. we learned a bit of Lemuel's life. He was born in Massachusetts and moved with his family to Kansas when he was young. He grew up working with his father as a carpenter near Kansas City and met and married his wife there. She introduced him to books, and he fell in love with them, and over the years gradually got into the business of selling them. When Pa had taken me to Kansas City one time, I remember Lemuel's bookstore, though I never met him.

When his wife died he decided to move west to begin a new life. He closed the bookstore and began a meandering trip westward, selling books from his wagon as he went and stocking up with shipments sent to him at various stops along the railroad.

Along the way he had made changes to the wagon and the result was a practical vehicle that served them as a way to travel, a place to sleep, and even a place to cook if it was raining, as well as a store to sell books.

The box of the wagon was about six by ten feet with sides framed with iron and paneled with thick wood planks. The door fitted into the rear was stout and heavy and in the front were hinged doors that could be closed at night, and a roof over the front seat. Looking it over I thought it would take a shot at close range to hole it anywhere.

Because of the weight of the wagon he had a matched pair of chestnut draught horses pulling and another pair trailing behind, and they had gotten him this far with no issues.

They traveled from about April till October and then picked a place to winter. He and his daughter, Gretta, had taken three years to cover the distance from Kansas City to Salt Lake, but they had made it this far and planned to begin the trip to their ultimate destination of San Francisco in the spring.

They stopped at Sarah's place to work on the wagon and, when the opportunity arose, joined her on the trip to Salt Lake City. The plan was for them to spend the winter at Sarah's place, helping her set up a new store and selling such books in town as he could. He also wanted to talk to us about joining our group for the trip west.

His daughter was blind from a childhood accident, but she knew the contents of the wagon so well that she could lay her hand on most any book desired. For the last three years he had read to her almost every night, either by campfire or in the homes of many of their customers. They really seemed to be happy with their life.

When I pointed out that we might not be the best traveling companions because of the likelihood of violence along the way, he climbed into his wagon and retrieved a twelve-gauge sawed off shotgun and a new Winchester carbine.

"I won't be a burden to you, I promise," he said. "We wouldn't have gotten this far if we were afraid or unable. I think you'll find I can be a help in a difficulty. I rode with Sheridan during the War."

"I'll talk to the others and see what they say about it," I said, but I liked the idea. An extra gun would be good, and I thought having Lemuel along would make for much more interesting conversations around the fire.

Pa was a well-read man, and it didn't take long for me to realize Lemuel was much the same, if not a little more so. He had been selling books for almost fifteen years, and since it was the kind of business where many times you were just sitting, he had had time to read most of what passed through his hands. The routine they followed on the road was to stop for the night early and after the chores and dinner were through, he would sit and read to her.

I think maybe because she was blind, Greta had an amazing memory, not only for where each book was, but she remembered most of what her father read to her. She could already find her way around the house. Lemuel had made her a long, slender pole she carried with her sometimes to help her learn new places.

Watching Gretta learn her way around the house made me wonder about the difficulties she had faced and overcome in a life of travel. She was fourteen and pretty, with long blonde hair and that solid look I'd learned to associate with German women.

Later that night I had a chance to talk to Sarah alone and I asked her about Lemuel.

"I know he don't look it, but he don't back up," she said. "There were a couple of rowdies from back in the hills in the store one night and one of them said something to Gretta that was out of line." She shook her head. "Suddenly he had that shotgun in his hand pointed right at that fellow's forehead, and when he cocked those hammers everything just stopped. He said something like, 'the only thing keeping me from blowing your head off is the idea I'd have to help this lady clean the blood and such off the wall. Now you get along.'" She smiled. "That fellow was suddenly sober. He left as he was told to and didn't come back."

She cocked her head at me. "He wouldn't have gotten this far if he didn't have sand, Johnny."

I hadn't seen Handy much since Rebecca got in town, but that night he rode back to the farm with us. When we were sitting on the porch with Wash enjoying his pipe, I brought up Lemuel's request.

Handy immediately liked the idea. "I agree with Sarah," he said. "They wouldn't have gotten this far if he couldn't handle himself. Did you say he'd been in the cavalry?"

I nodded, "He didn't say whose but being from Kansas City, he was likely with Grant. He might have known Pa and maybe even you," I said looking at Wash.

"I don't recall him," said Wash, "but hell, it's been twenty years and a lot of water's gone under the bridge since then. None of us look like we did then."

"As far as them going along, I'd say yes. If you told him he could get into the middle of a fight and he still wants to go, that's fine. And that wagon's a damn fort on wheels which could be useful."

He was quiet for a minute and then continued. "We'll want to move at a right good pace through some of that county but with the extra horses he has we should be OK. Don't want to wear them out."

"That's a good idea," said Handy. "We'll have to carry extra water and feed for them, but with the wagon, that shouldn't be too hard."

We sat quiet for a while and finally I said, "Let's make sure we include him in any talks we have about going. With all the traveling they've done he's probably got some good advice."

The next day after we finished work, we all rode over to Sarah's, which was becoming a kind of headquarters for us. Annaliese was there and she, Sarah and Rebecca were working on the details for the wedding on Saturday. After I kissed her hello, I told her about Lemuel and Gretta joining us in the spring on our trek west. She was a little skeptical but after I explained our thinking, she saw that it was reasonable.

After lunch Wash and Lemuel sat on a stump in the back field and watched Handy, Jed and me work out with our pistols. Since we were in the city limits, we didn't use any ammo, just went through the drill of draw and point. I was feeling more and more comfortable from the left side and had almost caught up with Handy on getting it out and level. Jed was improving and seemed to have a knack for it. I could see him using a Colt soon with no trouble.

"You said yesterday you had been in the cavalry during the war," I said to Lemuel. "What outfit were you with?

"I started out in Sherman's headquarters and later went east on Sheridan's headquarters staff," he answered. "By then I was the General's chief clerk and wrote out most of the orders for the division, later the corps."

"My Pa was a scout for Sherman from Shiloh right through to Johnson's surrender after Appomattox," I said. "Did you know him?"

"After I met you last night I thought about those days, and I do remember him. He was a little fellow and young, if I remember right. Everyone thought he was under-age, but he was such a good rider they let it be. He sure knew what to do with a Henry rifle, though, and he was smart as a whip." He looked a question at me.

"He died before I left Junction City on this trip," I said.

"Seems to me he had a brother, didn't he?" he asked. "Usually didn't see one without the other when they were in camp."

"That would be my Uncle Bill," I replied. "He lives in Sacramento. That's where we're headed."

Sarah, Gretta and Annaliese followed Rebecca around the corner of the barn and joined Wash and Lemuel sitting in the shade.

While they were talking about the wedding and all they had to do to get ready for it, Annaliese and I, with Jinx following, took a walk under the trees to a small pond in the far corner of the field.

"Are you working on the details of the trip?" she asked.

"Yes, some. Mostly we were talking about army days. He remembers my Pa and Uncle Bill from back then."

We sat down on a grassy bank out of sight of the others, so we lay back and kissed, then nibbled on each other's lips for a bit.

Finally, she sat up and asked, "Why do you practice with your pistol so much?"

"It does seem like a strange way to spend time, doesn't it?" I replied. "Whenever I practice, I think about Pa because we did it together so much when I was growing up. Whenever he had a gun to work on, he always let me watch, and then we would go to our range out by the river and try it out."

I sat sucking on the stem of a piece of grass I had plucked. "It's a skill and I seem to have a knack for it so I want to be as good as I can. Back in Julesburg it saved my life." I shook my head. "When that cowboy went for his gun, I didn't even think, I just drew. If I wasn't as good as I was, he would likely have killed me. It's like Handy said later, 'it's all right to have ethics about shooting someone just don't let them get you killed.'"

"Since the accident I can't use my right hand, so I want to practice with my left until I get back to where I used to be."

"Doc told me he had never seen anyone better with a gun than you, unless it was Handy," she said. "Do you think you'll ever get back to where you were right-handed?"

"I think I'm right close to it now," I answered. "But let's talk about something else, like how much I love you and how would you feel if I dragged you down and made love to you right here?"

She had stood up and when I reached up to grab her, she backed away, teasing me.

"First you need to answer a question." She pointed out to where we could see the grass waving where Jinx was chasing grasshoppers. "Do you love that cat more than you love me?"

"Is this one of those questions that no matter what I say, I'm in trouble?" I responded. She pounced on me and we wrestled for a bit before she ended up on top of me and suddenly, we weren't wrestling anymore and the pressure of her rubbing against my pants was almost too much for me.

"Stop," I said in a strangled groan.

"You know you don't mean it," she said and began to unbutton my pants. All I could see when I looked down was a mantle of dark red hair shining in the sun and moving rhythmically. It didn't take long. Afterwards we were lying hand in hand when Jinx hopped on my chest.

"Meow?" he asked. We were still laughing when we heard someone coming and scrambled to arrange our clothes before they arrived.

The rest of the day we couldn't look at each other for fear we'd start laughing.

By the time we rode away from Sarah's that evening the sound of women planning a wedding was everywhere.

"I'm sure glad all I got to do tomorrow is show up, say 'I do' and kiss the bride," said Handy. "The way my head's spinning lately I couldn't remember much else."

"Going to be some dancing and such at the Doctor's place afterwards," said Jed. He was going with us rather than stay behind with a house full of women. We had an extra bunk.

"You planning on much dancing?" I asked Handy with an innocent expression on my face.

He just smiled and looked dreamy.

CHAPTER TWENTY-FIVE

⟨⟨© ©⟩⟩

One of the nicest things about Sarah's place was that the front porch wrapped around to a nook on the east side of the house. One night Annaliese and I were sitting in the swing in that nook, hiding from everyone, looking up at the night sky and watching the full moon come up over the mountains to shine on Salt Lake City. Since I left Kansas, I had seen many pretty things but nothing quite like that.

We were snuggled under a blanket and there was light enough, even in the shadow of the porch roof, for me to see her head resting on my shoulder. We hadn't spent much time together lately and she was tired from long hours at the hospital. A wagon accident the day after the wedding had kept her busy, so for the last two weeks she had been caring for six people from the same family, including three children and a grandmother. I thought she was asleep when she surprised me by sitting up and turning toward me.

"There something we need to talk about before things get much farther along," she said.

"What things?" I asked.

"Us getting married," she replied.

She smoothed down the front of her dress and began. "I want you to listen to what I've got to say and then we can talk," she said. "The plans I had for my life were pretty much settled before you came along. I planned to go with the Doctor to Carson City and Sacramento, help him set up the clinics and stay when he returned. In the fall, I plan to enter medical school in San Francisco."

I started to remind her that I knew this, but she held up her hand.

"Just listen," she said and went on. "I'll be in school for two to three years and when I graduate, I'll have to decide where I want to practice. Which means that our life together will be pretty much dictated by what I'm doing and where I decide to do it."

She sat quiet for a moment. "When I begin my new career there will be many times when my patients' needs will come before your needs as a husband. I guess I need to know how you feel about that." She went on. "Of the four woman doctors I correspond with, one has never married and two have lost their husbands, one to divorce and one where he just got tired of it and walked away. The fourth is married to a doctor and they work together so he seems to understand"

We sat quiet for a minute and then she continued. "Do you have any plans about what you want to do when we get together in Sacramento?"

Actually, I do," I replied. "Since Wash got me thinking about the future, I've been talking to Lemuel about it."

"Why Lemuel?" she asked.

"Cause I'm thinking about going into business with him. We'd like to open a bookstore in San Francisco; I put up some money and he'd put in his stock and his knowledge of books and teach me the trade."

I got up and stepped to the porch railing to gaze up at the moon, too high now to be seen from the swing. I turned back to her. "By the time you finish school, if you want to move somewhere else, I should have learned enough to open a store of my own."

"I talked to Doc before he left," she said, "and he said nice things about the area around Los Angeles. The weather is supposed to be nice even in the winter. It sounds like a nice place to grow up with.

She sat for a moment and when I didn't say anything continued. "So, you've been thinking about this yourself, have you?"

I pulled her into my arms. "I realize what marrying you would be like. I'll just have to learn to be a different kind of husband if I want us to be happy. And I will because I want to keep you more than I want to be like every other husband." I kissed her and after it lingered for a bit, it became more than a kiss. When we finally stopped for breath, she whispered, "I'm glad you love me Johnny Fry, cause I love you and want you with me always."

We quickly found out that making love in a swing on a cold November evening, while it sounds romantic, is not too comfortable, so we retired to the bedroom.

A winter's day in Utah is many ways different from what I had known in Kansas. Not so much the temperature or even the snow, but in Kansas the wind was always there and a still, cold, sunny morning after a snow-storm was unusual. From the porch on the bunk house, I stood looking up at the west wall of the Rockies and felt like I could stand and stare at it for hours. The sunshine on the snow was almost blinding and the air was so clear that the mountains sort of jumped out at you.

This was my first winter since Pa had died and I felt it. Most nights of my life, especially winter nights, had been spent sitting around a stove reading or talking to him. These days I spent most of my time with Wash or Handy or Annaliese.

Now that Handy was married, he and Rebecca lived in the cottage behind Sarah's. He came out to work with us at the farm most days and last night bunked with us because it was snowing heavily about the time he usually left.

I heard him come out on the porch behind me and without turning I asked, "Do you ever miss home?" He didn't respond right away so I continued. "I feel a little bad some time because I don't think about it much."

He brushed snow off the swing, sat and stretched before he answered. "No, I don't usually. I guess it's because I'm happy and healthy so life's pretty good right now. I love my family and I'd love to see them, but I'm glad I'm right here right now."

I sat down beside him, and we began to swing. "When is Annaliese leaving?" he asked.

"She tells me they can't get to Sacramento until the snow in the passes melts enough for them to get through. They'll probably go to Carson City about the first part of April, open the clinic there, wait until the passes are open and head to Clarksville and set up the clinic when they get there. From what I hear they probably won't get through the mountains until sometime in mid-May."

"When will we be leaving?" he asked. "How early does the desert begin to heat up? Got any ideas about what you're going to do when you get there?" Handy had the darnedest habit of asking three question at once. I asked him about it one time and he told me it was probably because, with such a large family, sometimes he couldn't get a word in edgewise at home, so he had to make up for lost time when he did.

"Well that's not just up to me, so we need to sit and talk about it," I replied. "Answering the other questions, probably mid-March or so and, yes I have an idea about what I'm going to do out there."

"This is your trip Johnny, so when you think it's best, we go; and by the way, Wash feels the same. We can talk but it's your say so. As far as talking, why not today? Doesn't look like we'll be doing much anyway."

Wash had come to stand at the door and was standing, listening. He nodded his approval. "Sounds like sense to me."

I stood up and walked to the porch rail and stood looking at the mountains for a full minute before I turned and said, "First you've got to tell me why you two are still happy to let me run the show. Besides the fact that I've been off my feet for almost four months. I mean both of you, especially you," I nodded at Wash, "know so much more about life and things than me and have done so much more."

Handy looked at Wash and nodded his head. Wash sat down on a bench by the door and smiled at me. "We've talked about this before and it's like Handy said. You got a lot in your head and I like the way it comes out. Also, I'm a soldier, so I'm used to taking orders, but more important, I know that any group needs a leader. This is your trip so that's you. But also, I know I'm free to leave anytime and that helps me decide to stay." He looked at Handy as if to say, "Your turn."

Handy just grinned and said, "That says it all."

We watched Lemuel come trudging toward the house, widening and improving the path through the snow as he came. He had volunteered to see to the animals and make sure they had enough food and water to last the weather. He came up on the porch and stomped his feet to get the snow off.

"If we're going to talk a bit, let's go in by the fire. My feet are cold," he said.

Jinx had just come out on the porch and we watched as he took a mighty yawn and stretch. I scooped him up and shortly we were all sitting around the stove talking, me with Jinx purring in my lap. For some reason I always thought better with him in my lap.

"Ok Wash," I said. "Let me know what you think about getting to Sacramento? How long do you think it will take to get there? How much time should we plan to spend in Carson City?" Apparently, I had picked up Handy's three question habit myself. We had already talked a bit about things like this but I wanted to put everything on the table so we could put together a complete plan and all knew what it was.

Like always he sat for a minute and then said, "First thing will be to make sure we have a plan on how to deal with this gambler fellow. I think we'd be best off to keep doing what has worked up to now. That would be me outriding; trying to find them and keep from being seen. We'll be leaving early enough to beat the hot days across, but water might still be a problem. There are seeps and springs along the way, and I know some of them. After we make the Carson River, we should be ok."

He stopped to fill his pipe and, in the silence, Handy asked, "How long till we get to Carson City?"

Wash applied a brand from the stove and blew out a cloud of smoke before he answered. "We need to plan to make good time across that section of the country," he said. "Don't get me wrong, it's right pretty out there, but the sooner we get across the better. I'd say ten days to strike the Reese River and then another four to the Carson and then a day to Carson City."

"So if we leave here the first week in March we should get there the end of the third week in March," I said, "and from what I've heard it will probably be the middle of May or so before the passes through the mountains are open for horses.

"Any place in particular we're liable to run in to the Gambler?" I asked.

"About twelve every day," he answered with a smile. He went on, "We need to set up a marching order and try to watch everything, every day. If we all keep an eye out for trouble we can hope he won't catch us napping. I believe if we shake him leaving Salt Lake, we probably won't see him till Carson City. Then we'll see what happens. But we can't count on that. We'll need to be alert evert minute."

He went on. "One time I remember hearing a general say, 'Don't plan on what you think the other fellow will do; plan on what you think he can do.'" That's the way we have to think. If we figure he's going to wait till Carson City, and he don't, then where are we? For the two or three weeks we're on the way to Carson City there are dozens of places where a good ambush could be laid. We need to make sure we have a plan for every day we're crossing that desert and talk every night about the plan for the next day."

I cleared my throat, and everybody looked at me. "I've thought of something that might defuse this problem," I said. "I'm going to wire the newspapers in Carson City, explain the problem, and ask them to print a full-page message that will let this fellow know we have no use for the papers, and he can have them."

They were all quiet for a minute to let that sink in and then Handy said, "I vote yea for that idea and I'll chip in if they want to charge you."

Wash and Lemuel both nodded in agreement.

After that we talked about supplies and what extra equipment we might need in the desert. The big thing was to use the wagon to make sure we had enough food and water for the four of us and the stock.

We hadn't heard Lemuel's plans for the wagon before but like him, they made sense. Greta was going to leave with Annaliese and the

Doctor, help them with the set-up at the clinic in Carson City and then on to Sacramento to do it again.

It looked like we'd be a couple weeks ahead of them, and I decided then and there to send a letter to Uncle Bill in Sacramento letting him know how things stood and giving him an arrival date of the last week in May or the first week in June.

Lemuel planned to ship all his books and stock to Sacramento on the train with Annaliese and them and use the space in the wagon to carry things we needed to get across the desert safely, most especially water, food for us and fodder for the animals. He would also carry plenty of ammo and whatever tools we thought we would need.

In addition to our mounts, we decided that Handy and I would each buy a horse so Lemuel's stock could be spelled every other day. When we got where we were going, we could sell them or keep them as we chose. Wash was buying another mule in case one of our horses came up lame. In the desert, the fewer chances the better.

Lemuel also wanted to reinforce the folding doors in the front of the wagon with an iron bar and make sure the tires and spokes were in good shape. He already had a spare wheel thrust up underneath.

We usually ate with Ephraim and his family in the house, but with the snow and all, this time we used our own tucker and heated it on the stove right next to the coffee pot that was always there. Afterwards, sitting on the porch letting lunch settle, we began to talk about our futures, since when we got where we were going we'd have to begin to make choices that didn't have a thing to do with riding across the country on the Pony.

Handy and Rebecca had decided to contact Bill Cody and see if he would include Rebecca in the offer to be in the show. If so, they planned to spend a couple of years at it and then come back out west and find a place to settle. "It'll probably be somewhere close to you," Handy said nodding at me. "At least that's the plan right now. You know Rebecca and Annaliese are at least as close as you and me so that just seems natural. Of course, planning that far into the future seems more of a hope than anything, but it's always good to have a plan."

Wash had a couple of things he was thinking about and hadn't decided which was best. He was inclined to go as far as San Francisco with us when Annaliese started school and then maybe head south and spend some time with Doc down near the border with Mexico.

Lemuel and I hadn't discussed our projected partnership with them and now we did. The idea was to get premises somewhere around San Francisco, open the store and set up housekeeping somewhere close until Annaliese finished school.

While she was helping to set up the clinic, I would go to San Francisco with Lemuel to get the store up and running. I could come back to Sacramento every couple of weeks to spend time until she was ready to come back with me. That's about as far as we could plan because by then we would have to decide the best way to order our life while she was in school.

I had some new ideas about our venture and now when I talked about them, Lemuel heard them for the first time. I wanted to use part of the store for a leather working shop to make and sell tack and other leather products.

I was also thinking about a gunsmithing operation in the back room with sales up front. This would allow me to use the skills Pa had taught me and continue the reading and learning I'd always been so passionate about. Granted, I was passionate about other things now, but I didn't think a new passion would interfere with the others. Of course, one of my passions was asleep in Handy's lap, but I think my lady understood that one.

CHAPTER TWENTY-SIX

In the winter sunshine of Salt Lake, the snow was gone in just a couple of days. One afternoon a week later Annaliese and I were back in our nook on the porch looking out at the mountains, talking.

"I want to ask you something," she said, "but I want you to understand that I'm just curious. The question is about the trip and I don't want you to think I'm trying to keep you from doing it. I'm just curious. Why do you want to finish riding the Pony to Sacramento?"

A habit I'd picked up from Wash was to think for a minute before I answered a question, so I didn't say anything right way. I sat and lined things up so I could say them right.

"When I was a kid Pa told me stories of the days when he rode the Pony and I listened to him talk about it to others," I said. "When he died it just seemed natural to remember him by doing it. But I've gone a long way beyond the place where he rode so I don't feel this part of the ride is for him. This part is for me."

"All sorts of new things are happening to me right now. My new life began when Rusty fell in Emigration Canyon and I somehow think that finishing this trip is a part of the life I woke up to." She sat up and turned to face me, looking deep into my eyes.

"Since then, things happening to me are shaping my future and maybe the kind of person I'll be. I guess I want to be the kind of fellow who finishes what he starts."

The best kind of kiss is one you get because you said something she really likes.

A few minutes later we came up for air. She snuggled up against me, my arm around her.

"Sounds like you've been thinking about things," she said. "Have you fellows been talking among yourselves?"

"Well, with the four of us stuck in the bunkhouse with nothing to do but talk and read for a day and a night, we got a lot of talking and reading done," I replied. "And thinking," I added.

"So, have you been thinking about being married?" she asked. "I have."

"Yeah, I have too." I admitted. "Let me tell you what I've thought about."

She sat up in that listening pose she had, and I began. "What you told me the other night has given me some ideas on how this would affect me - you being a doctor, that is. I think for us both to be happy I need to be doing something important too. I don't know what just yet, but something."

"The bookstore idea is a part of it. If it all works, I can make us some money, so I won't have to spend so much of what Pa left me. From what Lemuel says, running a bookstore is not normally a full-time business for two people, so I should have some time to pick my direction and go."

"I think I'd like to be a scholar or a teacher, maybe even a professor, though I'm not sure what's needed to be one. I'm sure there's likely some college and a lot of reading and studying in it, but I think I'd like to point in that direction."

"I want you to be happy and to find what you need as a student and a doctor afterwards. I don't want you to think about what I need as much as what you need to get that done. I'll find some way to keep busy and stay out of your hair. One thing I've learned on this trip of mine is how to take care of myself."

"I've talked to Wash about it some. He'll probably hang around for a while and likely he and I will do some traveling together. I'd like to head south and scout out the area around Los Angeles and maybe San Diego and down into Mexico, and I'd like to see what Oregon is like. I think I can keep busy while you're in school. One thing about the west there's plenty for me to see. As far as me being gone occasionally, think of how much fun it will be when I come home."

I paused for a moment, "So what do you think?"

"I think it should work out for us. What you propose is for us to each live our own lives and when we can, we'll live them together, is that right?"

"Pretty much," I replied.

"It will be a different kind of marriage, but we're different kinds of people, so we can make it work." She snuggled down under my arm again and we resumed looking at the mountains which were slowly disappearing into darkness. "Besides," she said, "eventually we'll settle down and live together like normal people, although I suspect normal for us won't really be normal at all."

I bought Jed a Colt for his fifteenth birthday and the next time we practiced together I gave it to him. His face lit up and he immediately wanted to fire it, so we did.

After an hour he could hardly lift it. Between the more powerful kick and the additional size and weight his arm was sore and tired, so we sat on a hay bale and talked.

"Other than practicing with a gun, what are you doing to keep busy lately?" I asked,

He hung his head a little and I could have sworn he blushed. "Greta and I are working together doing things for Ma and Lemuel."

"Things?" I asked.

"You know, I do lift and carry stuff for Ma at the store and Greta does things around the house and at the store. She's sort of an assistant. I'm helping Lemuel do some work on the wagon too and we're moving his books into the store to display and sell them. He's planning to have them shipped out to Sacramento on the train this spring, so we're building boxes to ship them in."

He shook his head. "He sure has a lot of books in that wagon. I can see why he's got it built so stout. Those things are heavy."

"They are an amazing pair, those two," I said. "It's hard to believe she can learn so much so quick. Sarah told me Greta knows where everything is in the store and the house. And that Lemuel." I shook my head. "I like to watch Wash and him bicker over what's the best way to do something to the wagon."

"She's the first girl I've ever been around much," he said. "Sometime there would be girls with the people that stopped at the store, but they were never around long enough for me to get to know any. I look at some of the things she does, and I can't believe she can't see. She's a year younger than me and a little taller but I sure do like her."

"Does she know that," I asked.

"I guess not. I'm too afraid to tell her in case she doesn't feel the same," he replied. "I do feel strange when I'm around her."

"I'm not one to give advice on girls," I commented, "seeing as how I've only had one girl and I'm going to marry her. What does your mom say?"

"She thinks I should write her a letter, but if I do that then someone will have to read it to her, and I don't want that."

"Why don't you read it to her yourself?" I said.

He looked at me straight-faced for a moment, then a slow smile spread across his face. "Yeah," he said. "Why not?"

Sarah's kitchen had become the center of our social life in Salt Lake. It was centrally located, large and cheery and always seemed to have a pot of coffee on with some sort of baked goods close to hand.

The next day I sat down with Sarah and, over a biscuit with butter and honey and a cup of hot tea, brought up a question Jed had put to me before he left the farm the previous day. "Jed wants to go with us when we leave in the spring. How do you feel about that?

"You mean on the trail across the desert?" I nodded.

She sighed. "He's mentioned it a few times this winter, so it doesn't surprise me."

She took a sip of tea, and a biscuit from the plate, and spread some butter on it. "You know he looks up to you." I must have looked startled, but she continued. "He hasn't had a man around regular for a long time, and even though you aren't much older, he feels the need to have you approve of him."

I hadn't thought about that, but now that she mentioned it, I was kind of surprised at him telling me about how he felt about Greta. The idea that I could be to him what Pa was to me took me aback for a minute.

"I'm not sure how I feel about that," I said.

"When you talk to him, just make sure you think about what you're going to say before you say it, and always be straight with him. You should do fine."

"I haven't mentioned it to the boys yet, but I think they'll say Ok," I said. "You know there might be a fellow out there trying to shoot me, don't you?"

"I've heard that," she said, "but I believe the four of you will get him through." She sat quiet for a minute. "We live in a world where men wear guns, and there's reasons for that. You've been teaching him how and, more importantly, when to use a gun and I believe you'll go right on being a good teacher for him."

I stood and walked out on to the porch to think about that for a minute. When I returned I said, "I'll do the best I can, but I'd feel better being an older brother than a father, if it's all right with you."

"Absolutely," she said with a smile.

One morning later that week I had stopped by the livery stable near the hospital when I noticed a fellow working there I thought I recognized. When I walked up to him, he turned, and I saw it was Jason Redbird from Kearney. He had helped us take the Gambler and his friend from the livery stable there to Sheriff Joe's office. I remembered him charging out of the back with a large hammer in his hand, ready to deal mayhem if need be. Now he held out that hand. "I've been hoping to run into you," he said.

"Why's that?" I asked.

"You know, I heard you fellows talking about riding the Pony and all. Well, I thought about it, got some cash and an outfit together, and decided to see if I could catch you here and join up."

Since it seemed to be a popular idea amongst younger fellows, I wasn't too surprised. I invited him to Sarah's the following night so we could all talk it over and he accepted gladly.

Handy's uncle had told us a bit about him in Kearny. His mother was Kiowa, captured in a raid. His father was a Cheyenne brave, and Jason was born and raised in a Cheyenne village. After his father was killed in a raid, he followed his mother when she returned to her own tribe. When she died, he was eighteen and already wise enough to see the future of his people.

His life among whites had been difficult at times, but his skill with horses and his straightforward manner earned him a place of respect and a decent living in Kearney by the time he was twenty-five.

He was a quiet man, friendly and co-operative with most folks. He had been at the livery stable in Kearny for about five years, and by the time we showed up he was getting itchy feet, so it didn't take much to push him to action. He saved a little extra, packed up and took the train, hoping to catch us before we left Salt Lake.

I could see right away that he was a good addition to our bunch, and the rest agreed the following evening. That night, Jed was with us for the first time. Now that he was going, I wanted to make sure he was a part of every talk we had so he would understand how we wanted to move forward in getting ready to leave and how we planned to travel.

The next afternoon I was hiding on the side porch at Sarah's again, but this time by myself. Annaliese was busy at the hospital, so I just sat and looked at the mountains, thoughts floating around in my head like wind-blown autumn leaves.

The meeting the night before had been a good one. I started it by suggesting we get together a couple times a month and spend the time between thinking about the trip and how best to make it work. I also pointed out that with six of us now, it made sense to assign tasks so that we could make things run more smoothly, get more things done. Since they had pretty much appointed me leader, I was coming to them with some suggestions I'd like them to chew over.

Wash's role was his alone. He would be our outrider and shield us from surprise. The rest of us should ride in a formation of sorts, me on the left front of the wagon and Handy on the right front, with Lemuel in the middle driving the wagon. Jason would be riding on the left rear and Jed on the right.

Each of us would have a place to watch in a circle, with the wagon in the center, Lemuel straight ahead, me the left front quarter, Jason the left rear quarter, Jed right rear and Handy right front. If we each concentrated on our section, we were most likely to see anything there was to see. It didn't mean we had to watch our area all the time, but we would be more likely to see something different out there if we knew what was there in the first place.

The idea wasn't for everyone to always ride in the same place. Part of Jason's and Jed's job was to watch our back trail, and that could be best done by sometimes riding to promontories behind us to look for dust or other signs of someone following. Same with Handy and me in front - riding to high places in our quarters to spy out the trail before us.

"Another thing," I said. "Should we ride at night some of the time or even all the time?"

"I don't think we need to think about that because of the heat traveling this time of year," said Wash. "March in the desert is nice. But from the standpoint of someone not being able to see us as well, it's something to think about. The moon will be full come the middle of March, so if we start about the first week and finish up the end of the third week, we will have some moon all the way. Let's think about that and talk next time."

After that we talked about the little things we'd need to arrange and how to go about them.

While I sat there, I thought about the people who'd come into my life since I left Junction City. Before this trip I had known only Pa the way I know all these people around me. Annaliese, my sweetheart, someone to walk through life with; Handy, solid as the mountains before me, always there when needed; Wash, my mentor and protector, ready to give me wise words and loyalty; Lemuel, a good man and part of a bright path I saw to my future; Jed, someone to help me grow and look at myself while helping him grow up; Jason who I somehow felt was a solid man and good friend to have around; and, finally, Sarah, a fountain of warmth and hospitality that brought us all together.

These people were important to me, part of my life. I felt I was a better person when I was around them, somehow stronger, smarter, a different person altogether than the Johnny Fry who had left Junction City in another lifetime. The best way for me to repay their friendship was to be the best person I could be, and they were all there to help me.

CHAPTER TWENTY-SEVEN

After considerable editing, I finally got the message I wanted and telegraphed it to several newspapers in Carson City.

Rene' Paul

The papers you want are of no use to me.

Contact me by telegraph in Salt Lake City and we can arrange a meeting to pass them to you with no further trouble.

Johnny Fry

General Delivery

Salt Lake City, Utah telegraph office.

I hoped this would do what I thought it would. Three men had died over these papers and rather than risk more violence I felt this was a reasonable way to resolve the problem.

Of course, the issue was, would he get the message, and would he want to resolve the issue without violence? I had no idea if he had revenge on his mind and wanted to settle a score or not but, at this point all I could do was try. I know Wash was glad I went on practicing with the gun just in case.

With the weather such as it was, much of the work on the farm and all the farms around Salt Lake had slowed to a crawl and there were many dances and celebrations around town. Though I wasn't much of a dancer, I enjoyed watching everyone have fun and besides, the food was good and plentiful.

On this evening I had Jinx with me, and he sat on my shoulder while we watched the festivities from the front door. Occasionally Sarah, Handy and Rebecca or Annaliese would dance by and to my surprise I saw Greta dancing with Jed in one corner away from everyone else.

The musicians were taking a break and people were just standing and talking when I noticed a tall, distinguished looking, grey-haired man crossing the floor. The crowd parted like a wave in front of him and he was nodding right and left to people as he walked.

After a moment I realized he was coming toward me. At this point the music began again and when he stood before me, I couldn't hear what he was saying so he leaned forward and spoke directly into my ear. "I'd like to talk to you, tomorrow if at all possible. I'll be in my office at ten in the morning if that's convenient for you." He pressed a card into my hand and slipped through the doorway behind me.

Annaliese left the group she was talking to and came over to where I was standing reading the card. "What did the Elder want?" she asked me.

"He just said he'd like to talk to me and asked me to come by tomorrow at ten. Who is he?" I asked

"He's one of the Twelve Apostles of the Church," she replied. We were talking into each other's ear because of the music, so she took my hand and led me off the porch and into the shadows out by the horses and buggies. Out here we could not only talk but, hold hands and even kiss if we were careful.

"And he didn't say what about or anything?" she asked.

I shook my head. "It wasn't the best place for a conversation."

"The Elders know pretty much everything that goes on in the Valley," she said, "so you can be sure they know about us and probably that we're stepping over the line by spending time in bed together before marriage. But my father is important to them and I'm not a Saint which means they only have so much power over me. They know you won't be here much longer so they've probably taking an attitude of prudence. Which is good because when they're not prudent, strange things can happen."

She went on, "He probably knows much of your history and I'm sure he believes you have no problem attitudes. I'll bet he just wants to learn things, like your plans for the trip and what you think of the Mormons and their efforts to join the Union."

I took her by the shoulders, "This is not the conversation I want to be having with a lady under a tree in the dark," I said and gave her a long slow kiss. When we broke, she whispered against my chest, "You brute," and then, "I think I love you." We decided then and there it was time to go home.

The next morning, I stood at Temple Square at the requested time after having sworn to come to Sarah's as soon as possible after the meeting and tell all. In bed the night before, after making love, Annaliese told me some of the background of the man I was going to meet and talk to. Like many of the Saints, he was originally from England. He was twenty-five, in 1843, when he stood with Brigham Young and heard hm pronounce, "This is the place."

Now, forty years later, he sat at the right hand of the President of the Church and helped guide and direct the affairs of the Saints, in

Utah and elsewhere. He wielded great power every day. I felt as though I was going to speak with one of the Founding Fathers of the Nation.

His office was easy to find and shortly I was ushered in where he made me welcome. We sat in easy chairs placed across a small table from each other with drinks and rolls within reach.

"So, you'll be leaving us in the Spring." It was a statement not a question and I nodded in assent.

I knew he was aware of all this and probably much more but since he seemed to want information, I decided to make it easy for him. "I was carried into Salt Lake in a wagon by my friends and Dr. Crawford and his daughter from the site of an accident having suffered many injuries when my horse shied at a rattler and threw me. I recovered under their care and now live and work at a farm with my friends, awaiting the spring to continue our trip."

"And you plan to marry your nurse." Again, a statement.

"Annaliese and I plan to marry in Sacramento where she will help her father set up a clinic to serve Saints in that area after having done so in Carson City." Again, short and direct.

"Have you enjoyed your time among us?" His eyes were a deep blue and they held me in a direct gaze.

"Yes, I have." I replied. "Because I always planned to stop in Salt Lake, I did some reading about the people and the place before I left Junction City."

"You seem to be well read," he said. "What did you learn about us?"

I sat and thought for a minute. "I was raised by a learned man," I said. "Most nights while my Pa was alive, we read and talked and when we ran out of things to read, we'd take a trip to Kansas City and get something else. He made sure I had all kinds of things to read and when need be, he'd order whatever books we needed to find out what we wanted to know. When I had questions, he answered them. So, when I wanted to learn about the Saints, I found things about them in our home or ordered others from printing houses around the country."

"I know of the problems and violence you suffered in the east and of your decision to migrate to a place where you could get away from the people who seemed to hate you for some reason or other. I've seen the place where Brigham pronounced and spent time in the library since I've been here so I'm familiar with how you have built your Zion."

"I've also found out that it's difficult to get a straight view of the Saints. Most people who write about them are either Saints themselves and so favor them, or people who dislike them, for any one of a hundred reasons, and so, paint them black as night."

He sat quiet for a bit, staring into the fire. "There have always been those among us who, since the war with Mexico and our being joined again with the gentiles who have persecuted us, have believed we should migrate again to a new place where we can believe and live as we choose without the threat of their violence hanging over us."

"Most of us, however, follow the ideal of Brigham Young and believe we must make some sort of peace with the world around us lest we run out of places to run to. And so, we are trying to reach an accommodation with the government, but there are certain knotty issues that make it difficult."

"From what I've read, they are polygamy and the dominance of the church in civil affairs, two difficult knots to untie, I'm sure." I waited for him to go on.

He looked at me and smiled. "You have done your homework," he said. "Yes, those seem to be the problems, and neither side has moved much off their original positions; so things have been stalled, and we sit and watch the territories around us enter the union while we lie becalmed, blocking the wind with our own stubbornness." He looked at me steadily again. "How do you see the issues?" he asked.

I took my time answering. "One of the reasons Annaliese and I have decided to seek our future elsewhere is because the church is so dominant in the affairs of the territory and we don't want that in our life. As for polygamy, I can see the advantages of it in terms of growth but, the question is, is it worth what it's costing?"

"The Saints see these things as part of our belief system, and in both cases, don't wish to give them up," he replied.

"And yet here you sit surrounded by the nation you have been seeking to join since the early 1850's, if I remember right, and are now no closer to the benefits you seek from it than you were then. I guess you don't have quite as much power as I thought you did."

"We have only the power granted by God and the people we lead," he said solemnly and a bit gloomily, shaking his head.

He was quiet for a moment and then stood and said, "Thank you for stopping by. I enjoyed our chat and if you ever visit us again you will be welcome."

At the door he brought up something I had expected to hear sooner. "Speaking of God and his word; of the things you have read and talked about with your father, how many of these things have been about the word of God?"

"Well Sir, we never talked too much about that, and though I've read some, it never really held my interest," I said. "I don't want to upset you or argue about it, but I don't feel the need for religion in my life right now and doubt if I ever will."

"We all need help sometimes, son," he said, "and it's nice to know someone is there."

We stood for a moment and looked out at the growing center of the city. The Temple was the heart of things in Salt Lake. Brigham Young had paced out the dimensions of it on that first day in 1843, and it had been building ever since. I had come to believe it was one of those buildings that would never be finished - would always be growing, like something alive.

"I remember reading about that 'still, small voice' in all of us and I've come to believe it's just me talking to myself. Pa taught me to look for things to enjoy in life and handle the problems when they come up."

"The idea of spending this life worrying about the next one never made sense to me, nor did the idea that I needed someone else to tell me what was right and wrong or how to live my life." I turned and extended my hand. "I hope to spend my life trying to do what I think's right, and come judgement day, if that's not enough, I guess you could say, 'I backed the wrong horse.'"

Looking into my eyes he grasped my hand and said, "I say again, you're always welcome."

CHAPTER TWENTY-EIGHT

Spring was coming and we spent our remaining few weeks getting ready to leave. Since there would be six of us now that meant the whole thing would be more complicated than when Jinx and I left Junction City the year before.

Pa and I talked a lot about the war and life in the army, and I remembered the word logistics. He said it meant keeping the army in beans and bullets and on the move, which seemed like what I had to do now. While sometime everyone would take care of their own personal needs, there were things that would work better if we thought them out together.

At our next meeting I brought that up. "Of course, some things will take planning and organization," I said. "The last things we load before we leave should be the food, fodder and water. Lemuel has some ideas for the wagon that will allow us to carry what we need and still have a good amount of usable space inside."

"He also has a way he lets down some planks in the rear of it and makes a kitchen of sorts where we can cook and store salt, flour and whatever spices and such he might need. And, most important, he has volunteered to do the cooking while we're on the trail. We can all take turns helping him. He's also going to buy what supplies we need and try to open space in the wagon so we can get the best use from it."

"I'd like Jason and Handy to take care of the stock; fodder, new shoes and such, before we leave, and we'll want a system for watering them when we don't have a spring or stream handy, plus any tools we might need out there. We'll have ten horses and two mules along, so there will be a lot to do. If you need help, ask."

"Since the idea is to get us all to Carson City in one piece, it seems like we should agree what needs to be done and then divide up the chores to make sure it gets done." I looked around at everyone nodding in agreement. "Jed will work with me, sort of tying the whole thing together. Making lists, checking things off and looking over everyone's shoulder to help get done what needs to be done."

"Wash, I'd like you to spend your time finding out things about the trail and how best to get where we're going. Talk to people, go over maps and such, and let us know what you find out. Any ideas you have, share them around. The more we all know about things the better."

Later, when everyone was getting ready to leave Handy said, "Johnny, I'd say you're getting pretty good at this leading thing." When they all agreed, it was the best I'd felt in a while.

With five weeks before we left there was no reason to rush. It felt like we had plenty of time, and yet why was I so busy?

We made our checklists by committee, with Annaliese and Sarah helping Jed and me figure out what we might need and where to get it. Once a week Jed and I chose one of the travelers and checked and repaired all his leather goods and weapons.

He and I still spent a few hours every week drilling with the Colts, with target practice once a week. Occasionally Handy, Jason or Lemuel showed up to watch or participate and we all improved. Jason proved to be an exceptional rifle shot and I had pulled just about even with Handy when it came to drawing a Colt and putting a bullet where I wanted it.

I also talked with each of them several times a week about his chores; how he was coming along, did he need any help? Sarah's store was the place where we would all see each other. There was always a good reason to go, always a pot of coffee on, and each of us was in there almost every day for one thing or another.

Then there was time with Annaliese. Her work at the hospital came in spurts. She would sometimes be around most of the time, and other times she be gone for days at a time. We had pretty much stopped even pretending, and when we could arrange it, I could wake up and kiss her good morning and sometimes more.

She and I generally met at Sarah's. One of us would walk in and the other would be sitting drinking coffee and talking to Sarah or Rebecca or Jeb. She knew everything I knew about the trip and some of my best ideas came from her. Sometimes when I walked in and saw her, I would feel warm in my chest as though I had a sun inside me. Suddenly it was a better day.

Lucky for us, Sarah understood about the 'I've missed you so much' kind of kisses when we hadn't seen each other for a week.

All in all, I was amazed at how the days went speeding by, and then suddenly one day they seemed to stop.

Lemuel, Wash and I were in the barn at Sarah's working on the wagon when Handy came in waving a telegram.

"It's from Carson City," he said. He handed it to me and stood looking down to where I had just slid out from under the wagon.

I read it through and then again and looked up at the three of them staring down at me. "It's from him," I said. I took Handy's outstretched hand and let him pull me to my feet, dusted myself off and said, "Let's go in and sit down."

As we emerged from the barn, Jason and Jed drove up in a wagon. Jason had fitted all the stock with new shoes and had made extra ones. These, along with some tools, were to fit into one of four boxes Lemuel and Wash had built beneath the floor.

The others held ammunition and extra dry good and general equipment and clothing. The way they were fitted, we could use the floor for other duffel and still have room if need be. In a few minutes we were all sitting around the stove in the long dining room drinking coffee.

"This sure is the best organized, best equipped outfit I was ever with," said Jason. "When is the bill coming due for all this stuff?"

"I've arranged with the merchants in town that we will settle up before we leave." I looked at Lemuel. "How does the bill look?"

"I'd say we got most everything we need except some of the food and water," he replied. "We'll load that up last, just before we leave. But we've already got a reckoning about the food, so it looks like about $300.00 or so will cover it all."

"I'm going to pay half of that, and you fellows split the rest," I said.

"Why you paying half?" asked Handy.

"Cause I've got the money and you'all don't have so much. Save it for later," I answered.

"Now about this telegram." I took it from my pocket and handed it to Handy who read it and passed it around the circle. When Wash handed it back I said, "As you can see, he seems to have accepted that we want to give him the papers and has agreed to meet us in Carson City right after we get there to work it out. I want to hear what each of you thinks about it." I looked at Wash to start because I really wanted to hear what he had to say.

"While Wash is thinking about what he's going to say, I want to say something," said Handy. "Because we believed someone might try to shoot at us on the way, we've set things up so we have a good plan for dealing with that. I'm not sure I trust that man enough to believe what he says. I'm for keeping on being careful all the way to Carson City."

Wash nodded his head vigorously. "Couldn't have said it better," he said. "We need to stick to the plan no matter what he says. He might have an idea to catch us napping because we believe he's not behind that next rock."

"Does everyone agree with that thinking?" I asked. I looked at each and got the same nod. "OK, then we stick to the plan."

"Besides," said Wash, "it's the best way to travel the kind of country we'll be passing through whether someone's gunning for you or not."

"As far as dealing with him when we get there, we'll just have to wait and see what happens. Can't make plans until we know more."

The more Jinx was around Brutus the more they seemed to like each other, and I was glad Jinx had someone on his own level to spend time with. During our meetings the two of them played together or lay down together in a bed Sarah had made for them in the corner of the kitchen.

Later that day Annaliese and I were sitting in Sarah's dining room when she held up a bag she had brought with her. "My diary is in here and some of the letters from that doctor in Colorado I told you about. We were going to read them together, but we never got around to it, so I'm going to let you take them with you, so you'll have something to read on the trail." She looked me in the eyes for a moment and continued.

"When we see each other again you can ask me all the questions you'll have, and we can decide if we still want to get married."

That night we all gathered in the barn at Sarah's to double check our gear and supplies and make sure everything was done and ready to go. Then we locked the door and joined the festivities in the house. The following afternoon we would move into position just south of the Great Salt Lake and begin our trek at dark.

The Doctor and some of his family joined us, as did some of the Mormon friends we had made since we got here.

We were drinking punch and eating little bits when I noticed a strange man standing by the door. He was unshaven and had the dusty look of someone who'd been on the trail for a while. He was looking around the room, and when he recognized someone he came in to where Annaliese was standing. She greeted him with a big smile and introduced him as Brad Flaherty, brother of a patient the Doctor had saved when he was bitten by a rattlesnake the year before.

He bent his head toward me and said into my ear, "I need to talk to you."

Annaliese looked puzzled, then led us into the next room where she seated our guest by the fire and left to bring him refreshment.

I had motioned to Wash and Handy. They joined us and we all sat waiting for him to speak.

"My brother Frank and I sometimes work as guides for hunters and such out west of here. A couple weeks ago he was hired by some fellows from back east who wanted to find a place to hole up while they waited for somebody. Usually when we have someone like that we just listen for a bit, and if we don't like what we hear, we disappear."

He accepted a cup of coffee from Annaliese, took a sip and went on. "When a fellow showed up in their camp with a newspaper, they decided to go to Carson City and didn't need Frank anymore; but he heard enough to realize this bunch was up to no good, so he skedaddled and told me about it when he got home."

Annaliese had picked up Jinx and seated herself on the floor in front of me with him in her lap.

"If I've got this right, these fellows are after you and your friends," he said. "You must have something they want but that's not the whole of it. There's this one fellow who's got a grudge on you," he nodded at me, "and he plans to take what you give him and then shoot you. I remembered hearing about you and how you was marrying Annaliese. Considering what we owe her and her father, I felt I ought to tell you."

When he stopped talking we were all quiet, and then Wash said, "I'm not surprised. I've been expecting something like this from the first time you told me about this fellow."

"Me too," said Handy.

"That makes it unanimous," I added.

"That's not all," Brad continued. "He's hired a fellow who's going to meet him in Carson City. His name is Glenwood Coe, and from what I've heard, he shoots people for a living."

CHAPTER TWENTY-NINE

Suddenly the stakes were higher, and I wanted to talk to all the people who had a hand in the game we were in. Jason, Jed and Lemuel had seen us leave with Brad, and they soon joined us with the women in their lives, so there were nine people sitting around waiting for me to say something.

After Brad left, I said, "Let's talk about how this changes the plans we've made."

"Since the plans so far are about us getting to Carson City in one piece, I don't see how it changes things at all," said Handy. Everyone agreed with that, so we began to talk about what to do when we got there and how we'd deal with the Gambler and his murderous cronies.

"We don't yet know where or when we are to meet him, so it strikes me we just need to be ready," I said. "One thing I want you all to think about. It seems like this is suddenly a more deadly game, and anyone around me could well be a target, or at least be in the line of fire. We leave tomorrow night, so anyone who wants to get off this train better do so now."

I looked around the circle, but my friends all seemed to want to stay the course, though I was not so sure about some of the women who loved them. When bullets began flying no one knew who would get hit, and everyone in the room knew that. I tried to think the problem through, but there were so many unknowns I couldn't find the answers to, so I quit trying. All I could do was to be ready when the time came and hope for the best.

That night I didn't sleep much. We tried to make love, but my mind was elsewhere, and it just didn't happen. Finally, she curled up under my arm and we talked.

I had to come to grips with the idea that I might soon be facing a professional killer in a gunfight. It was unnerving. The last time someone drew a gun on me I didn't have time to think. I just acted and then stood staring at the body of the man I had killed.

It was not something I wanted to do again, but I might be forced into a corner and need to. And if I didn't handle it right, I could be dead. Right-handed, I had been drawing and firing a gun for years, but from the left side I had only been practicing a few months. Was I good enough to survive such a showdown?

I would need to try to shade things in my favor as much as I could, but if he set the meeting place then he would call the shots, and I would have to play the game his way. The two times I had faced the Gambler, Jinx had entered the picture giving me an edge, but I didn't think I could count on him again.

After a while she drifted off to sleep, but with these thoughts chasing each other around my brain I couldn't, so I lay there and stewed.

Tomorrow we would begin moving toward a showdown and I felt a certain responsibility for the ones who had joined me. Granted, they were all with me because they chose to be, but that wouldn't make me feel any better if one or more ended up dead.

On top of that there was the special responsibility I felt with Jed. I felt like his teacher and protector and I'm sure his mother felt the same. What would I tell her if he was killed? How would he feel if he killed someone? I had felt that and knew it was a burden to carry especially for someone his age. Also, I would need to help him fit in, feel a part of the group.

And then there was the future, if I had one. When I kissed Annaliese goodbye the next day it might be the last time we would see each other. The question of our marriage hadn't been finally settled, so I woke her up and kissed her cheek. "I still want to marry you," I said.

"Good," she said, then smiled and went back to sleep.

The next morning I kissed Annaliese goodbye in our little alcove on Sarah's porch and rode away without looking back. Inside I felt like I was tearing in half. One part of me wanted to go back to her and never leave, the other was excited at the adventure I was beginning.

The plan was that she would see me in Carson City in early April, but that would probably be after we confronted the Gambler and his gang, so whether or not I would be alive and well was in a future we couldn't yet see. Things were already in motion, and the closer I came to the rendezvous Wash had selected for us, the more excited I was.

The idea that I was going to ride with men who had chosen to ride with me to finish what I started when I opened the door to the livery stable in Junction City the year before excited me and made me glad for some strange reason. We were likely riding into a fight, but that was alright because we were doing it together.

There were six of us, and though we were all friends, we settled into pairs on the trail. Handy and I were riding front. He was my closest friend and we just naturally made a pair. In the rear, Jason and Jed made another, and Wash and Lemuel, close to the same age, were also a pair, though Wash spent most of his time outriding ahead and to the side of our cavalcade. When he was with us, he was usually in the wagon or riding beside it talking to Lemuel.

The plan was to be on the trail early, ride till noon or a little after, find a place to rest and start again in the late afternoon. We could ride into the night and ride as long as we wanted, although I thought it was up to Wash as to where and when we stopped for the night. He was the wagon master and it was part of his job, that and finding water and graze and leading us to it.

The country we rode through at first was the outskirts of Salt Lake. Farms and pasturage stretched away on both sides of the trail, but gradually they faded, and we began to see the country we were to cross. From what Wash had told us we would be riding through a series of valleys made by ridges that ran across our route.

The first time we crested a ridge and I looked into the valley below, I thought I'd never seen anything so beautiful, but according to Wash, it was like this all the way to the Nevada border and beyond, one beautiful valley after another.

Wash rode between Handy and me for a while and talked about the tricks he used in looking over a new piece of country. Listening to him I came to see that beauty sometime hid danger; that looking and seeing were two different things; that we needed to see what was there and not just look at it. The first time Jed and Jason rode out a way to look over our back trail, Wash rode along and then disappeared until it was time to halt.

Wash spent a lot of time out of sight, and out of curiosity, one day I ask him what he did when he was gone.

As always, he took his time answering. "I scout and look over as much country as I feel we need to be safe. Look for water and graze and good places to stop for a while, but you know all that, don't you? So, I guess you're asking me is why I'm gone so much." I nodded and he thought for a minute, then continued. "Sometimes I take my meal and sit afterwards, just looking at what's around me and feeling free. I never seem to get enough of that feeling. I guess I still got some free to catch up on."

I sat thinking about that for a moment then said, "I don't figure there's any way I can understand how you feel, but I think I can see why you'd feel it."

He had picked our first rest spot earlier in the day and we spent some time getting used to camping again, and all the chores that needed doing first day or night on the trail.

We had seen the kitchen part of the wagon before. Lemuel had it down and open in a few minutes and food on our plates before long. While we were eating breakfast: biscuits and jerky with coffee, he made some extras we could carry with us to eat while we were riding. It was near dark when we took to the trail again, and when the half-moon rose over our shoulders it turned the desert into a hard-to-believe picture of light and shadows.

"It's really something to look at, ain't it," said Wash. He was riding between Handy and me again.

Earlier he had come out of the night in his dark suit and everyone was amazed at how hard it was to see him. Like he said, if he didn't smile, he was invisible in the dark, just like Jinx. I remembered the last time I'd seen him in it, and the idea of him being out in the night, Bowie in hand, still made me shiver a little.

The third night we camped in a circle of rocks around a spring, and when supper was over, Jed and I went off to practice with the Colts. We had gotten to the point that some of our practices were almost like tumbling matches. With guns unloaded we would draw while falling, or diving or spinning one way or another. Some of these tricks left us a little winded and a bit bruised. After a good session that night we sat on a rock and talked for a while.

"Can I ask you something?" he asked.

"Sure, anything," I responded.

"Do you worry about that fellow who's supposed to be waiting for you in Carson City?"

I looked out at the desert for a bit, at all the pale shades and shadows of the moon. "Jed, I don't think I'd be normal if I didn't think about him," I finally said, "but I'm not afraid of him, if that's what you mean."

"Pa and I talked about such things, and he understood I might have to face something like this. His advice to me was, "Don't hurry." He believed that a lot of human mistakes and accidents happened because people were upset or nervous or afraid," here I nodded at him, "and trying to hurry something they're doing that would be a natural movement if they weren't upset or nervous or afraid."

"You know how much you and I practice. We do that so that drawing and firing a Colt will become a natural motion, like walking or scratching your nose. Pa and I were doing that together for close to ten years, if not a little more. He taught me that having the first shot hit what you need to hit is more important that a faster shot that doesn't. So, when I meet Mr. Coe, I'll try not to hurry and hope it's fast enough."

"Will you let him draw first?"

"I have no notion how the whole thing will shape up," I said. "Once we're face to face, I'll have to see what happens and then do what

I need to do. This is not a time to worry about being fair, it's a life or death situation. I'll take any edge I can get and hope I'm good enough."

"Let's talk about something else. How are you getting along with Greta?" I asked. I could understand if he was a little reluctant to talk about her, but he didn't seem to mind.

"We talk a lot and she's taught me a lot. You know, Lemuel reads to her every night." He shook his head. "And she seems to remember everything she hears. I think she's listened to as many books as you've read. And she only stumbles once when she's in a new place or doing something new. She always remembers where things are once she's been shown. She's really something."

Though I couldn't see his face in the shadow of his hat, I guessed he was smiling when he said all this.

"Did you know Lemuel's asked me to help him stock up the bookshelves when we're a going concern again and learn to be his assistant?" he asked.

"He mentioned it to me. I guess that means you'll be working for me too, cause he and I are going to be partners," I answered. "And of course, Greta will be around most of the time too, so there's that." This I could see his grin, shadow or no.

CHAPTER THIRTY

$\langle\!(\mathbb{C}\ \mathbb{O})\!\rangle$

Back home Jinx never paid much mind to other people. Now, with him being in close contact with so many, he was learning to be sociable. He naturally had a good relationship with Lemuel, since he was the cook and the source of treats and such. Handy and he had bonded from the beginning and he occasionally rode with the big fellow, sometimes even on his shoulders.

He loved to play with the rope toy when Handy would drag it across the ground for him to pounce on and he and Brutus had many a fierce struggle over it, sounding for all the world like they were trying to maim each other. He tolerated Wash and the feeling was mutual, but he sat with Jed and sometimes Jason around the fire while they petted and scratched him and gave him occasional treats Lemuel had provided.

With Brutus around now he had to share some of the attention when he used to get it all but didn't seem to mind. I was glad he had someone to play with, and sometimes even sleep with, and he was spending more time in the wagon with the bulldog. Of course, that could be because that's where all the treats were, which would be in character for him.

With Annaliese in my life now, he had a rival for my affections for the first time but seemed to have accepted the idea and tolerated her attentions. Others that came and went around me, he kept a wary eye on, but seemed to be at peace with most of the changes in our lives since we left Junction City.

The next morning I was up early, and while Jed helped Lemuel with breakfast, Jinx and I rode out with Jason to look at our back trail in the morning light. I had already seen enough of the desert to know it would look different from the evening before. The same rocks and trees we had passed were there but seen from a different place in a different light it was a different world.

We could see some dust along the trail, but the glasses told us it was just a couple of water wagons sent out by the railroad when it was especially dry to fill the water tanks that kept the locomotives running. They were pulled by oxen, were painfully slow, and usually traveled at night and rested in the shade somewhere until the cool of the evening.

Handy's uncle had told me a bit about Jason, and I was curious as to what it was like growing up in two different Indian cultures. Like most Indians I had met, he thought for a bit before he answered me.

"It was hard sometimes. Things that were done in one tribe sometime were done differently in the other, so I felt like an outsider until I learned the new way. It was a while before I was accepted by the other children and even my mother's other children she had with her new husband always seem to know I was somehow different."

"They stayed behind when I left the tribe after my mother died when I was eighteen, and I don't believe anyone missed me." He was quiet for a moment and then said, "I think it helped me when I came to live among whites. They always treated me like an outsider, but I was used to it, so I got along pretty well."

"Where'd you learn to shoot a rifle like that?" I asked. "Pa was a fair hand with a Winchester, but I'd say you're a sight better."

He chuckled, which was unusual among Indians. "When I first came to Kearney," he said, "I was about eighteen and I worked for this old fellow who had a ranch north of town. His wife was dead, and his two daughters had left the ranch and moved to town, so he was alone most of the time. "

"When I showed up looking for work, he took me in and treated me like a son. We sometime spent the whole day without saying anything to each other, other than something like 'hand me that hammer', but we got along well."

"Anyway, he had a bunch of guns, so he gave me a nice Winchester and taught me to shoot. I had done some before I left the tribe, and I just took to it natural."

"We used to have shooting matches and he would get mad when I beat him most of the time." He smiled a rueful smile. "When he died, his daughter's husband came around and let me know I wasn't needed anymore, so I got a job at the livery stable where I was when you met me."

"Do you ever miss the tribe?" I asked.

He shook his head. "No, I don't," he replied. "I never felt at home with the Kiowa. I guess I'm a Cheyenne after all." After a moment he continued. "Or nothing, maybe. I don't know, but when I'm with you fellows I feel at home." He gave me a steady look.

"I'm glad," I said. "I reckon you're part of the family."

It's easy to look at the desert, day or night, and believe there was nothing much alive out there. Then you look up at the birds and realize there must be something for them to hunt or they wouldn't be there. Hawks and other hunters must eat and since there were plenty of them in the sky most days, they must find enough to keep them going.

At night, owls and night hawks were out, and one evening we saw thousands of bats streaming out of a cave mouth we could see south of the trail. Mostly what we saw were lizards of one kind or another and all kind of insects, but no other small animals. I guess they were good at staying out of sight.

I had seen some beautiful sunrises and sunsets back home and on the trail, but what we saw here was marvelous. Sometimes I just sat on Black and watched a slow explosion of colors and shades turn into a blue morning sky or saw the colors of the rainbow reaching down toward the setting sun. I could see why folks wanted to put it behind them because it was barren and dry at times, but they would never forget what they saw here.

Wash had told me of the danger of flash floods that would sweep away everything in their paths, and it was easy to see in the dry washes where they had run.

He also told me of the flowers that bloomed suddenly after a downpour and how the desert became a carpet of colors from horizon to horizon. All in all, the desert was a place I wanted to get to know better and considering the talk Annaliese and I had back in Salt Lake, it looked like I might have a chance to do just that.

Pa would sometimes talk about having my cake and eating it too. The idea of being married to the woman I loved with all the good things that meant while getting to travel around and see the country at the same time sounded like what he was talking about. It gave me a lot to think about. Wash said he'd be glad to show me the country anywhere, anytime which made the idea sound even better.

Annaliese's diary in my saddlebags gave me something to read and then to think about during the time I spent riding ahead of the caravan. She had begun it shortly after her brother had told of the massacre and even then, at age eight, it seemed to influence her thoughts and ideas about the people around her and how she was different. There were gaps in it when she put it aside for a while, but she always came back.

Once she began working with the Doctor, she began to keep it on a regular basis and sometimes would write long entries about her work and the people she cared for. I skipped over most of these parts, but when she wrote about her brother and what she felt about the Doctor I paid attention.

These two men had shaped her life, and as she grew older, they turned her loose and let her grow in the direction she chose. She never had any real problems with her sisters and the Doctor's wives but seemed to draw a line around herself as she grew older and spent more and more time in her room in the hospital wing, and finally moved into it completely.

When her lover, Jean Paul, entered her life she filled pages with thoughts and hopes that came crashing down as she came to realize he was one who would come and go but never be a constant presence. She wrote about the time they spent in bed, and how the Doctor accepted that as a part of her estrangement from the people around her. He seemed to feel it was necessary for her happiness, since marriage was probably not in her future.

When it was my turn to help Lemuel, I was up early and stayed busy cooking, serving and cleaning up after breakfast and then making a lunch we could eat in the saddle. In the middle of the day we didn't have much to do, so we talked.

My joining him in the business had made him think about some new possibilities and how he'd like to spend his time once we got the bookstore up and running.

"Fact is, I love traveling around selling books to people, so I think I'll find a way to keep doing it. Once we get the store working, I'd like to hire someone to run it and go back to traveling."

"The store will be what we make it and it will provide us an income, but it can also be a warehouse we can wholesale books into and out of for other stores. I could order books from our own warehouse same way I order books from back east. That way we'd have two stores, if you count the wagon, and probably make enough to open a few more stores up and down the state."

"We could come into a new town, set up a store, get a good man to run it, and then go back to traveling and open up another one if the opportunity come along." Apparently, he'd been thinking about it a lot because he had some pretty detailed plans, including some new ideas for making the wagon better suited to live and travel in.

"I've talked to Jed about it and he'd like to travel with us for a while, at least until he decides what he wants to do. And I'm beginning to see that he and Greta might have a future together." He stopped and smiled to himself. "I have been wondering if and when something like that would happen and it looks like it might just."

He looked at me. "Since you're sort of his guardian, how would you feel about it?"

"I think it's a great idea, but I'd say you'd need to ask them, wouldn't you?"

"Well, I know how she feels, and while he's bashful, he's not stupid, so it seems he'll probably get around to the idea before long." He seemed to ponder his hands for a while then continued. "Besides, it would be great to have someone along to help us as I get a little older. I took a bullet through my hip in a scrap in Georgia back in '64 and I can feel it most mornings, plus the arthritis in my hands is pure misery some days, especially when it's wet."

"A pair of strong, young hands would be a blessing on the road, and who knows, maybe I'll have some grandchildren after all." He grinned with all his teeth showing and winked at me. "Yes sir, that would be fine."

He thought again for a minute and said, "Of course losing Greta will be a blow." His voice trailed off and he shook his head. "I guess we'll just have to wait and see."

The next day Handy and I were leading when Wash rode in.

"It looks like a storm coming up, so we need to get off the trail and onto some high ground." He shouted so we could all hear him. "The way those clouds are building it looks like we're in for a gulley washer. It will probably come on suddenly so let's move."

Behind him we could see what he meant, and we scrambled to get the wagon and stock into a protected place he had found a little north of the trail. When everything was as secure as we could make it, we sat and waited, but not for long.

A stiff wind struck first and then the rain in buckets. We were all either under the tarp attached to the back of the wagon or inside, and once the wind stopped blowing, the rain came almost straight down, so we all managed to stay mostly dry.

Lemuel had made some coffee and sandwiches, so we hunkered down and waited till it stopped. Below us, back on the trail, we could see the water level rising where it crossed what had been a dry wash a few minutes before. Within minutes it was a raging torrent and we were glad we had Wash along for the umpteenth time since we left Salt Lake.

Half an hour later it stopped as suddenly as it had started. The clouds disappeared and it was as though it had never happened, except for the waterfall pouring over some rocks that had been buried in dry sand a few minutes earlier, and a new river raging across the desert sweeping everything in its path.

"The real danger is when you don't see the rain." Wash had come up behind where Handy and I were standing watching small puddles disappear before our eyes, sucked up by the thirsty ground. "There'll be a storm up in the mountains somewhere and suddenly the water comes rushing down a dry wash you're standing in the middle of. The only warning you get is the noise. It's one of those sounds you hear once and remember the rest of your life." He grinned at me. "Like the buzz of a rattler ready to strike."

It was easy to visualize what he described because we had just seen it. "Sounds like we should stay out of dry washes," I said, "and get across them in a hurry."

"It's not a good place to stop for the night, that's for sure," observed Handy, indicating the rushing waters.

"We could get bogged down in a hurry if we try to move too soon," said Wash. "Believe it or not, that will be gone in an hour or two, and within a couple of hours it will look just like it did before. We'd best stay right here for the day and start early in the morning. Won't hurt us to take a day off. I know this is hard to believe, but tomorrow we'll be riding through fields of wildflowers." He shook his head. "You've never seen anything like it."

He was right. The desert we awoke to was not there when we went to sleep. Green plants were everywhere, and when the sun got up high enough to touch them, flowers exploded before our eyes. No matter where you looked there was color - bright in the sun, muted in the shade, but color still. For the first time in my life I wanted to be an artist and be able to put this in a painting so I could see it again and again.

Where the water had raged the day before, now there were just puddles here and there. The water had stopped moving and was disappearing and the desert floor, already drying up was showing cracks again. The dust was gone for the present and the air was fresh and clear for a while, but we knew that wouldn't last; dust and desert travel go hand in hand.

CHAPTER THIRTY-ONE

◄(❡ ❡)►

The next day we came to a regular river. The Reese River flowed across our path and fording it was a bit of a problem because of the rain the day before. It wasn't because there was a lot of water in it; in fact, back home it would have been considered little more than a creek.

The problem was that the rush of water had changed the bottom and some of the surrounding land, so it took Wash and Jason a while to find a crossing place with a firm enough bottom for the wagon. When we crossed we could see the new banks carved by the scouring action of the runoff and we had to ride a little way upstream to escape the small canyon it had created.

We filled our water bags at the Reese. The next sure water was the Carson River, four- or five-days west, though there was probably a spring closer we could use if need be. That meant we were about five days from Carson City, and we began to talk about what we would do when we got there.

Riding up front with Handy was great at times, but when we started the trail all he would talk about was Rebecca and the things they'd do together when he saw her again. Though this got a little tiring after a while, I did learn about what they had decided to do about the opportunity Cody had purposed the previous year. We had both read news accounts of the show's doings and we sometimes speculated about what it would be like to do that for a living.

"If it's the same offer as before, we should be able to save a lot, and after a couple of years we'd have a pretty good stake, especially if he can use her in the show."

It was a day after crossing the Reese, and we were riding across the heart of the Nevada desert. "Now that I can handle a gun and I've learned a bit about riding and such, I think there's a chance I can be what he wants in the show. The trouble is, I don't have a notion about what the job is really about."

We were stopped at the crest of a ridge and the desert stretched out beneath our feet for maybe thirty miles to another ridge just like this one. Behind us the double-teamed horses strained to pull Lemuel's heavy wagon up the steep grade.

Lemuel's wagon was heavy and slowed us down quite a bit, but with six of us it was handy as a shelter at need and carried extra supplies and water that made our trek more comfortable and certainly safer.

On top of that, it seemed like his and my futures might be joined at the hip, and likely it wouldn't have been prudent to refuse to let him join us, especially since we were going to the same place. He did his share and more, and I believed if danger threatened, he would be right there with his twelve-gage.

We had decided the best way to use the horses was four, all the time. It gave a better day's travel and the horses seemed to handle the work fine. Lemuel was constantly checking over the wagon to make sure it was rolling as easy as possible and he treated the horses like his children. They got oats while the other stock did without. Every morning he was out with the grease pot, lubing wheels and joints. The smell of the petroleum didn't improve the taste of breakfast.

Increasingly hot days made traveling in the cool moonlit night seem the better choice, and just before dawn one morning we sat on a rise and saw the lights of Carson City in the distance.

"It looks closer than it is," said Wash, who had been riding with us the last hour. "This clear desert air fools you."

"How long, you reckon?" asked Handy.

"Let's sit down for the day and then about six, set in to ride all night. That should put us in town in the morning around dawn. We can get a bite, find a place and settle in. We can rest and then sit and talk about what's next." He turned his horse and dropped back to let the others know.

"Don't recall ever feeling so two ways about coming into a new town," said Handy. We sat our horses and looked over the land. I'd never get tired of the desert, but I did feel like I'd like to see some real green for a change. There's green in the desert but it's usually covered with dust, so it doesn't look like the green of a pine or an oak. Unless it's just rained, that is.

"Do you think we should find a rooming house or start out at a hotel and take some time to look around?" I asked. "Personally, I'd like to sit down to a nice breakfast for the first time in a while."

"Let's stop at the first place we see that serves something besides biscuits and beans," said Handy.

"We're going to need to see the sheriff early on," I said, "and I want to make sure the wagon is secure, and the horses are in good shape."

We could already see the Sierras rising from the desert floor and we needed to make sure we had the horses it took to pull the heavily built wagon over them. Of course, we did have some problems to deal with before we got to the mountains. That thought seemed to pop up into my mind regular lately.

"We'll need to check the telegraph office to see if he's sent us anything, and we need to find some rooms," I said. "We could be here for a month and a hotel wouldn't work for that long. We'd all go broke."

Wash had ridden up behind us. "I used to know the sheriff here, but Carson City is a rough place; he might not still be around. Name was Henry Grossman. Had a big dog he took everywhere with him, even to church."

"Wash, I swear," exclaimed Handy, "I believe you know someone everywhere."

Wash grinned. "I have been around," he said.

Lemuel had a fire going when we got back to the wagon and we all sat around drinking coffee and speculating about things.

I'd already shared my ideas about the hotel and the safety of the wagon. Of course, everyone wanted to talk about the Gambler and his gang, but I pointed out that until we heard from him we could make no plans, so rather than talk about that let's talk about other things. So we did.

The solitude and the camaraderie were two nice things about the three weeks crossing the desert. If that sounds strange, it's not really. For hours at night you ride by yourself, looking around, watching, listening, thinking.

But there were just as many hours sitting around a campfire talking, or lying in your bed roll looking up at the stars and finding new things to know about your friends, new things you'd have a chance to think about that night in the dark when you're riding along watching, listening, thinking.

That night I finished reading Annaliese's diary. The last entries were about me and then about us. It was strange to read about myself from her point of view. I could see how her feelings changed and could almost pinpoint when she began to love me, which was about the same time I began to love her.

I took up the letters from the doctor in Colorado and then decided to wait until we were settled in Carson City before I read them.

Carson City was just waking up and stretching when we rode in. First thing we went to the Carson House, signed in and led our stock to the hotel stable in the rear. We had more than they could handle, so Lemuel took his team to a livery stable close by.

When they were undressed and comfortable with food in their mangers, we trooped into the hotel dining room and ordered breakfast. While that was cooking, I walked across Carson Street to the sheriff's office. A deputy was seated at a desk in the front room.

I introduced myself. "We're new in town and would like to talk to the sheriff about some things," I said. "There are six of us so rather than clutter up your office, if you could ask him to join us in the hotel dining room for a cup of coffee we'd be grateful."

We had just finished eating and were talking over coffee and smoke when the sheriff came in, followed by an enormous mastiff. Jinx disappeared under the table, but the dog ignored him, and everyone else for that matter. He touched noses with Brutus and then sat looking at his master.

The sheriff nodded at Wash and smiled, "Good to see you Wash. Are you traveling with this bunch?"

Wash rose from his chair with outstretched hand and then seemed to change his mind in mid motion. "Just remembered," he said. "You don't shake hands, do you?"

"No, never thought it made much sense to let the other fellow get his hands on you." He stopped smiling and looked carefully at each one of us round the table, then said, "So who was it that wanted to talk to me?" About that time Jinx jumped up on the table. Apparently, he had decided the dog wouldn't bother him and he was curious, as always.

I lifted my hand. "That's me. My name is Johnny Fry and last spring I had a set-to with a fellow back in Kansas. He tried to rob me, but it didn't work out and I got to keep his horse and this gun," I said. "I can give you the name of the sheriff I talked to after it happened. I explained the whole thing to him, and he said it's my horse and my gun."

I nodded at Handy. "His Uncle Joe is the sheriff in Kearney, Nebraska and he can vouch for us, and so can Sheriff Bob Risley in Marysville, Kansas. The fellow broke out of jail in Kearney and has been chasing me across the country. While we were in Salt Lake, I found some papers he had hidden in his saddle. I put an ad in the paper here several weeks ago, and we have arranged to meet here to give him the papers."

"I remember that ad. People were talking about it." He turned to Wash. "How long you been siding with this bunch?"

"Joined up in Casper. We've had one brush with this guy and I, for one, think he's got some kind of killing grudge against Johnny here."

"What's this fellow's name?"

"To tell you the truth, I'm not sure what his name is," I answered. "The papers are made out to a Rene' Paul but we've never been introduced. He was dressed like one when we first met, so I've always called him the Gambler."

Handy chipped in. "I saw him in Salt Lake and he's a bit scruffy now, and he's got a bullet scar across his right cheek. Dark hair, not quite six foot I'd say. Skinny guy with a slick way of talking."

"I think I know of him," the sheriff said. "He and some others are staying out at the no name saloon on the North Road. I heard they're waiting for someone."

"Before we left, we had someone tell us he overheard this fellow say he's got a hired gun coming in to shoot me after he gets the papers," I said. "A man named Glenwood Coe."

The Sheriff's expression didn't change but he was quiet for a moment. "I know Coe. He's dangerous and likely a killer. What would you like me to do?"

"Nothing really," I said. "I just wanted you to know where things stand. I'm not looking for trouble." I looked around the table. "None of us are. He's supposed to contact me here to set up the meeting where I can give him the papers and there may be gunplay. It's your county so I figured you ought to know."

He sat for a while, apparently thinking, and scratching the dog's ears.

"Just keep me informed as best you can. I know these kinds of things happen pretty quick, but the more I know the better." He smiled at Jinx." Never saw anyone travel with a cat before. He come all the way from Kansas with you?"

"Yes, I've had him since he was newborn," I said. "He's pretty smart; smart enough to stay out of trouble all the way. Wash said you had this dog with you all the time so you must have had him for a while."

He stood and nodded to everyone. "Actually, he's the second one I've had. The other one died a couple of years ago and I had someone send this one from England. I raised him from a pup. His name is Max."

We got into our rooms, unpacked and tested the beds, then dispersed in pairs to do various things around town. Wash had surprised us by not joining us in the hotel.

"There's a lady here I stay with when I'm in town. She got a place just east of town and we've known each other for a while. I wrote her from Salt Lake, and she invited me to stay. She works at the hotel, helping out. Lost her husband a few years ago in a mine accident. Her place is not far from the hotel, so I'll see you for breakfast most mornings I suppose."

Handy and Jed found the telegraph office and the post office and came back with news and mail. I had three letters from Annaliese and one from Sarah. Handy also had a wire from Bill Cody and a half a dozen letters from Rebecca. Everyone there sent letters to everyone here. For the next hour we all sat and read our mail.

Annaliese, the Doctor and Greta were planning to leave Salt Lake the day after tomorrow and be in Carson City the next morning. She sent me the address of the clinic and asked me to go by and see if it was ready. The other letters were about how much fun we were going to have when we got our hands on one another again. Stuff like that.

She also wrote about Greta and how effective she was as a helper at the clinic. She had been working with Annaliese to help organize the moving of equipment needed so the new clinic could get opened for business.

They were planning to stay here a month or so, get the clinic open and working, then make another move of equipment to the clinic in Sacramento. If all went as planned, they should be in Sacramento about the last week in May or the first week in June.

Sitting there thinking about it made me realize that no matter what else I was thinking about, I always came back to the showdown with the Gambler. Annaliese was writing excitedly about a future I might not even be a part of. Eventually all I could do was ignore it.

After that, whenever it entered my mind, I'd try to go back to what I was thinking before. Sometimes it worked and sometimes it didn't, but as least I stopped thinking in circles so much, where I always ended up back where I started.

The next morning Handy and I rode by to look at the place where the clinic was going to open, and it seemed ready for whatever they wanted. There were several people working there, carpenters by the sounds, and probably local Mormons, so we had a chance to look around.

It was not going to be a hospital but would provide treatment and medication to locals, with Mormons able to receive care whether they could pay or not. They could also arrange to move patients to hospitals as necessary and would travel to miners' camps in the area to treat Mormon miners and their families. One thing about the Saints, they always knew where each Saint was, probably because that's where they were told to be.

When we got back to the hotel a telegram was waiting for us from the Gambler. His name really was Rene' Paul and he wanted to meet us the next afternoon at the saloon north of town. I stood looking at the paper for a moment, then handed it to Handy.

"Well," he said, "it looks like tomorrow's the day."

CHAPTER THIRTY-TWO

The next morning at breakfast we had a visit from the sheriff and Max.

"Coe got in yesterday," he said. "I imagine you'll be hearing from them today, if you haven't already."

"He must be in a hurry," said Handy. "We got a message from him yesterday afternoon. Supposed to meet him at the no name saloon out on the North Road.

"He said after lunch," I said, "so we'll probably go out around two."

"I'll try to be in the vicinity if I can, and if not, a few deputies will be. I've also let the doctor and the undertaker know there might be a need for them." He stood and looked down at me for a moment. "Good luck, Fry," he said. "Don't worry about giving him an even break or anything like that. If he makes a mistake and gives you an edge, take it."

We had passed the saloon without a name on the way into town the week before. It was a seedy looking place with several outbuildings to one side and behind, and a dilapidated stable across the road. Wash had scouted the place, and now he took a spot in the loft door of the stable with his Sharps.

The plan was for Handy and me to go inside and deal with what was there, and the rest would watch the front to cover our backs and make sure no one interfered. Jason scouted the back of the place, then stood at the end of the front porch to cover the door while Lemuel sat on the front seat of the wagon by the hitchrail, twelve-gage across his lap. He had locked Brutus inside the wagon to keep him out of the line of fire just in case.

Jinx had disappeared. He probably sensed the tension and since it was likely followed by gunfire he was probably under the porch. Jed stood on the far side of the wagon watching across the road. Inside was as bad as we expected. There were few windows and the smoke from pipes and such made it very dim. It was a good thing they didn't open up on us when we walked in, because we couldn't see much.

When our eyes adjusted, we could see our two men sitting at a table near the back of the room, and several more standing at the bar, which was to our right.

Jinx surprised me. He had come in under the batwings and sat just inside the doors, looking around. There was no time to get him to safety, so I put him out of my mind.

We moved forward around either side of a table and stopped, a few feet apart, in front of where they sat.

The Gambler nodded at some chairs scattered to one side and said, "Have a seat."

"No thanks, let's just do what we came to do and then we'll go about our business," I said. I had no desire to have a conversation with this man or accept any of his hospitality. I just wanted him out of my life.

"Here's what you wanted, I believe," I said, and tossed the leather pouch on the table.

He slowly and carefully untied the thong, opened it and glanced at the papers he drew from it.

"What about my horse and my gun?" he asked, and he smiled at me. "You see, I figure you owe me for taking my gun and my horse and making me chase you all the way across the country to get them back."

Since I knew he didn't really expect an answer, I didn't give him one, just stood looking at him.

"I hired this gentleman to help me collect," he said, glancing at the man sitting beside him. "His name is Coe, Mr. Glenwood Coe. I figure you might want to meet the man who's going to kill you."

When he said this, suddenly some of the men who had been standing at the bar left through the front door, but though I couldn't tell for sure, I believed at least one stayed where he was.

Coe slowly slid back his chair and stood, facing me, a slight smile on his face. He nodded at me and we stood looking at one another. I noticed he had narrow shoulders and long arms and his right hand hung just below the butt of the gun tied down on his right leg.

Out of the side of my mouth I muttered to Handy, "Where's Jinx when you need him?"

About that time Jinx jumped onto the bar and knocked over a bottle. Coe's eyes flickered toward the noise and I drew the Colt. It was almost level by the time he started his draw, and I could see the panic in his eyes when my bullet hit him.

Suddenly, all around me there was deafening gunfire. I triggered another shot to make sure of Coe, then pivoted to the man to my right, but there was no need. He had fallen against the bar, blood showing on his shirt and his gun pointed at the floor. When I turned to look at the door, Jed was standing there, arm extended, gun in hand, like a finger pointing.

Handy was down with a bullet in his left thigh, but the Gambler was in worse shape. Like me, Handy had gotten off two shots and either one would have been enough. One hit just above his right nipple and the other in his mid-section, but he was alive. His eyes found mine and he tried to speak.

"There's nothing we can do for you," I said, shaking my head. "Are there any kinfolk anywhere we should send that to?" I nodded at the pouch still lying on the table. He accepted the verdict in my eyes and nodded. "In New Orleans," he whispered; "my sister Claire."

I shook my head at him. "I hope she's a better person than you." I said.

I could see he was trying to say something, so I lowered my ear to his mouth.

"So do I," he whispered.

A few minutes later I was standing outside, leaning my head against Black, trying to catch my breath and wondering where Jinx was when he jumped down from the hayloft in the stable and came racing across the road.

Lemuel and the local doctor were inside the bar watching Wash bandage Handy's leg. The bullet had gone through the meat of the thigh without hitting the bone so all that had to be done was to stop the bleeding with a firm bandage.

Wash had taken one look at the doctor's shaking hands, smelled the whiskey on his breath and decided to do it himself. Jed and Jason were standing on the porch keeping an eye out in case there was someone else who wanted to make trouble.

Jinx stopped in front of me and I picked him up and held him for a minute, then put him on my shoulder. "Sure am glad you showed up again, little buddy," I said, scratching his ears.

Behind me Jason chuckled. "When all the guns were going off in there, he came out the door like he was shot from a cannon. Didn't stop till he was in the hayloft across the road."

"He doesn't like gunfire, and if I remember right, there was a lot of that going on right about then," I said, "but I'm sure glad he was there when I needed him." He purred loudly while I rubbed his head. "You always are," I said, just to him, and kissed him between his ears.

The batwing doors opened, and four men came out carrying Handy on a stretcher, followed by Wash. The doctor had apparently stayed at the bar. Jinx hopped into the saddle and I leaned over Handy.

"It's a little different when someone's shootin' back at you," he said grinning up at me. I wasn't surprised it took four men to carry him. Before he left to join Cody, I wanted to find out how much he weighed. They loaded him into a wagon to take him back to our rooms and the rest of us mounted up to follow.

The man at the bar had been drawing against my back when Jed's bullet hit him on the point of his shoulder and came out the front. His friends had patched him up and helped him to his horse. When he was in the saddle, he looked at Jed and me standing with everyone and said, "He hired me to cover his back. I was just doing a job. No hard feelings?"

I looked at him for a moment, then said, "No hard feelings. Are there any more of you around?"

"No, it was just the three of us," he said. "The boys here are just friends."

As we were turning toward the road to leave, men came out of the saloon carrying two bodies. You know, I believe all undertakers look alike, as least the ones I've seen.

On the way back to town I asked Jed, "How did you get inside? I thought you were covering the road."

"When those three fellows came out, I could see the one at the bar. He was behind you and I figured you might need help. All of you at the table were so busy you didn't notice when I came in."

"I'm sure glad you did." I reached across and put my hand on his shoulder. "Thanks," I said.

I looked at Jason. "How about the other fellows out front? Were they part of it?"

"If they were you couldn't tell," he said. "With a Sharps, a Winchester and a twelve-gage looking at them when they came out the door, suddenly they were downright peaceful. When Lemuel explained to them the necessity of sitting on the edge of the porch for a while, they took right to the idea." He paused. "What all happened in there?"

"Jinx hopped up on the bar and when Coe's eyes went to that, I drew." I answered. "The first shot would have been enough, but I gave him another for good measure, and by the time I turned to the third one at the bar, Jed had already got him. Handy put two into the Gambler, which was more than enough. He died while I was finding out about next of kin."

Halfway back to town we met Sheriff Grossman and Max, trailed by a couple of deputies.

"Since you're alive, I'm thinking maybe Coe's not," he said. When I nodded, he continued. "If this had been in town the marshal would have had to take you before the local judge, but since it's in the county, you just have to stay in town until I check things out. I'll let you know when you're cleared to go." So saying, he continued down the road with Max easily keeping up with the horses.

We took Handy to the new clinic were Wash examined the bandage and decided it needed to be changed, even though the bleeding had stopped. While he was doing that, I wrote out wires to Rebecca and Annaliese and delivered them to the telegrapher.

CHAPTER THIRTY-THREE

The next couple of days were busy. With Handy down, I had to find places for the four of us. Greta would be living at the clinic most times and Lemuel slept in his beloved wagon. Jason and Jed found a place a couple of doors down from us. We all got settled and were on the platform when the train from Salt Lake pulled in.

Rebecca was the first one off the train, and leg wound or no, Handy picked her up and hugged her, then kissed her. Annaliese was close behind and I hugged her, but she stayed on the ground.

After all greetings were done, the Doctor led us to a flatcar father back on the train, and while we all talked excitedly, he supervised the unloading of a special-built carriage wagon to be used at the clinic and the supplies and equipment needed to get the clinic going.

"It's for carrying patients who can't ride or walk to the clinic, or to the station to go to hospitals in Salt Lake or San Francisco," he explained. "We can also use it for around town things like carrying supplies and just taking the staff where they need to go."

Everyone seemed to understand when Rebecca and Handy and Annaliese and I left after breakfast for private places.

After the first hurried frantic coupling we lay there holding hands and looking up at nothing. After a while I kissed her gently and began my favorite pastime of counting her freckles with my tongue.

"Get away from me, you brute," she said pushing me away playfully. We wrestled for a while and then she sat up in her listening pose and said, "Tell me what happened."

For a long moment we looked into each other's eyes, then I dropped mine and said "I knew from the minute I walked in the door who he was and what he wanted. He and I were looking bullets at one another when Jinx jumped on to the bar. When Coe's eyes went to the noise I drew and shot him before he could shoot me. I fired again and then swung to the other man at the bar but there was no need. Jed had gotten him from the doorway."

"Handy had drawn against the Gambler and got two in him but took one in the leg. When I turned back to Coe, he was dead. Either one of the two shots would have killed the Gambler and he knew he was dying. He gave me the name of a sister in New Orleans to send the papers to. The fellows watched outside and covered our backs."

"Did the one Jed shot die?" she asked. She seemed to hold her breath till I answered.

"No. He took one in the shoulder, but his friends got him on a horse afterwards and he left ok," I answered.

"Thank the Lord for that," she breathed. "I'd hate to think he killed a man at his age."

Another long moment and, "What about my age?" I said.

"Tell me what you're thinking, Johnny," she said. "That's the second time you've had to kill a man. Does that bother you?"

I don't think Wash ever took so long to answer a question. "I think about it some, but I have to go back to what Handy said after Julesburg."

She smiled, "What did Handy say?"

"He said, 'Have all the conscience you want but don't let it get you killed," I answered. "If I hadn't beat him, that would have been me they carried out of that saloon and he could have gone on killing till someone finally stopped him, the way I did." I paused for a moment, then, "It's one thing to say that, but is getting past it that easy? Don't get me wrong, I feel no remorse at his death. He surely wouldn't have mourned me."

"No, my problem is what kind of man does it make me? Will I get the reputation as a killer, someone who kills easy and often? Someone who hunts trouble and enjoys the thrill of a gunfight just for itself? Will I become a target for any and all who want a reputation or a family member who wants revenge?"

She buried her head in my chest. All I could see when I looked down was that glorious red hair. "I'd love to take off my gun, but not carrying it at this time and place could be just as dangerous. I guess all I can do is stay away from saloons and hope for the best."

I took her by the shoulders and held her at arm's length. "And now madame, if you don't mind, I have been deprived for too long." We were both laughing when we fell back on the bed.

The next couple of days were spent moving things from the train station to the clinic and tacking up signs around town for an open house the following Saturday evening where the citizens of Carson City could meet the new doctors and nurses.

The Doctor knew the Mormons involved in the clinic would be looked at with suspicion by some, so the staff had been recruited with that issue in mind. One of the new doctors was Mormon and the other wasn't. Of the three nurses, one was a Mormon from Salt Lake, one a Mormon from Carson City and one gentile from Carson City. And of course, Annaliese, Greta and Rebecca who were doing most of the setup and training weren't Mormon.

The Elders had followed the guidance of Brigham Young in trying to live among gentiles in peace by searching for accommodation instead of confrontation. They and other men in the middle understood this, but there were people on both sides who still got their dander up over the issue. The idea was to give them no cause by meeting them halfway or even more.

Annaliese had told me the Doctor had the same plan in place for the clinic in Sacramento, and over the next few weeks two doctors from Sacramento, one Mormon and one Methodist, were coming to work here to learn how to set up and run the operation there.

In the first few days Annaliese and I were able to use the clinic carriage to take trips into the surrounding hills and canyons and found again the joys of making love under a blue sky. But as the clinic became busier, she spent more time at work, and I had to find other things to do.

Handy was healing rapidly and was ready to mount a horse again so he, Jed, Jason and I went on long rides exploring the area and rode as far as the south end of Lake Tahoe to see the beginnings of the trail into and over the Sierra Nevada range. It was a little overwhelming for a flatlander to see those great, grey, snowcapped peaks towering even higher than the Rockies, or so it seemed. I knew the Rockies were actually higher, but these looked so much bigger. We also took a trip to Reno, which was a day's ride north, and explored the areas to the south and east of the city.

We made our plans to leave Carson City a week or so before the Doctor and his bunch. With the clinic doing well, he now turned his attention to Sacramento and getting the equipment and supplies there so they could repeat the success of this one and then get back to Salt Lake where his hospital was limping along without him and Annaliese.

Her plans were to stay at the clinic in Sacramento until she was ready to start school in San Francisco or until she wasn't needed at the clinic, so we really didn't know when she'd be able to leave.

Which left me with the question of what to do while she was becoming a doctor.

We talked about it on our last picnic in the mountains. "I should be pretty busy for a while, helping Lemuel get the shop set up and putting together the leather working and gunsmithing end of it. I'll also be traveling between Sacramento and San Francisco and trying to find us a place to live while you're in school."

"It's nice to have the railroad. Just a couple of hours and you're there," she said.

"That's good, because I'll want you to look at any place I find to rent and pick out the things we'll need to have a proper home," I said.

"Have you thought about life after the clinic is open?" she asked. "How long do we wait in Sacramento before we move to San Francisco? Have you and Lemuel any ideas about where you want to have the shop?" She was getting as bad as Handy with the three question questions.

"Lemuel has a friend there and he wrote him from Salt Lake just before we left asking him to look at some places, so he's hoping that will help us get located and open within a few weeks, if not sooner." I stopped and looked out over the view of Carson City below. "Have you decided if you want to marry me or not?" When I turned back to her, she focused on my eyes.

"Tell you what let's do," she said. "I want you to tell me how your life's different since we met, and I'll do the same. Then we can talk about getting married."

We continued to gaze at one another for a while and finally I said, "Loving you gives me something to think about, and all most every thought I have leads back to you. You've taught me so much about love and loving, about friends and friendship, about giving and caring, about the importance of a belief that drives you to spend your life caring for others. Learning these things has helped me grow into being a man. I feel like I am a man now, and much of what has made me one has come from you."

We stood, eyes locked on each other's eyes, then she kissed me on the nose. "I love you," she said, "and I believe you love me. I've thought a lot about how we can make this work so we're both happy with the way it must be between us. I've come to believe the things that bring us together are stronger than the things that might drive us apart."

She took my hands and pronounced, "So yes, Johnny Fry, I will marry you and I believe we will live happily ever after."

We made love again, and the sight of her lying naked on a blanket in the light of a summer evening was something I would remember always.

We planned to cover the 130 miles to Sacramento in about a week. The heavy wagon would slow us a bit, and we would need to take it easy because of some of the grades we would be pulling, especially after we left Tahoe. As we had once before, we met outside of town near the trail, checked our supplies and equipment, and sat round a fire talking about what was in front of us.

"You don't push yourself in the mountains," said Wash. "Never wait until you're tired to stop for the night. That altitude will take the starch out of any man. Remember, the idea is to get there safe and healthy, so keep something in reserve just in case."

"No one's out there lookin' for us that we know of, but keep your eyes peeled and your gun close to hand just the same."

For much of the time we would ride in sight of the Union Pacific tracks, and many times our route was on the road built to help railroad construction in 1865-67.

Our biggest problems would come from having to go around the eleven tunnels that had been necessary to conquer the Sierra Nevada, including one at Donner Pass that had been blasted through 1659 feet of granite rock. From what Wash told us, some of the road was ill kept, and we might have to make some improvements to get the wagon through.

The next day I was struck again by the beautiful shade of blue water in Lake Tahoe. For the several hours we rode along its southern shore I could seldom take my eyes off it. It was the first of many wonders we would see over the next few days.

Thick stands of evergreens, towering grey snowcapped peaks wherever we looked, and hundreds of rivulets, all snow born, eating away at the road we were traveling. And waterfalls. We had seen many forms of running water since we left the plains, but nothing like the waterfalls that were constantly appearing, dropping off the side of sheer walls, usually falling to a place out of sight and sound and looking like silver threads on a green tapestry. Time and again I stopped just to stare at them.

We passed people on the road several times a day, mostly railroad workers of one sort or another, and the second night we were on the trail we slept in a bunkhouse built into the side of the mountain to house section hands away from home overnight or longer. Several hands bunked with us that night and we shared grub and talked into the night.

There were also occasional freight wagons, and one train of about ten wagons carrying goods to Carson City. We passed through several villages, some just collections of huts on the right of way and saw one place bigger than the rest that seemed to be a whorehouse, though how a whore out here would make enough to live on puzzled me.

The major town between Sacramento and Carson City was Placerville, California. In the days of the gold rush, Placerville had been known as Hangtown, for reasons easy to guess. But now it was buzzing with respectable looking people going about their business and looked like a nice place, if a bit raw.

While we were checking into a hotel, the desk clerk informed us that there were over 2000 people living in Placerville, and at the rate they were growing they would soon be as big as San Francisco.

We ate a nice dinner and were up early to get started. Jed and I had gone to the livery to saddle our horses and when I stepped out onto the boardwalk afterwards, a voice came from somewhere behind me.

"They let any young sprout carry a gun around here don't they?" When I turned toward the voice, I saw a man standing loosely, hand near his gun, poised to draw. When he opened his mouth to say something else, I drew my Colt, and it caught him flatfooted. Instead of controlling the moment, he was suddenly looking down the barrel of a six-shooter. He stood with his mouth open in surprise.

CHAPTER THIRTY-FOUR

When I looked at him a little closer I could see a family resemblance. "Your name wouldn't be Coe, would it?" I asked. He nodded and I continued. "You look like your brother. Act like him too. So, what are you going to do now?"

He looked at me without speaking for a moment. "I heard you killed Glen, using some trick to get the drop on him and then shot him down. Where I come from we don't let that kind of thing pass, so I came to even the score."

He carefully lifted his hand to scratch his chin. "But to tell the truth, I can see you would have beaten him anyway. You're pretty quick with that thing."

I didn't answer him; just kept the Colt trained on his midsection, so he continued. "That being the case, I guess Glen got what he deserved, so I'm going to get my horse, ride away and forget about it. If that's alright with you, that is."

I nodded slowly and again didn't speak. Handy and Jed had come out of the stable, and Jason was leaning against a pole that was holding up the porch roof. Coe looked at me for a minute and then stepped into the street and headed across to where his horse was tied.

I turned to Jed who was standing behind me when I heard Handy say sharply, "Watch it Johnny." Suddenly gunfire erupted around me as Jed and Handy both drew and fired; behind me Jason fired once and jacked another round into the chamber of his Winchester. When I turned back to where Coe had been standing, he was on his knees trying to lift his right hand with his left. As I watched, he tipped over and sprawled on his face in a small puddle near the water trough.

We crossed the street and Wash came out of the barber shop where he had just gotten a shave. He shook his head, and said solemnly, "I can't leave you alone for a minute, can I?" Then he knelt at Coe's side and began to work on his wounds. Within a minute another man appeared, introduced himself as the local doctor, and began to work on Coe's wounded right wrist.

There looked to be three wounds; one in the left shoulder that had gone through and out the back, one just above the left elbow that had gone through and ploughed a furrow in his back, and the one at the wrist. Coe was conscious and the pain hadn't started yet. He looked at Wash, then the doctor, and asked, "Am I going to make it, Doc?"

The doctor kept working, ignoring the question for a bit, then said, "Looks like it, but you won't be using this hand to fire a gun again for a while, if ever."

"Looks like you better find another line of work, friend," said Handy. "Doesn't look like you're very good at this one."

"Well, Glen was always a little better than me," he answered, trying to grin, but the pain was coming on, so he didn't quite make it.

Several men appeared with a stretcher and Coe was moved to the doctor's office with such efficiency it was easy to see they'd done this before, frequently.

"I'll get him patched up OK," said the doctor. "Unless infection sets in, he'll be back on his feet before long if you men want to prefer charges." He nodded at the man with a badge crossing the street from the sheriff's office.

Over the next hour we all gave statements to the deputy. He asked us to wait until we talked to the sheriff, who was due back from the capital that afternoon. Given the fact that Coe was the one who ended up bleeding all over the street, we didn't see any need to add to his trouble by having him arrested. The deputy was still adamant that we talk to the sheriff before we left town though, so we killed time drinking coffee and eating at a small café and reading the local newspaper.

Shortly after lunch we saw a man carrying a valise from the station to the sheriff's office, and within a few minutes the Sheriff of El Dorado County was sitting with us having coffee and scratching Jinx's ears.

He had heard of our fight with Glenwood Coe and knew of the family and their roots in the mountains of southern Missouri, so he wasn't surprised at the family's reaction to his death.

"I've known some of those Bald Knobers to track people for months to avenge a cousin or brother. I had a wire from Grossman in Carson City saying you were headed this way and he has checked you out with someone he knows back east, so I have no problems with you leaving as soon as you want to." He looked at Wash. "Weren't you through here a couple of years back with some fellows headed up north to Oregon?"

"That was me," answered Wash, nodding his head. "We split up and I picked up with this bunch last summer in Casper. Figure to travel with them for a while."

The doctor came in, caught my eye and came over to the table. "Mr. Coe wants to talk to you, if that's all right."

I was a bit puzzled at that, but after we said goodbye to the sheriff and paid our bill, everyone followed me to the office across the street. Handy and I went into a small room where Coe was propped against a wall with pillows behind him.

He had a little trouble getting his words out. The doctor had given him some laudanum and he was half asleep. "I just wanted to tell you that we have a clean slate as far as I'm concerned. I figure anyone who has friends like you do must be ok. It looks like Glen just bit off more than he could chew."

"Are there any other Coes around nursing a grudge?" asked Handy.

"No, most of the rest are still in the hills back home. I don't think you need to worry about anyone else looking for you." He didn't say anything for a minute, and we thought he had fallen asleep, but he finally opened his eyes and said, "I'd shake hands if I could, but so long, and I hope we run into one another again one day." He tried to lift his right hand but couldn't make it and fell back onto the pillows.

"Your wrist and hand look pretty bad," I said. "You might have to find a way to get along with what you've got left, maybe use your head instead of your hands so much. If I were you, I'd pick out a good book and read it. Might find something you like."

I reached out and squeezed his shoulder. He was asleep before we were out of the room.

We left shortly after, and by nightfall had covered almost all the twenty miles we aimed for each day. Now that we were out of the mountains we planned to move faster and figured on reaching Sacramento within a couple of days, or three at the most.

The clinic was in Clarksville, on the western edge of Sacramento, but we would pass Uncle Bill's place on the way in, so I decided to stop there first and let him know I was in town.

The last night before the end of our trip, we sat around the fire and talked about what it meant and what we planned to do once it was over. Lemuel's plans were to find a secure place to park the wagon and then do some things to it that might require the assistance of a good carpenter and some tools. I had come to believe he would always have things he wanted to do to that wagon, and they were all aimed at making it better for what he thought was his, and now our, future.

We had decided to stay in Sacramento for a couple of weeks after the Doctor and Annaliese showed up and would then take the cars into San Francisco to search for premises that fit what we wanted for the shop. We hoped to have things ready for opening by Independence Day which would help us start off, as Lemuel put it, 'with a bang'.

Annaliese would be free to leave the clinic shortly after the Doctor returned to Salt Lake, though she could stay longer if need be.

We planned to marry before we moved to San Francisco, but just when that would be was still not clear.

Wash planned to ask Bill if he needed any help and wanted to be around to help Lemuel with the wagon. I knew Wash needed to work, but he was good at so many things he shouldn't have any trouble finding something to tide him over.

Jed was going to stay with me for a bit and then move into the wagon. He liked sleeping there, and felt he was learning things spending time with Lemuel. Besides, when Greta arrived with Annaliese, he would be where he wanted to be; that is, close to her.

Jason planned to find work at one of the livery stables in town. Lemuel and I had discussed hiring him and teaching him the book business. He was bright enough and we believed he was a solid man we could trust.

Handy had gotten a wire in Carson City and was expecting two tickets to somewhere would be waiting for him at the telegraph office. Cody had made an offer that included them both, and he was all on fire to grab Rebecca and get on the train.

I knew I would miss them, but I could see why he was so excited and wished him Godspeed. His idea to save enough to settle down with their own place didn't surprise me. He was after all raised in a family of farmers, and had ties to the land that I, raised in town, would probably never have.

Our way that last day led us along the American River. We had been warned not to water at the river and we could see and smell the reasons why when we got close. For years mining operations upstream had dumped waste into the river, for want of a better way to get rid of it, and the result was easy to see.

From what Wash had told us, the use of powerful water cannons to blast dirt from canyon walls upstream had created other problems by washing tremendous loads of mud and rocks into the American, changing the way the river ran, even to causing changes in the direction of the main water flow.

Between the two problems, most of the fish in the river were gone, and whether or not they would ever return was something no one knew. All of this had created major problems for people living downstream, and the state was finally beginning to step in to curb the power of the big mine owners.

It was easy to see that cleaning the river up to the point where people downstream could use it safely began with facing the problem at its source, but the political power of the mine owners in the state legislature and in the Congress in Washington D.C. was making it difficult. People living downstream from the mines were beginning to confront the issue with votes and political pressure of their own, but progress was slow, and it looked like any solution was a long way off.

My letters from Bill told us he lived at a place called Hangtown Crossing, about four or five miles from the capital, and that anyone in town could direct us to his lumber yard.

It was early one morning the first week in June, 1885 when we rode passed the front entrance of the yard and tied our horses at a small café down the street. While the others trooped inside and ordered coffee and breakfast, Jed and I walked across to the yard to see if we could find Bill. His yard foreman told us he had needed to stop at a job site for a little while but had expected us any day and would be at the yard shortly. Before we left he had already dispatched someone to let Bill know of our arrival.

We were just finishing breakfast when he drove up in a wagon, and after checking in at the yard, came rushing across the street, burst into the café and crushed me in a bear hug. I had forgotten how much bigger a man he was than Pa. He was somewhere between Handy and me in height and had the lean, spare look of a man who worked hard every day. After he put me down, I introduced him to my friends, and he joined us at the table.

"We've been expecting you for the last couple of days," he said, "so Jess has a couple of rooms made up for you at the house. You won't get to see the kids for a day or two. They are out at Jess's mother's farm north of town. Jess volunteers at the miner's mission in town two days a week and they go out to Grandma's in the summer while she's working there."

He looked at me for a moment. "You sure do look like John, except you're a bit taller. It's been ten years since I was there, so I didn't know what to expect." He turned to Wash. "Johnny said you might be looking for work and we can sure use you if you want, but my father-in-law also needs someone out at this place. You might want to ride out there and talk to him before you make up your mind. If you come over after we finish here, we can talk to Ben - he's the foreman at the yard - and see what kind of spot he might have for you."

Lemuel spoke up. "I'd like to find a secure place for the wagon while we're here and will likely need some of your boys to help Wash and me with some things we plan to do."

"That won't be a problem at all," said Bill. "We usually lock up the yard at night and never had any trouble with anybody bothering things. As far as the boys helping you, just let us know what you need, and we'll take care of it."

"Most of the time, I'll be sleeping in it and sometime Jed here will join me," said Lemuel.

"Must be some wagon," said Bill, looking interested. "I can't wait to look it over."

I sat back and listened to him talking with my friends and volunteering to help them get settled in. I was looking forward to meeting his family and having a nice talk about Pa and years past, and about the future and what I planned to do with it. Jinx finally came out from under the table to meet Bill, and he assured me that Jess and the children would love having him around.

Now I sat petting Jinx, thinking about how my friends would all scatter and that this was the end of one part of my life. Although people tend to drift apart, I felt this group of men would stay close and that somehow the roads we all traveled would be entwined.

Bill needed to go back to work, so when he took Wash and Lemuel across the street to the yard, the rest of us rode into town. After dropping Jason and Handy at a rooming house recommended by Bill, we found his house without a problem and were welcomed by a young girl who helped Jess around the house.

She called for the stable boy and once our stock was cared for, showed us to our rooms. Jinx who had already examined the kitchen, was waiting for me on the back porch and was first on the bed when we got into our room.

That night Bill, Jess and Jed and I sat in the parlor and talked until after midnight; and later when Jinx followed me to our room, he hopped onto the windowsill and out on the roof while I got ready for bed.

As I expected I was too excited to sleep and for a while I lay in the dark, moonlight coming in through the curtains, and petted my little buddy, purring on my chest. He had come through so much with me over so many miles. I thought about how much I had gained and how much I had changed; how I had found a love to carry with me through my life, and friendships more valuable than all the gold ever dug out of these hills and valleys.

"Well, Little Buddy, looks like we made it," I said.

EPILOGUE

1908

At the end of the week I liked to have my desk clean, and here it was Friday afternoon and it wasn't. Little Jinx was sitting patiently on the windowsill watching me work diligently toward that end when Jason, my assistant, stuck his head around the door and said, "There's a fellow out here wants to see you. Says he's not a constituent, just an old friend."

Considering Jason knew most of my old friends, it was unusual he didn't recognize this one. "What's his name?"

"Sebastian Coe," replied Jason.

I leaned back in my chair and glanced at the hat rack standing by the desk; at the old gun belt with its strangely canted holster, and the ivory handled Colt pistol it held. I cleaned and oiled it every week and though I hadn't used it in over fifteen years, for some reason, I wanted it lying loaded on the desk in front of me when this visitor came through the door. The last time I had seen anyone named Coe, he was lying wounded in a doctor's office in Placerville, California, having just tried and failed to kill me.

I resisted the urge and met Mr. Coe at the door, and when he reached out his left hand to shake mine, I realized who he was.

When he was seated in the easy chair by my desk, which I kept for constituents, he began, "You don't remember me do you?"

"When you reached out with your left hand, I realized who you are. Last time I saw you, you were pretty shot up."

He lifted his right arm and I saw the shortened sleeve with the stocking covered end of a stump projecting from it. "It got infected and they had to take it off," he said.

"So, how has it been with you?" I asked. "Did you ever pick up that book I mentioned to you?"

He smiled at me. "I did, and a few more. I grew up on a farm, so I started reading about farming and then read some more. A year or so after our set-to, I got on a train to Bloomington, Indiana. Met a fellow there who got me a job cleaning the labs in the science department at the university and later taking care of the animals at the university stables. Started school and found out I could do it, and furthermore loved it.

I graduated in agriculture, came back here and found a job traveling the state helping farmers be better farmers. Loved the job so much I wrote a couple of books about the topic, left-handed of course, and now my family and I are on our way up to San Mateo where I will become the assistant to the new head of the California Agricultural Extension Service."

My smile had been getting wider as he continued his story and by the end I was grinning broadly. "Well, I'll be damned," I said. "Mr. Coe, that is the best thing I've heard in weeks."

"Call me Seb," he said. "I've known you were here for a while, and I didn't want to leave without seeing you and telling you my story"

"Well, I'm sure glad you did. Did you recognize the fellow outside here?" I asked.

He shook his head and I rang a bell that was sitting on the table beside me.

Jason appeared immediately, looking tense and ready.

I waved my hand at the seated Coe. "Jason, meet Seb Coe. Seb, this is Jason Redbird, the man who shot you in the wrist twenty-five years ago."

Seb's grin was as broad as mine when he stood up and offered his left hand to the startled Jason. "Best thing that ever happened to me," he said, to Jason's slack jawed amazement.

"Mr. Councilman, I wondered if we might step across the street and talk for a while over a cup of coffee?" He turned to Jason and added, "You're invited too, if you'd like to join us."

I still had a few things to finish before I left but told them I'd be there shortly, and they left together.

After they'd gone, I sat for a minute thinking about Seb's story, petting my little black kitten, second copy of the original, and ignoring the clutter on my desk. Finally, I got up, and from the hat rack took the gun belt, slung it round my waist and settled it into place. It felt like it belonged there and yet it didn't, not anymore. The world I lived in had moved past the need to carry it and I had moved with it. I unbuckled it and put it back on its peg, put on my coat and stood looking at the three framed pictures on my desk. Annaliese and the children smiled back at me.

Finally, I looked at the painting of Jinx hanging on the wall by the door and said softly, "This is the end of it, Little Buddy. That day back in

Kansas, when you and I kept the Gambler and his friend from robbing me was like a stone dropped into a pond. That pond was my life, and this was the last ripple."

I turned off the lights and, with Little Jinx on my shoulder, walked across the street to join my friends.

THE END